They moved as one, their bodies rubbing together, creating heat everywhere. Ann felt Casey's warm breath on her neck, Casey's hands caressing her butt, her own hardened nipples rubbing against Casey's chest. Ann's heart was racing with excitement, her breath coming in short gasps; she was losing control of herself. It had been so long since she and Kathy had been this close, and lately they hadn't even been able to be in the same room together without fighting. Concentrating hard on the image of Kathy's face, she was able to pull away from the embrace.

"Casey," she mumbled, still just inches away from Casey's face. Casey traced Ann's lips with her fingers. Ann felt swallowed up in the dark brown eyes. Casey leaned in to touch her lips to Ann's.

Ann had to regain control.

"Casey," she whispered as she pushed herself away. "I need you to leave."

Visit

Bella Books

at

BellaBooks.com

or call our toll-free number

1-800-729-4992

Out of the Fire

Beth Moore

2006

Bella Books, Inc.
P.O. Box 10543
Tallahassee, FL 32302

First Edition

Cover designer: Stephanie Solomon-Lopez

ISBN-10: 1-59493-088-0
ISBN-13: 978-1-59493-088-1

To Veronica

Acknowledgments:

My deepest gratitude and love to Veronica and Matt, who probably felt ignored as I worked on this latest book but still provided me with unlimited support. To Rachel, who made it possible for me to have a weekend or two of much needed silence. And always, to those of you who love and encourage me continuously, it's been a rough road, I can never thank you enough.

A special thanks to my editor, Christine Cassidy, for unlimited patience and understanding. To Linda Hill, who gave me the extra time that I needed to make this book possible.

About the Author

Beth Moore was born, raised and continues to reside in the San Joaquin Valley in California. She splits her time between working in the business world and sharing time with her family and friends. Her passions include softball (watching, she was never coordinated enough to play), football, gardening, and cozy nights by the fire. Writing has also become an important part of her life and she hopes to complete many more books in the future.

Chapter One

"I'm not going to have Casey Duncan star in a lesbian film," the actress's agent, Sandy Sinclair, exclaimed. "She's the hottest thing in Hollywood right now. I won't let her ruin her career on some fly-by-night lesbian movie!"

"But the public knows that she's a lesbian," Ann Covington argued.

"Who knows? Those that read the tabloids?" Sandy waved her arm. "Those who've heard it on the talk shows?" She waved her other arm. "The public never 'really knows' until they see with their own eyes her kissing another woman."

"But you know the film will really only be seen within the gay and lesbian community—" Ann tried to remain calm but was rudely interrupted.

"But what if not? What if the film catches on with the media and it flies to the big screens?" Sandy was not backing down. "There goes her career!" She flailed her arms again. Then, as if to recognize she was losing her temper over some petty item, she calmly sat back down, placed her elbows on the desk and firmly stated, "I will not let Casey make this film. That is my final answer."

Ann gritted her teeth at the use of the now overused phrase. "Then I'd like the script back," she said coldly.

The agent punched the intercom button. "Jill, find Miss Covington's script, please. She'll wait out in the lobby." Turning the intercom off, she went to the door and gestured for Ann to leave.

"Thank you for seeing me," Ann said sarcastically. She heard the door shut behind her and made her way to the lobby.

Moments later, Ann sat in the lobby of one of the most prestigious talent agencies in the nation waiting for her script. She wore many hats—attorney, writer, screenwriter. Today she was the casting director. She still couldn't believe her novel was being made into a movie, a small movie, but nonetheless a movie. The project was so small that she doubled as screenwriter and casting director. And as casting director, she was here to try and hire Casey Duncan. Casey was a well-known lesbian actress and a hot name in the movie business lately. Ann's script had been sent to her agent months ago, however, and no matter how many times Ann had phoned Sandy Sinclair, the agent never returned her calls. And this was the reason Ann had insisted on seeing her. She had been bound and determined to get an answer today. Unfortunately, the answer was no.

There were so many beautiful people coming in and out of this lobby, Ann wondered what they thought of her sitting there. She was attractive, yet by no means beautiful. Her mousy shoulder-length brown hair had highlights of blond woven in. She was a thin five foot five. Her skin was lightly tanned thanks to the Los Angeles sun. In San Francisco, she only saw the inside of her office and home.

She watched as Jill, Sandy's assistant, approached, looking remorseful. Jill had managed a way for Ann to see the agent today. Jill sat down next to Ann and handed her the script.

"I'm sorry about Sandy's attitude," Jill said softly. "I personally loved it." She stared at Ann for a minute as if trying to make a decision, then stated boldly, "I think that Casey should get a chance to look at this. I think that she might have a different opinion."

"Yes, that would be nice." Ann looked Jill in the eye. "But I wouldn't know where to find her."

"I may lose my job for this." Jill took a deep breath. "She usually hangs out at this bar called The Place. You can find it in the phone book."

Ann stood and shook Jill's hand. "Thank you so much." Jill began her way back to her office when Ann called after her, "Are you friends with Casey?"

Turning, Jill smirked. "We were once. Yes, that would be the word, *once*." She smiled and continued walking. "Good luck, Ann. Tell Casey hi for me."

Ann turned the key on her hotel room door, glanced into the empty seating area of the suite and sighed. No sign of Kathy, her partner of ten years. She looked at the closed bedroom door, knowing on the other side Kathy was probably still in bed, at four o'clock in the afternoon. She leaned against the couch for a minute, deciding what stance to take this time. Kathy used to be so energetic, so loving, so . . . fun. For the last couple of years, she had become exactly the opposite—critical, barely wanting any sexual contact, a workaholic. She'd once been a beautiful woman. Thick dark brown hair graced her long fit body. But she had aged in the last few years. Her face had wrinkled with frown lines, her body shriveled as if she was existing only on coffee. Ann still loved her dearly, and every once in a while she saw the old Kathy creep out. She longed for those times, and that was what had kept her from leaving.

She slowly opened the bedroom door. Kathy wasn't still in bed. Instead, she was freshly showered and packing their suitcases. Ever since Ann had gotten involved in the movie, there had been constant commuting between San Francisco and Los Angeles. Several times, Kathy had accompanied her. The suite had been a second home for Ann, and she'd reserved it for an indefinite period so that she could go and come as she pleased.

"Kathy, I've got great news!"

Kathy glanced up while she continued packing. "The picture's been canceled?" she said dryly.

Ann tried to remain upbeat. "Casey's agent declined the script."

"Yeah, I told you so, but you had to go get your idea slapped down in person," Kathy grumbled.

"But here's the good news. A woman at the agency told me that I should approach Casey in person—"

"So what? What are you going to do, search all of Los Angeles?"

"No." Ann crossed her arms. Kathy's bad attitude wasn't going to ruin this for her. "I was told where Casey hangs out, a bar called The Place."

Kathy continued packing. "Too bad we're flying out in a couple of hours. You'll have to wait until your next trip."

"Kath, I want to go there this evening, maybe around seven or eight o'clock."

"Well, I guess I shouldn't have packed your suitcase. You'll still have to drop me off at the airport."

"Do you mean you want me to go alone into a bar filled with who knows what kind of women?" Ann whined. "God, who are you?"

Kathy looked Ann in the eye, then went into the bathroom and slammed the door.

Annoyed, Ann sprawled out on the couch and flipped through the channels on the television. She tried to relax so that her headache wouldn't turn into a migraine. She wanted to go to the bar tonight, not be sick in bed.

A few moments later, Kathy sauntered into the living area and sat down. She caressed Ann's face. Ann looked at this Jekyl and Hyde person and closed her eyes. *How many times do I have to put up with this?* she asked herself.

"You're right, babe. I don't want you going to that bar all alone," Kathy said softly. "Let's go out to dinner, and then we'll find the bar."

Ann nodded, kissed Kathy on the cheek, then went to take a shower.

"Gee, not really what I expected." Ann reviewed the outside of The Place in West Hollywood. She had expected some lavish building. What was before her was very ordinary and somewhat rundown. Same ol' neon beer signs that you would find in any bar, she thought.

Kathy shrugged. "Maybe this is where she's always hung out with her friends, even before she was famous." She opened the large wood door for Ann, then escorted her inside.

Ann felt like she had just walked into the stereotypical bar, low lit, alcohol ad decorated, loud music. The pool table in the corner was surrounded by several women, only a couple of them actually playing the game. The remainder of the bar was filled with tables around a small dance floor. The jukebox played a country song that Ann had heard before. They took stools in front of the bar. The tall, slender bartender looked as if she could be a model, but her muscular arms convinced Ann that she must be a female body-builder. She nodded toward Ann and Kathy, acknowledging their presence.

They perused the bar as they tried to locate their target, Casey Duncan. It was Ann's lucky night as she suddenly spotted the woman making her way to the bar. Ann elbowed Kathy and smiled. Kathy nodded and almost pushed Ann off her stool as she nudged Ann to go to her.

Casey looked exactly like the pictures Ann had seen. Supposedly, the camera adds ten pounds, but this was clearly not the case. Casey's blond hair shone even in the dim lighting. Her lean tan body could not be mistaken in the tight jeans and shirtless vest. Her black cowboy boots looked worn and comfortable.

"Casey Duncan?" Ann asked, leaning toward her. The brown eyes before her were mesmerizing.

She glanced at Ann, then turned toward the bar as several glasses of beer were set in front of her. "Depends on who wants to know."

Ann stretched out her hand. "Ann Covington."

Casey dug her hand into her pocket for the money to pay for the drinks.

Ann held out enough money to pay the tab. "Can I pay for a minute of your time?"

Casey shrugged and nodded as she attempted to pick up all of the glasses. Ann handed the money to the bartender, picked up several of the glasses and followed Casey over to a crowded table. Setting the glasses down, Ann took a seat at a nearby empty table.

Casey pulled out a chair, flipped it around and sat down across from her. Leaning on the back of the chair, she impatiently said, "Shoot!"

Ann set the script down on the table. "I have a script that I'd like you to look at."

Casey shook her head and started to stand. "All scripts go through my agent."

Ann placed her hand on Casey's arm. "I've already seen her. She said that she wouldn't let you do a lesbian movie. Said it would ruin your career."

Casey shrugged. "That's what I pay her for."

Ann nodded. "Yes, I understand that. It's just that when I was leaving, I ran into Jill—"

Casey nodded and impatiently motioned for Ann to continue.

"Well, Jill said that maybe I should let you decide for yourself and told me where I might find you."

Casey laughed and shook her head. "She's getting even with me."

Ann smiled. "Haven't you learned not to have a one-night stand with someone you're going to run into on a day-to-day basis?"

"I guess not." Casey grinned and looked at her curiously. "How about you? Interested in a one-night stand?"

Ann shook her head and looked over at the bar. "See the woman in blue at the bar? We've been together ten years."

Casey nodded and lifted her hands in surrender.

Ann scooted the script toward her. "Look, here's the script. You can toss it as soon as I walk out the door, or you can take it home and read it. If you find that you're interested, the director's number is inside the cover. If you can't get in touch with her, you'll find my number at the hotel in there too." Standing, Ann extended her hand. "It was nice meeting you. Jill was wrong. You aren't the bitchiest person I've ever met."

Casey shook her head. "I guess I deserved that." Ann turned to leave, but Casey stopped her. "Hey, where's the part where you tell me that I'm your favorite actress and that you've loved all my films?"

Ann looked at her. "I'm going to be honest with you. I've only seen a couple of your movies—well, actually only one in its entirety. The other one was so bad that I walked out."

Casey looked shocked by her honesty. "I guess that you're not really big on flattery, huh? So why—"

"I said that the movie sucked, not necessarily your acting." Ann smiled, collected Kathy from the bar and walked out the door.

Chapter Two

Casey awoke the next morning still regretting her actions from the night before. She couldn't believe that she had snubbed Ann Covington last night. This woman was one of her favorite authors. By the time she had opened the script and realized who had approached her last night, it was much too late to call. First thing this morning, she was going to rectify the situation. She glanced at the clock, a little after ten o'clock. Pulling a robe on, she grabbed for the phone.

Ann sat at the desk looking through a pile of 8 by 10 photographs. If Casey wouldn't take the part, which was pretty apparent from last night, they needed to start calling in other actresses. She sighed. Casey would've been perfect for the role. Ann was even more certain after meeting her in person. The ringing phone broke her from her trance. She grabbed the receiver, not wanting to wake Kathy.

"This is Casey Duncan. I hope I'm not calling too early."

Astonished, Ann almost dropped the receiver. "No, it's not too early. I'm an early riser."

There was a moment of silence on the other end as Casey gathered her thoughts. "I . . . I took a look at the script last night. Can we meet somewhere to talk?"

Ann was still in disbelief that she was even hearing from Casey. But, she thought, maybe Casey wasn't interested at all and just wanted to politely decline in person.

"Yes, of course," Ann answered. "What's your schedule like?"

"Well, I'm free this morning. I could come over right now."

Ann looked at her watch. "That would be fine. I have to be somewhere at one o'clock, but we should have plenty of time."

"So where should I meet you?"

"Would you mind coming to the hotel?" Ann gave her the address. "I know that it's probably not very professional but . . ."

"That's fine. I'll see you in about half an hour," Casey said.

Ann hung up the receiver and ran her fingers through her hair. She shouldn't get her hopes up. Even if Casey was interested, Ann knew that they wouldn't be able to afford her usual salary. Turning off her laptop, she wandered into the bedroom to change. She was glad that she had already taken a shower. As she pulled on a pair of jeans and a T-shirt, Ann saw Kathy stir in the bed, roll over and instantly fall back asleep. Kathy looked so peaceful lying there, why couldn't some of that peacefulness flow into their relationship? Ann finished applying her makeup and crept back to the living area, quietly closing the door.

Just then she heard a knock. She looked at her watch. Had it been a half an hour already? Unfortunately it was room service with her breakfast cart. *Shoot.* She had forgotten that she'd ordered breakfast but was glad as her stomach growled from the mere sight of the food. Tearing off a piece of a croissant, she stuffed it in her mouth and signed the tag. As she handed the pen and paper back to the attendant she glanced over at a figure standing in the doorway. She quickly swallowed in embarrassment and extended her hand to Casey, who was holding the script.

9

"Good morning. I hope you don't mind. I forgot that I had ordered breakfast."

Casey shook her hand and smiled. "Not at all. Looks good."

Ann shut the door and motioned to the food. "Please, help yourself. I can't possible eat all of this." Then, remembering Kathy was still asleep in the other room, she lowered her voice. "We do need to keep our voices down though. Kathy's kind of a late riser."

Casey looked over at the closed door of the bedroom.

"You'd better save some of this for her," she said, looking back down at the cart.

Ann shook her head. "She won't be up for quite a while. She'll want lunch, not breakfast."

Casey set the script down on the coffee table and broke off a small bunch of grapes from the fruit tray. Ann placed a few items on her plate and poured a glass of orange juice. She plopped down on the couch, watching Casey pace in front of the fireplace.

"This is a good script," Casey began. Meeting Ann's eyes, she continued, "I think it could be as good as the book."

Ann was taken aback. "You read *The Charade*?"

Casey seemed to relax and popped a grape in her mouth. "I can't believe that I didn't recognize your name last night. I love your books."

Ann blushed. "I'm flattered that you even read them."

Casey smiled and sat down in the overstuffed chair by the window. "I just wish that you had liked my movies as much as I enjoyed your books."

Ann felt bad about the comment that she had made the night before. "I like the characters you chose to play," she explained.

"They were all strong women. I refuse to play a character without any substance."

"I know. That's why I thought you'd be perfect for this role." Ann paused before asking, "So, are you interested at all?"

Casey leaned forward and placed her elbows on her knees. Tucking her hair behind her ear, she sighed and raised her eyes. "My agent will probably kill me, but yeah, I am interested."

Ann took another bite of croissant and then swallowed, trying to hide her rising hopes. "I probably don't need to say this, but I'm sure we can't offer anything closely comparable to your usual salary. I mean, look, I'm the writer and I'm doubling as the casting director."

Casey popped another grape into her mouth. "Sometimes it's not about the money." She chuckled. "Don't get me wrong. Sometimes it's all about the money." Then with a shrug she continued, "This time it's not."

Ann took a sip of orange juice and nodded. "Okay, now the biggest problem. Your agent had this script for months. I finally had to camp outside her office for an answer. We need to start shooting within the next couple of weeks. I'm not sure what your schedule is like."

Casey grimaced, then massaged her temples. "Well, actually I'm supposed to be taking a break right now. But technically, my next project doesn't start for several months."

Ann took the last bite of her croissant. "So, I guess it's up to you then."

Casey searched through her jacket pocket, pulled out a pack of cigarettes and walked over to the window. Turning back toward Ann she brought her lighter to her cigarette. "Do you mind if I smoke?"

"Actually, I do," Ann admitted.

Casey lowered both the lighter and the cigarette and searched Ann's face. "I can't quite figure you out. You're giving off mixed signals. Do you want me to do the movie or not?"

Ann ran her hands over her face. "I'm sorry. I just never quite realized how stressful all this movie stuff was. I mean, if it's not the actors, it's the money. If it's not the money, it's scheduling problems." Looking up at Casey, she softly smiled. "I'd really love for you to do the movie. The truth is that you're my first choice. But even if you decide that you want to do this, the director still has the last word."

Casey smiled mischievously. "Then let's go see the director."

Ann looked at her watch. "That's who I'm meeting with at one o'clock."

Casey grabbed her jacket. "Let's go!"

"Okay." Ann smiled. "Let me tell Kathy that I'm leaving."

Casey watched Ann as she opened the bedroom door and lightly pushed it closed after entering, leaving the door ajar just enough for Casey to eavesdrop on their conversation. She had picked up this habit years ago, and it had come in handy in several situations.

"Babe, I'm leaving now."

Kathy rolled over and moaned. "What time is it?"

Ann combed the hair from Kathy's eyes and smiled. "It's a little after noon. Are you getting up?"

"No. I'm still tired," Kathy said gruffly.

"I ordered some breakfast a while ago, and there's still some croissants and stuff left."

"You know I don't want that stuff. I'll order lunch later," Kathy said, jerking the covers back.

"Remember that we're having dinner with Leslie and Debbie at seven, okay?" Ann kept her voice soft.

Kathy rolled away abruptly. "Yeah, yeah. I won't forget!"

Ann sighed and stood. "I'm leaving the car for you. I'll call you later."

"Whatever!" The blanket was pulled over Kathy's head.

So much for peaceful.

"Thanks for letting me ride with you. It will be a lot easier later if Kathy has the car." Ann led Casey into the building on the Universal Studios lot that housed Leslie Walker's office. Ann had told her the sound stage was also here, but it was small and at the very end of the lot. It was all they could afford due to the low budget of their movie. Casey had been here before but not in this section of the building. As they approached the office Ann stopped and turned to her. "Give me a minute with her first, okay?"

Nodding, Casey took a seat and motioned for Ann to go on ahead. Ann knocked on Leslie's door and entered. Casey listened carefully to the sounds coming through the office door. Her eavesdropping skills made it easy to decipher their words.

"I hope it's a good surprise. We could use one."

"Well, I think it's a good surprise . . ." Ann sounded hesitant. "I finally got in touch with Casey Duncan."

"Ann, I told you, I don't think—"

"She's right outside," Ann interrupted. "Leslie, she's interested in the part."

"Look, Ann, we've discussed this. Her reputation precedes her. Everyone says that she's a real bitch. The last thing we need on this movie set is someone like that!"

Ann must have lowered her voice because Casey couldn't hear the rest of the conversation. Did everyone really think that she was a bitch? She was still trying to deal with that question when Ann poked her head out of the office, gesturing for her to join them. Casey slowly stood. Part of her wanted to go in and prove Leslie wrong, part of her wanted to run. She chose to take her chances. Putting on her best smile, she walked through the door. "Hi. Casey Duncan," she said, feeling confident. She extended her hand.

Leslie stood and shook her hand. "Leslie Walker." She gestured for Casey and Ann to sit, then took a seat herself. "Well, Casey, I've seen a lot of your work," Leslie said as she removed her half-glasses. Her reddish brown hair, which looked like it had been recently curled, was pulled back away from her face and secured by two pencils. By the way her sleeves were rolled up, Casey wondered how long she had been there.

Casey looked straight back at her and said cynically, "I hope you thought more of my work than Ann did."

Leslie laughed. "Ann's a writer. She actually believes there should be a plot."

Casey looked at Ann, who was smiling as she shook her head. "Well, I think there's a good plot in this script."

"So you're interested in the part?" Leslie asked. "Did Ann tell you about the money and time restraints?"

Casey nodded. "I'm sure we can work something out. Who else has signed on to this project?"

Leslie smiled. "Absolutely no one you've ever heard of before."

Casey smiled back. "Who's playing Chris?"

Leslie and Ann both sighed. Leslie sat back in her chair. "That's the problem. We wanted to cast the part of Lynn before we cast Chris. Therefore, we haven't been able to cast either of our lead roles."

Casey nodded in understanding. "So, do you want me to do a screen test or anything?"

Leslie raised her eyebrows, apparently impressed that Casey would actually be willing to test for the part. Most well-known actors, Casey knew, rarely would.

"Call me suspicious, but why do you want this role?" Leslie asked.

"No reason to be suspicious. I'm a big fan of Ann's writing. I think this could be a really fun experience." Casey smiled, feeling mischievous. "I'm always open to new experiences."

"You know your agent is going to be really pissed," Leslie said.

Casey laughed, picturing Sandy Sinclair's wrath. "Yeah, but that won't be a new experience."

Her laugh must have been contagious because soon Ann and Leslie were laughing along with her.

They spent the next few hours talking. Leslie showed Casey the pictures and biographies of the actors and actresses already cast. Ann explained the locations of the shoots. Even after all these discussions, Leslie had still not given the part to Casey. It was approaching seven o'clock.

"Casey, why don't you join us for dinner? That way we can get to know each other a little better," Leslie suggested. Clearly, she still was not convinced that the rumors about Casey were untrue.

"Leslie, I'm sure Casey has other plans on a Saturday night." Ann offered Casey a way out.

Casey shook her head. "No, actually I didn't have other plans. I'm really kind of a homebody."

Ann shrugged and looked at her watch. "Well, we'd better get going. Kathy will kill me if we're late."

The three walked out to the parking lot. Leslie looked around the area. "Where's your car, Ann?"

"Oh, I came with Casey so that Kathy could have the car," Ann replied.

Leslie nodded as she watched Casey unlock the passenger side door and open it for Ann.

"Thanks," Ann said as she slid into the seat and Casey closed the door behind her.

She climbed in behind the wheel of her Lexus RX Hybrid and watched Ann secure her seatbelt before she began pulling out of the parking lot. Even though she had only met Ann a few hours ago, she felt like she had known her forever. Usually she wasn't this comfortable with someone this quickly. She glanced over at Ann, whose mind was obviously somewhere else.

Ann softly smiled, trying to remember the last time Kathy opened the door for her. "It's been so long since anyone has opened a car door for me. You know, after ten years, you forget the little things. You're happy if your partner doesn't forget your birthday." Kathy had been so absentminded lately, Ann wondered if she would remember her birthday this year.

Casey laughed. "I wouldn't know about that. I think the longest relationship I had was . . . two weeks."

Ann's smile widened. "So, are you one of those women afraid of commitment, or do you just like to play the field?"

Casey paused for a moment then grinned. "I guess I just haven't found anyone that I've wanted to make a commitment to."

Ann nodded. "Yes, I was lucky to have found Kathy."

At the restaurant, Casey put the car into park and placed her hand on Ann's knee. "Stay there."

Confused, Ann looked at her but understood as soon as Casey came around and opened her car door. Ann smiled and thanked her.

Casey returned the smile. "I believe it's the little things that count."

The two approached the restaurant. Casey opened the door for Ann but didn't follow her inside. Ann turned around. "Aren't you coming in?"

Casey pulled out her cigarettes and lighter from her knapsack. "It's been about three hours."

Ann nodded in understanding and made her way through the lobby. The two couples had eaten here, at Chan's Dynasty, before. The food was delicious and the place was impressively decorated with what looked like priceless Chinese vases and gold etchings. The bamboo trees set off the deep colors with the light green of their leaves. The owner had spared no expense.

Peeking around the hostess counter, she immediately spotted Leslie and her partner, Debbie, sitting with Kathy at a table near the window. *Had Debbie's hair been cut even shorter?* Ann asked herself. Since she had first met the couple, Debbie's black hair had lost several inches. The style made her look thinner and older than Leslie. But both women were in their early forties.

"Where's Casey?" asked Leslie.

"She's having a cigarette," Ann explained as she sat down.

Kathy rolled her eyes. "What a disgusting habit!"

"Actually, I just quit about three years ago, when we had our kids," Debbie remarked.

"Hmm . . . it was all right to destroy your health, and Leslie's, but heaven forbid you hurt your kids?" Kathy said sarcastically.

Ann ran her fingers through her hair and looked apologetically at Leslie. Leslie caught the glance and took a sip of her white wine as if to avoid shooting back. Ann felt a little apprehensive to see Casey approach the table. She had the feeling that Casey would not be as polite as Leslie and Debbie had been.

Casey pulled out her chair as she extended her hand to Kathy. "You must be Kathy."

Kathy shook her hand. "I hear you have a bad habit."

Casey looked confused, then realized what she was referring to. "You know, I've tried to quit several times, but then I end up in a movie where I have to smoke and it starts all over again."

"So, don't agree to play parts where you have to smoke. Seems simple enough to me," Kathy quipped.

Casey looked around the table at the three other women, then smiled politely. "Yeah, if it were only that easy."

Leslie gave the conversation a break. "Casey, this is Debbie."

"Hi, Debbie." Casey smiled and shook her hand across the table. "I feel kind of like a fifth wheel here. I know Ann and Kathy have been together ten years. How about you two?"

Debbie smiled as she took Leslie's hand. "Eight years and two kids."

"She always says it that way. Our oldest is three. Three plus eight is eleven. We've been together eleven years," Leslie explained.

"Wow, two kids!" Casey exclaimed. "That's great. How old is your youngest?"

"A year and a half," Debbie replied. "Would you like to see pictures?"

Casey smiled and nodded. Debbie withdrew her wallet from her purse and opened it, exposing several pictures.

"The oldest is Kenny, then there's Emily." Debbie passed the wallet to Casey.

Casey admired the array then handed it to Ann. "So, who was the lucky woman to carry them? Or, I'm sorry, are they adopted?"

"No, not adopted. I carried them both, but Leslie was part of the entire process, if you know what I mean," Debbie said.

Ann smiled at the pictures and tried to show them to Kathy, just to be waved away.

"And you know, Casey, Debbie quit smoking just for the kids' sake," Kathy said mockingly.

Irritated, Ann looked at Kathy. "Just drop it, Kathy, okay? I mean, we all have our vices. For example, mine is lobster smothered in butter. And, Leslie, I know that you couldn't live without your cookie dough ice cream."

17

Leslie laughed. "I admit it. I'd die without it!"

That seemed to break the ice for the rest of the evening. They filled the table with orders of brandied chicken wings, ginger beef, sweet and sour shrimp and several different types of rice and noodles. The five women feasted not only on the delectables, but on stories of past adventures, mishaps and dirty jokes. Kathy's sarcasm was ignored again and again.

At ten o'clock, Kathy had had enough. "Honey, we need to call it an evening. I'm really tired."

"How can you be tired? You slept until after noon," Ann joked. Kathy shot her a look that could kill and the table fell silent. Standing, Kathy dropped sixty dollars on the table, moved to the back of Ann's chair and placed her hands on her shoulders. Ann swallowed the last bit of wine from her glass and rose.

"Well, I guess I'll see you Monday," she said to Leslie. Then, turning to Casey, she hesitated, then looked back at Leslie.

Leslie seemed to understand the unasked question and turned to Casey. "Casey, you've got the part. That is, if you still want it after seeing the wacky women you'll be working with."

Casey's eyes lit up. "Thank you. I'd love to work with you wacky women!"

"Well then, I guess I'll see you Monday too," Ann said. Responding to Kathy's obvious impatience, Ann waved good-bye and followed her to the door.

Casey took some money out of her wallet, wondering what Kathy's problem was.

"I guess we'd better get going too. We have a new babysitter tonight," Leslie explained.

"You mean a babysitter for the kids that you quit smoking for?" Casey said sarcastically, remembering Kathy's refusal to look at the pictures. Did Kathy not like kids? She wondered if Ann wanted children of her own, and if she would ever be able to have them if Kathy didn't. Casey's heart had skipped a beat as she caught Ann's gaze when the wallet was handed back to her. *Whoa, what was that feeling?* she'd asked herself.

Debbie handled the check and left some money for the tip.

Casey shook her head. "What does Ann see in her?" she asked.

Both women responded with a shrug.

"I'm sorry," Casey apologized. "Maybe I just caught her on a bad night."

"No, she's always like that. But Ann must see something that we don't," Debbie answered as she stood and pulled out her partner's chair. Leslie and Casey rose and all three made their way out of the restaurant and to the parking lot.

Casey watched as Debbie walked Leslie to her car, opened the door for her and kissed her. Casey remembered Ann's comment about a long-term relationship and the things that disappear after a while. Maybe Ann was wrong, maybe it wasn't all long-term relationships, maybe it was just hers.

Chapter Three

Ann sat in her car waiting for Leslie to arrive on the lot. Mondays were always bad for Leslie because Debbie taught an eight o'clock class at UCLA. That meant no help with the kids. This morning had been quiet since Kathy had taken an early flight back to San Francisco on Sunday. She felt refreshed as she had gotten quite a bit of work done yesterday, including some research that she had put off for way too long. Thank God for laptops and the Internet.

At nine o'clock, Shelley, the production manager, arrived with keys to Leslie's office. Ann watched as the stocky woman with curly brown hair climbed the steps to the building. She was doing a balancing act with one arm full of papers and files, and the other cradling a large plastic bag from an office supply store; all the while she kept trying to keep her thick-rimmed glasses from falling off her nose. Ann offered to help but was waved away. Casey appeared shortly after that, carrying flavored coffees for everyone. Leslie rushed in, grabbed a cup and thanked Casey profusely for her contribution.

"Okay," Leslie said as she straightened out all the head shots into one pile. "What we need to do during the next two days is go through these dozens of photographs, and all these tapes. Since Casey has graciously offered to help, we'll split into two teams. Shelley and I will take half. Ann, you and Casey take the other half. Organize them into two piles, yes and no. I think the first thing we should do is throw out all the actresses taller than Casey, which is what . . . five-seven, five-eight?"

Casey nodded as she picked up one stack and followed Ann into the next office.

"Let's throw out any actresses that look a lot like you too. I hate it when the characters look too much alike," Ann suggested.

She and Casey proceeded to go through each photograph. At one o'clock Leslie called them for lunch—she'd ordered up salads—and asked them to bring their selections thus far.

"I think this one definitely has possibilities," Ann touched her fork to a glossy picture of a woman with blond hair.

"Yes," Leslie agreed. "But she would have to darken her hair for the part."

The others nodded. "Well, we'll just have to ask her agent," Casey chimed in. "What about these others though? We need to call several in for screen tests."

"Speaking of screen tests, we have all of those tapes to watch," Leslie reminded them. "We'd better get to work."

At six o'clock, after watching dozens of tapes, Ann was worn out. At least they had compiled a list of potential actresses for the part of Chris.

"It's a good list," Leslie remarked, then sighed. "Next are all of the calls we need to make. We'll start on that tomorrow."

"Can't we start right now?" Casey asked. "I mean, we are behind schedule, right?"

"Well, I need to get going. I have a date tonight," Shelley said.

Leslie also declined. "Yeah, sorry, I need to get home to Debbie and the kids."

Casey turned to Ann. "I'm sure Kathy wants you back at the hotel."

Ann shrugged. "No, actually Kathy flew out yesterday. I'm free."

"Okay then. Let's stay and make a few calls."

Hours later, Ann sank back in her chair after accomplishing their task. Screen tests would begin in two days. The brief silence ended with the ringing of Ann's cell phone. Feeling lazy, she gestured to Casey to answer it.

"Hello. Ann's phone," Casey said. After listening for a few seconds, she spoke again. "Leslie, just calm down. Ann and I can be there in a few minutes . . ." She put her hand over the speaker. "Ann, do you know where Leslie and Debbie live?"

Ann nodded, wondering what was up, but Casey was back on the phone.

"We're on our way. Everything is going to be fine." The conversation ended and Casey immediately grabbed her knapsack and motioned for Ann to do the same.

"What's going on?" Ann rushed after Casey. "Is Leslie all right?"

Casey opened the passenger door. "Leslie's father had a heart attack. They need someone to watch the kids."

"And you volunteered us?" Ann exclaimed as she slid into the seat. "Kids don't like me. Do you have any experience with children?"

"My niece and nephew have provided me with plenty of practice." Casey started the car. "What do you mean, kids don't like you? How can anyone not like your sweet face?"

"Well, thanks, but for some reason, I just don't get along with them."

"I don't believe you." Casey stated.

"Okay, I'll give you an example," Ann offered. "My first and only babysitting job was watching three children for a couple I attended church with. The kids were always well-behaved on Sunday, so I wasn't expecting any different in their home setting. Everything went smoothly during the first half-hour or so, then they wanted to play outside. They lured, and I mean *lured*, me out into the backyard. Before I knew it, the kids had run into the house and locked me out. Of course, I didn't have any keys, so that's where I stayed—for hours. I was allowed back into the house only minutes before their parents came home."

Casey just laughed while she listened to Ann's experience. Soon they were parking in Leslie's driveway, where Leslie stood waiting for them. Debbie came running out to their minivan, climbed in and turned on the ignition.

"Oh, I'm so glad you're here. Come in and meet the kids. There's a list of emergency numbers on the refrigerator," Leslie babbled. "And lasagna in the oven."

Ann put her arm around her, trying to comfort her as she and Casey were shown around the house and introduced to the children, who had just been put to bed. Leslie then rushed off.

A few minutes later, Ann looked into the oven to review the lasagna inside. The aroma made her tummy rumble with hunger.

"I don't know how you can say that you don't get along with children. Kenny sure came running to you." Casey's voice came from behind Ann as she reached into the cabinet for plates.

Closing the cabinet door, Ann turned and chuckled. "Yes, the boys always seem to be running to me."

Casey laughed. "And at what age did you realize that you didn't want the boys running to you?"

"Not until my early twenties. How about you?"

"I started early. While most of my friends in high school were dating the football team, I was sneaking into the college dorm to sleep with an older woman."

Ann nodded. "I think everything is ready. Why don't you grab us something to drink?"

Casey opened the refrigerator and pulled out a bottle of wine. "This was probably meant for tonight."

23

Ann shook her head. "I think I'll stick with a soda."

The table already set, Casey filled the wineglasses with diet cola and handed Ann her glass. "To good food and new friends."

Ann smiled and touched her glass to Casey's. "Yes, to new friends."

The lasagna was delicious, and Ann's plate almost licked clean, when suddenly Kenny rounded the corner. Clearly he hadn't gotten to sleep yet. He shuffled over and pulled on Ann's sleeve.

"Kenny, what's the matter?" she asked softly. He looked so cute in his light blue airplane pajamas.

Kenny squeezed his blanket and hugged a children's book. "Can you read me this book?"

Ann reached out for it. "*Miss Piggly Wiggly Goes to Town.*" She looked at Casey, then down at the boy who hadn't been broken of his thumb-sucking habit. "Sure, I can."

"Go ahead and take him into the living room and I'll clean up here." Casey gestured toward the next room. Ann scooped up Kenny and headed for the couch.

Finished with the dishes, Casey turned the corner into the living room and stopped. For a moment all was frozen in time as she watched Ann on the couch cradling the little boy in her arms. Casey felt like she was in the sequence of a movie where a person sees another across the room finally coming to the realization that this was the person that they wanted to spend the rest of their life with. Casey could not move. She had only known Ann a few days. Was this the woman that she was meant to spend the rest of her life with? There was only one big problem. Ann had already promised the rest of her life to Kathy.

"Here, let me put him back into bed," Casey offered as she came into the living room.

As Casey leaned over to pick up the child, she caught a whiff of the perfume radiating from Ann. For a moment their eyes met, then Casey smiled tenderly as she continued to gently scoop up the child from Ann's arms.

"I can take the book too," Casey whispered, holding out her hand.

"No!" Ann whispered back. "I want to find out what happens to Miss Piggly Wiggly."

Casey couldn't stop grinning as she turned and left the room.

When she returned, Ann was busy working on her laptop. The script lay on the arm of the couch, Kenny's book on the coffee table.

"Do you work twenty-four hours a day?" Casey asked.

"No, I sleep about two hours," Ann joked. She threw the children's book toward Casey. "Here, catch up on your reading. It's a surprise ending."

Catching it, Casey dropped down next to Ann. Within minutes she had dozed off, her head on Ann's shoulder.

Ann felt the weight on her shoulder and sighed. Casey looked so peaceful, she could not wake her. But try as she might, she could not type with one hand, and she felt her own exhaustion set in and her eyes begin drooping. Last thing she remembered was the screen of the laptop getting blurry.

Casey heard the key turn in the lock but could not wake up enough to open her eyes. Her body felt like lead. She hadn't slept this good in a long time. She could hear Leslie and Debbie talking quietly but kept still.

"I hope that's not going to be a problem," Debbie commented.

"What do you mean?" Leslie questioned.

"Look at the two of them all snuggled up on the couch."

"Well, one good thing, it would get Ann away from Kathy the bitch."

"Yes, out of the fire and into the frying pan. You know about Casey's reputation as well as I do."

"Sometimes someone's reputation is all rumor. I haven't seen any proof and I've spent a lot of time with her this week," Leslie said in Casey's defense.

"Leslie, she's an actress. She could be acting this whole time."

Casey stirred, not wanting to hear any more. She felt a gentle touch on her head. "Hey, your job is over. Time to go home." She heard Leslie's voice.

Casey opened her eyes, sat up and massaged her neck. "What time is it?" Ann awoke from Casey's movement and rubbed her face.

"Two a.m. Sorry we're so late. I was going to call but didn't want to wake the kids. I tried your cell phone, but you must have it turned off," Leslie explained.

Ann closed her laptop and set it on the coffee table. "Yes, I probably did."

Debbie eyed her and Ann. "You guys look beat. You're welcome to stay the night. This couch pulls out into a bed, but you'd have to—"

"No." Casey stood and stretched. "I'm fine to drive."

"How is your father?" Ann asked Leslie.

"I think he'll be okay. We'll find out more tomorrow. Did you have any trouble with the kids?"

"No." Casey smirked and looked over at Ann. "Kenny took a real liking to Ann."

"Really?" Leslie responded. Casey wondered if Ann had told Leslie about her discomfort around children.

"Yeah, must have been a fluke." Ann shrugged and smiled.

"You ready to go?" Casey asked. Ann nodded, picked up her laptop and headed to the car. Casey opened the door for her, shut it and made her way over to the driver's side.

❧

Casey backed her SUV out of the driveway. She turned on the air and rubbed her face with her hands as if trying to revive herself.

"Are you sure you're okay to drive?" Ann asked, trying to hold back a yawn.

"Yeah, just talk to me," Casey said, still clearly trying to shake herself awake.

"What do you want to talk about?"

"I don't care . . ." Casey paused. "How did you finally come to the realization that you'd rather have girls running after you than boys? Was it one defining experience, or a series of events?"

Ann smiled. "Just a long line of meaningless encounters with men, and a growing infatuation with women, I guess." She tried to recall the real turning point for her. It hadn't been just one person or one experience. She remembered always wanting a boyfriend, but only basically because all of her friends wanted boyfriends. But there was never that emotional connection to men. She tried over and over again. The kisses, the snuggling, even the sex had meant nothing to her. Thinking back, the only time that she ever felt queasy about someone was when she thought about girls. Crushes, she thought. Her first encounter with a woman, at a friend's party, had been an awkward but pleasant experience. So pleasant that she began dating women in secret, while pretending to enjoy the company of men. Soon, she became tired of the charade. Her emotional and physical needs had only been satisfied by women. And so, she had taken the step out of the closet.

She told Casey all this and before long they found themselves in front of Ann's hotel.

"You know, you can crash on the couch in my suite if you'd like," Ann suggested.

Casey stretched, rubbed her eyes and shook her head. "No, I'm okay now. Really."

Ann was not convinced. "Call me when you get home so I know you've made it safely."

Casey agreed. "It should take me about twenty minutes."

"Give me your cell phone number, just in case."

Casey wrote the number on a piece of paper and handed it to her. "I just want you to know, you're one of only a handful of people that have this number."

Ann leaned against the car door and smiled. "I'll die before I give it out to anyone."

She hadn't been inside more than five minute when she decided to call Casey. Even though she'd said she was okay to drive, her eyelids were drooping.

"Hello?" Casey mumbled.

"Hey." Ann heard music in the background—Casey's car stereo. "Doing okay so far?"

"You must have ESP or something. My eyelids were just failing on me."

"I knew that I should have made you stay," Ann said, admonishing herself.

"Talk to me," Casey said.

"No. It's your turn. Tell me about the college woman who changed your life." Ann took a swig from the bottle of water on her nightstand.

Casey laughed out loud. "Not much to tell really. I was in this summer softball league along with some older girls. We would always go back to the dorm after a game and we'd order pizza and they'd drink beer. They never let me even have a sip. Anyway, there was this one girl that was constantly giving me a bad time. We were in competition for everything. The night we won the city championship, we all went back to her room for our usual ritual. It got pretty late, and she suggested that I crash on her roommate's bed. Everyone ended up leaving and it was just the two of us. She let me have my first beer. I don't remember why, but we started wrestling around. The next thing I knew, she had me pinned to the bed. I don't even remember who made the first move."

"So she got you drunk and took advantage of you?" Ann's question hung in the air as she tried to stop the images in her mind of Casey pinned to a bed.

"Oh, no." Casey sounded mortified. "I was not drunk. And

believe me, I was a willing participant." Ann didn't respond, and Casey said, "Hey, are you still there?"

Ann was having a hard time keeping the sexual images out of her mind. She cleared her throat. "Yes, I'm still here. So how long did this relationship last?"

"Oh, you know. She was older. After a while she found someone her own age and dumped me. I was devastated, to say the least."

"Hmm . . . it's hard to imagine you getting dumped," Ann mused aloud.

"It wasn't the only or last time, believe it or not," Casey admitted. "But I got even with her."

"How's that?"

"I ran into her, about a year ago, right after my first big hit movie. I simply pretended not to remember her at all."

Ann laughed. "I bet she regrets her actions now."

Suddenly, Casey announced, "Well, I'm home!"

"Okay," Ann said. "Go get some sleep."

"I will." Casey paused, then added, sincerity in her voice, "And Ann? Thanks for talking me home."

Chapter Four

"I never realized how much went into contract negotiations!" Ann whispered to Leslie after spending most of the day faxing Casey's contract back and forth between Casey's agent, attorney and their office. She wished that she could be out scouting locations with Shelley.

"I'm sorry, guys." Casey had apparently overheard Ann's whispers. "I'm really trying to work it out so that you don't have to pay an arm and a leg for me. It's those damn vultures representing me that are the problem."

"We know, Casey," Leslie replied. "I know it was a sacrifice to give up your own assistant, makeup and hair people. I really appreciate what you're doing."

"Well, it just makes me mad." Casey shook her head. "I'd do it for free if it wasn't for all these legalities."

Just then the fax machine began to print again.

"Ugh . . . here we go again." Casey moaned. "Let's hope the fiftieth time is the charm."

Ann placed the contract in the middle of the conference table for the three of them to review, just as they had time and time before. She sat up, rubbed her weary eyes and scrutinized the document.

"Okay, this part looks fine." Leslie pointed to a section of the contract.

Casey groaned as Ann tapped another section. "But this paragraph still reads wrong." Taking a black pen she began crossing out and rearranging words. "There, that should do it." She slid it over to Casey to review. Casey nodded, stuffed the paper into the fax machine one more time and hit the send button.

Looking at her watch, Leslie sighed and crossed her fingers. "It's getting late and I really would like to have some time with my father today. If the next contract isn't correct, we may have to continue this tomorrow."

Ann stood and stretched. They had run out of small talk hours ago and everyone seemed lost in her own thoughts. After several minutes, the machine began to whirl again. Pages were grabbed and read as each came through.

"Well, it looks like we finally have a deal." Leslie smiled as she reached out to shake Casey's hand.

Casey took Leslie's hand and then Ann's. "Let's make a movie!"

Leslie grabbed her purse and quickly headed for the door, then swung around and slapped her head. "Casey, have you gone over the scenes that we're testing on tomorrow?"

Casey's face dropped. "All of the time I've had today just waiting and I didn't even bring my script." She shrugged. "That's okay. I have all evening."

Leslie nodded. "Okay, guys, I'll see you tomorrow."

Her absence left the room still and Ann didn't know what to say.

Casey finally broke the silence. "I'll buy dinner if you help me run through the scenes."

Ann thought for a moment. She had really enjoyed Casey's company the night before, but she didn't want to give her the wrong idea. She was with Kathy—not exactly the perfect couple

31

right now, but still a couple. But running through lines . . . that was innocent enough. She was sure that Casey had no ulterior motive.

Casey released Ann's fingers and slid her free hand around Ann's back and down onto her other buttock. The two were rehearsing the dancing scene. Ann felt the strong hands against her taut muscles, pulling their bodies closer together.

"I don't think that's in the script," she whispered into Casey's ear.

"Maybe it should be." Casey's voice was low and sexy.

They moved as one, their bodies rubbing together, creating heat everywhere. Ann felt Casey's warm breath on her neck, Casey's hands caressing her butt, her own hardened nipples rubbing against Casey's chest. Ann's heart was racing with excitement, her breath coming in short gasps; she was losing control of herself. It had been so long since she and Kathy had been this close, and lately they hadn't even been able to be in the same room together without fighting. Concentrating hard on the image of Kathy's face, she was able to pull away from the embrace.

"Casey," she mumbled, still just inches away from Casey's face. Casey traced Ann's lips with her fingers. Ann felt swallowed up in the dark brown eyes. Casey leaned in to touch her lips to Ann's.

Ann had to regain control.

"Casey," she whispered as she pushed herself away. "I need you to leave."

Casey stepped back, a look of confusion on her face.

Ann answered the unspoken question. "I need you to leave before I do something I'll regret later."

"Regret?" Casey responded as if insulted.

Ann tried to explain. "Oh, God, Casey, you are a beautiful, intelligent, extremely sexy woman. But I just can't throw away ten years of marriage for one night!"

Casey stepped toward her. "It doesn't have to be just one night, Ann."

32

Ann ran her fingers through her hair in frustration. "Please, Casey, just go."

Casey put up her hands in surrender. "Okay, just let me stay. I won't touch you. I promise. I'll just stay as a friend."

Ann shook her head. "I just really need you to leave. We're still friends though, okay?"

Casey grabbed her jacket then turned as she headed toward the door. "See you tomorrow?"

Ann nodded and watched as the door shut on a very dangerous situation. She fell back against the door. *A few more minutes and it would've gone too far. I could have gone to bed with almost a complete stranger,* she admitted to herself. She posed several questions to herself as she readied for bed. Was she that starved for attention? Or was it something about Casey? How could she be so attracted to someone in such a short time? Ann was still pondering the answers as she drifted off to sleep.

Casey scolded herself as she entered the elevator and then made her way home. She had finally found a woman who actually interested her, both physically and intellectually, and she had to pounce on her. Well, she hadn't exactly pounced. Ann hadn't objected immediately. Remembering how their bodies felt together, how Ann's firm butt felt on her hands, made Casey wet. She jumped into a cold shower until she felt the heat inside subside.

"Hey, are we okay?" Casey asked as she stuck her head in Ann's trailer the next morning.

Ann looked over at her, smiled and nodded. "Yes. Let's just forget last night ever happened okay?"

Casey smiled back, nodded and shut the door. *Like forgetting is that easy,* she said to herself.

❧

The remainder of the week was grueling. It was one screen test right after another. And for Ann, it was particularly difficult as she sat watching what had occurred in her room that night, over and over again. Each time the scene played out, she remembered how her body had felt as it had pressed against Casey's. By the end of the week, she was mentally exhausted. She went back to her trailer to check her e-mail before heading back to the hotel. She heard a knock on her door. Casey stuck her head in Ann's trailer.

"God, you look terrible!" Casey exclaimed.

"Thanks!" Ann replied sarcastically, then explained, "It's been a very demanding day."

"What are you doing tonight?"

Ann shrugged. "Just going back to the hotel, I guess."

Casey shook her head. "No, it's Friday, and you need to get out. I'm going to a bar with a few of my friends. Why don't you join us?"

Ann tucked her hair behind her ear. "I don't want to intrude."

Casey climbed the steps into the trailer and took Ann's hand. Pulling her up she demanded, "You're coming with me. You deserve a little fun!"

Casey didn't have to do much convincing. Ann did need some fun. She allowed herself to be pulled out of the trailer and out into the parking lot.

"We'll come get your car later," Casey said as she opened the passenger side door of her SUV and gestured for Ann to climb in.

The bar was dark, loud and very crowded. Casey led Ann to a table where several women were seated.

"Hey!" Casey shouted hello to her friends. "This is Ann. Ann, this is Tina, Gail, Barb, Pam and Diane." The women all shouted their hellos as Ann and Casey sat down at the table.

Ann observed the table of women. Tina looked like a stick, probably only weighing one hundred pounds. Her blond hair was pulled back into a ponytail which made it easy to see her flawless skin. She wasn't wearing makeup, but it seemed to Ann that if she was, Tina could surely be a model. Barb, on the other hand, was a bit stocky with brown curly hair. She wore a Dallas Cowboys T-shirt and had her sleeves pushed up past her elbows. Ann noticed Gail's eyes right away. The blue eyes glistened like crystals even in the darkness of the room. Her white hospital doctor's badge hung off the green scrubs she was wearing. The colors offset her coppery African-American skin beautifully. Gail was, in Ann's assessment, the most attractive woman at the table.

Pam and Diane were the only two who appeared to be a couple. Pam had her arm around the back of Diane's chair and the two were sitting closer than the others. Pam's straight dark brown shoulder-length hair was pushed behind her ears revealing small diamond studs. The studs were completely different than the dangly gold and bronze ones hanging from Diane's ears. The colors seemed to almost match her short blond streaked hair which framed a thin face. These two fit together, Ann thought. With further examination, Ann could see the rings on their fingers. She examined her own as she heard a voice from across the table.

"So, you're the writer of that lesbian movie, huh?" Tina asked. "I can't believe you talked Casey into that."

"She didn't have to talk me into it. It's a great script!" Casey said in Ann's defense.

The waitress came and set down a round of beers.

"Is this okay? Or do you want something else to drink?" Casey asked Ann politely.

"No, this is fine," Ann answered. In fact, she liked the occasional beer. "I really need a drink."

Casey and her friends kept Ann entertained for the next hour with stories of their adventures. The group had been friends for many years and had some wild experiences. Finally, Ann could laugh no more without going to the restroom. Casey pointed the way. Ann was lucky; there was no line. She returned to the table

35

within minutes. Apparently, she was back before the group had expected. Ann hid behind a column next to the table and listened to their conversation as she heard her name mentioned.

"So Ann must have you head over heels. I've never seen you smile so much in my life," Gail teased.

"I hope you're remembering that she's a married woman," Tina reminded her. "You better not get your heart involved with that one."

"You're shaking your head no, but your eyes are saying yes, yes, yes!" Diane laughed.

"She's going to break your heart, Casey," Gail warned her.

Ann had heard enough. She stepped up to the table, really needing to set Casey straight about their relationship.

"Let's dance," Ann said to Casey as she took her hand. Casey was clearly stunned but allowed herself to be led to the dance floor.

Ann let Casey lead as they joined the bodies on the dance floor.

"I overheard you and your friends' conversation just now," she said to Casey. There was no response. "I hope our relationship isn't going to be a problem for you."

Casey looked at her. "It's not going to be a problem, I promise."

It was nearly midnight when they walked into Ann's hotel room.

"I really need a hot shower. Do you mind?" Ann asked.

"I'll just see what's on TV." Casey flipped through the channels as she lay on the couch. She heard the water turn off in the bathroom and the bathroom door open. Succumbing to temptation, Casey wandered over to the bedroom door and peeked in. She saw Ann's image in the dresser mirror as Ann walked into the bedroom from the attached bathroom. She watched as Ann let the towel drop, revealing her nakedness. Ann loosened the towel from her head and proceeded to towel-dry her hair. *She's just as I imagined*, Casey said to herself as she felt the heat grow in her body.

"I thought that this wasn't going to be a problem for you," Ann said out loud as she met Casey's gaze in the mirror.

Casey was stunned. She hadn't realized that she could be seen in the mirror's reflection. "I'm sorry. I guess my curiosity got the best of me."

Ann continued to stare at her. "So, are you done oogling or can I get dressed now?"

Casey smiled wickedly in response.

"Do you think that you can get the 'best of you' to get us a couple of cold drinks?" Ann said sarcastically.

Casey nodded, retrieved the drinks and sat back down on the couch.

Ann came out of the bedroom fully dressed.

Casey looked up as she approached. "I'm sorry about that."

Ann nodded. "That's okay. I'll get to see you when you do the nude scenes in the movie."

Casey laughed and shook her head. "I guess you don't remember the details of my contract. I have a nudity clause."

Ann grinned. "Do you have a bathing suit clause too?"

Confused, Casey frowned.

"You know, the scene that you're wearing a tiny little bikini, covered with oil?" Ann reminded her.

Casey chuckled and conceded, "I guess you got me on that one."

The two sat in silence as they watched *Who's Line is it Anyway?* The comedy finally sank in and Casey began throwing out her own humorous lines to make the show even funnier. It wasn't long before Ann's eyes were watering from laughing so much.

The show ended. Casey stood and stretched. "I think I'm going to get going. You exhausted me."

"What?" Ann chuckled. "You were the one making me laugh!" She stood. "But thanks, I really needed to relax and have fun."

"By the way," Casey asked, "why isn't Kathy here? Isn't she coming in this weekend?"

"No. She's behind at work," Ann answered. "Maybe next week-end." She shrugged.

Casey nodded and opened the door. How she wished that she could just crawl up in bed with Ann. She leaned forward to give Ann a hug and Ann looked apprehensive.

"Don't worry, it's just a hug." Casey embraced her and gave a gentle squeeze. "Sleep well."

Chapter Five

Casey awoke the next morning with the sun streaming on her face. Looking out her window, she was taken aback by the color of the sky. Had she ever seen it so blue? Reviewing the rest of the scene out the glass, all of the other colors were vibrant too. The next thought that crossed her mind was if Ann knew what a beautiful day it was. Maybe she should call her. No, maybe she should take breakfast to her. She caught herself. When did she start craving time with Ann? This sudden need for this relationship was shocking. *Yes, a relationship,* she told herself. *Not some roll in the sack, but a real relationship.* But then there was Kathy, she had to remind herself. Ann already had a real relationship.

She jumped out of bed. Well, friends it had to be then.

Ann pulled her robe on and wandered into the living room. Opening the curtains, she admired the blueness of the sky. She grabbed her laptop and slumped down on the sofa. Another day of script changes. She never realized the difference between writing a book and writing a screenplay. A knock on the door threw her back into the moment.

"Who is it?"

Ann opened the door at the sound of Casey's voice.

"What are you doing today?" Casey asked with a glowing smile.

"I have to get these pages rewritten." Ann gestured toward the living room where a slew of papers and her laptop sat on the table.

Casey followed her. "You can't stay inside on a beautiful day like today," she said, clearly exasperated. Grabbing Ann's hand she pulled her over to the window. "Look at that blue sky!"

Ann pulled away, sank down on the couch and smiled apologetically. "I know but—"

"But nothing!" Casey interrupted. "We're going to the beach and I won't take no for an answer. We'll take the script and your laptop and I'll help you finish those pages. We'll just do it out in the sun." She offered her hand. "Come on. Go change into some shorts."

Ann knew she wasn't going to win this argument. Taking Casey's hand, she allowed herself to be pulled up off of the couch. "Can we get something to eat first? I'm starving."

Casey nodded and shooed her on her way.

Although the drive to Santa Monica Beach was beautiful, Ann missed being able to walk almost anywhere as in San Francisco. Even if you couldn't walk, there were no highways or freeway interchanges to maneuver. In Los Angeles, even if you owned a car, it might take you hours to get to your destination. Fortunately, the travel time today was minimal. And being with Casey made the time in the car more pleasant than usual.

Ann frowned at the computer. They had settled themselves on a stretch of grass on the outskirts of the sand. A small tree shaded the spot and a cool breeze whispered through the leaves.

"What's wrong?" Casey asked as she repositioned herself on the blanket. She plucked a piece of grass and twirled it in her fingers.

Ann looked at Casey, then lowered her eyes. "Why couldn't Kathy be helping me like this? She's never there for me."

Casey reached out to touch Ann's arm. "You guys are just having a tough time right now. Come on, tell me one good memory that you have about your relationship."

Ann shrugged and picked at the fuzz on the blanket.

"Okay, tell me how you met," Casey prodded her.

"We met in a courtroom," Ann mumbled, remembering the first time that she had seen Kathy. The dark black suit. That was what had first caught Ann's attention. Kathy had been clad in the dark suit along with a gray blouse and a single strand of pearls. Ann was wearing a crème suit with a pale green blouse. The colors of good and evil had made Ann grin as she set her briefcase on the prosecution's table. Kathy's client had been charged with the sale of an illegal substance and the trial had dragged on for several days. Ann had grown to appreciate the woman's choice of clothing, always dark, and very classy. But it had been Kathy's air of confidence that had been the major attraction. Little did she know that the attraction was mutual. After the battle was over, Kathy asked her if she would like to discuss the case over drinks. Ann suggested the lesbian bar around the corner and was thrilled when Kathy accepted the location. That was the night of new beginnings for them. In contrast, Kathy's client was sent to prison for life under the Three Strikes law in California.

"A courtroom?" Casey asked in confusion.

Lost in the memory, Ann looked over at Casey. "Have we never talked about my life back in San Francisco? You do know that writing is just a hobby for me, don't you?"

Casey looked surprised and shrugged. "I thought you wrote for a living."

Ann laughed and shook her head. "I'm an attorney."

Casey was clearly taken aback by the statement. "Like someone who puts away the bad guys?"

"Well, I used to be a prosecutor. Now, I'm more like someone who helps people out of tax problems. I'm a tax attorney."

"And Kathy?" Casey asked.

"Kathy's still a criminal defense lawyer. She defends the bad guys," Ann replied.

Ann relayed the story of their meeting and then about how their relationship had began struggling lately because of Kathy's mood swings. Getting tired of her own sob story, Ann turned back to her work.

Casey lay on her back with her eyes closed, enjoying the peacefulness of the day. All she could hear was the sound of the seagulls and the soft tapping of Ann's fingers on the keyboard. Feeling the breeze turning cooler, she looked at her watch. The sun would be setting soon. Casey sighed. Their day was coming to an end. She felt her stomach twinge with hunger. Suddenly she had an idea that would extend their time together.

"Hey," she said as she looked up at Ann. "Can I talk you into dinner? I know this great place within walking distance."

Ann finished typing, looked down at Casey and shrugged. "I don't know. I still have work to do."

Casey rolled over and propped herself up on her elbows. Smiling, she knew exactly how to sway Ann's decision. "They have great lobster!"

Ann closed her eyes and smiled in a way that Casey knew her ploy had worked. "You know that I can't turn down lobster. That would be like you giving up cigarettes."

Casey gave her a sly look.

Finally it dawned on Ann. "Wait a minute. I haven't seen you smoke all day!" she exclaimed.

"It was a nasty habit." Oddly enough, she hadn't craved one since her first cup of coffee that morning.

"This doesn't mean that I have to give up lobster, does it?"

Casey laughed as she stood and offered her hand to Ann. "Come on. Let's go eat."

Ann closed her laptop and allowed Casey to pull her up. They walked to the car and dropped off the computer and bags in the trunk.

"Okay, which way to the lobster?" Ann asked.

"Just down the beach," Casey said and motioned for Ann to follow.

Casey loved the feel of the sand between her toes. She had always wanted to live next to the ocean, but she thought the prices of the homes were ridiculous. Especially for a single person . . . maybe someday when she had a family. This thought brought her back to the woman walking beside her. A writer, screenwriter and an attorney. Would Ann ever have time for a family? Casey smiled to herself. Ann would make a great mother. She hoped that she herself also would, someday. They could have a nice life together. Just then Kathy's face flashed into her daydream, shocking her back to reality. She remembered Ann saying, *This relationship isn't going to be a problem for you, is it?* Well, if it was a friend Ann wanted, then Casey was going to be the best damn friend she'd ever had. As Casey began climbing the stairs up to the restaurant, she decided to put away her thoughts and enjoy the moment.

They got settled and ordered a nice bottle of white wine. Ann looked across the table at Casey and smiled.

"What?" Casey asked, having already decided on the grilled halibut.

Ann put her chin in her hand and gazed at her. "You have the most beautiful smile."

Casey felt her body heating up, starting with her face and heading downward. She looked across the table into Ann's green eyes. "Be careful. I may think that you're flirting with me."

Ann smiled mischievously. "Hmm..must be the wine."

"Well, then, no more wine for you!" Casey said as she pulled Ann's wineglass to her side of the table.

"Can I ask you something?" Ann asked as she placed her elbows on the table. "Why are you giving me the full court press?"

Casey put down her glass of wine and looked at her. "What do you mean?"

"You know exactly what I mean." Ann leaned back in her chair and crossed her arms. "I've already told you that all we're ever going to be is friends. So why are you still hanging around with me?"

Casey was confused. She'd really been trying to respect Ann's terms. "Is it so hard to believe that I may just want you as a friend?"

"I'm sure you have plenty of friends," Ann shot back, still on the offense.

"None like you."

Ann squinted as she tried to read Casey's face. "I'm not quite sure how to take that. Can I ask you how I'm different?"

Casey shrugged and finished her sip of wine. "You actually laugh at my jokes." Then, suspiciously, she asked, "Unless you're just trying to be polite?"

Ann smiled and shook her head.

Casey concentrated on tracing the droplets of water sliding down her glass. "Most of my friends don't actually get my sense of humor." It had been that way since grade school. She glanced up. "Do you know what I mean?"

Ann grinned. "I know exactly what you mean. Most of the time Kathy asks me, 'Is that supposed to be funny?'"

"And you treat me like a normal person. A lot of my so-called friends, even my best friend, Pam, I don't know . . . They just treat me like I'm some special person."

"You are a special person."

"Yeah, so, you're an attorney, a writer and now a screenwriter. You make me feel like I've done nothing with my life," Casey replied.

"How can you say that? You touch more people with one movie than I could in my entire lifetime."

"Thank you, but I'm not quite sure just how deeply I touch them." Casey smiled.

"Don't fool yourself, Casey. Entertainment provides an escape. That's how I feel about my books. I mean, writing is difficult, but it isn't rocket science. I don't take it too seriously. I just want people to be able to escape into another world . . . if only for a few hundred pages. It's even an escape for me to write them."

"Hmm . . . and what is Ann Covington escaping from?"

"I'm just like everyone else. I need an escape from . . . a lot of things. You must need an escape too if you've read my books."

Casey was still pondering Ann's statement when their food arrived. Her plate of fish, rice and steamed asparagus looked and smelled wonderful. She found it hard to even look at Ann's dinner. It had always bothered her the way that they cooked the live lobster, and then the way it was eaten. Pulling the body apart with your fingers was so primitive. Fortunately, upon finally lifting her gaze, she observed the graceful way that Ann accomplished the task. It really didn't seem that disgusting at all.

Ann moaned with delight upon tasting her first bite. When a bit of melted butter trickled down chin, she quickly wiped it away. She took a few more bites before the conversation began again.

"So your family must be proud with all that you've accomplished."

Ann lowered her gaze and smoothed away the condensation that had developed on her water glass. "I don't have a family . . . other than Kathy . . . and her family."

"I'm sorry, Ann. When did you lose them?" Casey asked as she took another forkful of rice.

"The moment I came out. They pretty much disowned me, right then and there," she said, still concentrating on the glass before her.

"Now I'm really sorry. Was it just your parents . . . or siblings too?"

"I was an only child. The key word being *was*." Ann looked up to meet Casey's gaze. "Can you believe parents who disown their only child . . ."

Casey shook her head in disbelief. "No. I can't." She paused, trying to imagine life without her family. "How long has it been? Have you tried to contact them?"

"It's been twelve years. And yes, I sent them several notes. They all came back unopened." Ann shrugged. "Twelve years and it still hurts. Silly, isn't it?"

Casey reached out and touched her hand. "No. It's not silly at all. I can't even imagine it."

"Are you close with your family?" Ann asked, swirling her next bite in the butter.

"Very." Casey answered. "Well, as close as I'll let them. I've always been kind of a loner. My family has come to accept it. Kind of a 'don't ask, don't tell' policy. But I love them very much."

"So, how many in your family?" Ann reached across the table and snagged a stalk of asparagus from Casey's plate.

Casey slid her plate closer to the center of the table. "My mother died several years ago—breast cancer—but my dad remarried last year. She's a wonderful woman. I'm glad he found her. I have an older sister, Carol—she's an interior designer—and her husband, Phil, and their two kids, Nicole and Peter. Then there's my younger brother, Tony. He's one of those computer geniuses, been dating Rebecca forever. And me, the middle child, the wild and rebellious one."

"And they know that you're a lesbian?"

Casey laughed. "Yes. How could they not know? I am glad that I told them before it was public knowledge, though. They're pretty good about the whole thing . . . they love to tease me."

"Do they all live around here?" Ann cracked another lobster claw.

"Yeah, within about a ten-mile radius of my house. That's why I bought the house that I did. My family calls it 'within shouting distance.' It's really nice to be able to depend on someone being close if you need them."

"I have the feeling that you don't really need anyone that often." Ann smiled.

Casey nodded as she dabbed her mouth with her napkin. "You're right. That 'don't ask, don't tell' policy kind of flips around to the 'what they don't know won't hurt them' policy for me."

"So, they never know if you're seeing someone special?"

"Someone special?" Casey nearly choked. "I only seem to attract the bimbos."

"Are you sure you attract them?" Ann asked, finishing up her lobster. "Maybe that's all you look for."

"Hmm . . . you think that you have me all figured out, don't you?"

"Quite the contrary. I can't figure you out at all," Ann replied. "Why don't you try women with beauty and brains? There are attractive smart women, you know."

"Well, just because I may find them attractive doesn't necessarily mean that they'll find me attractive."

"What woman in her right mind wouldn't find you attractive?"

"You."

"I never said that I didn't find you attractive." Ann wiped her hands roughly with her napkin.

"But you won't—"

"Casey, I'm a married woman. Married women don't fool around. At least that's my belief." She set her plate toward the end of the table.

"I understand. It's just that I find you so beautiful and intellectually stimulating, I like being around you."

"And I feel the same for you," Ann confided as she twisted the napkin before her. "But I treasure my marriage, and so, friends we'll have to be."

"Well, you certainly have a friend in me." Casey smiled.

Suddenly, the waiter broke into their conversation. "Have room for dessert, ladies?"

Casey glanced at Ann. "You know, you're looking pretty tired. Are you ready to go?"

Ann nodded and gave instructions to the waiter to bring the bill. There was a small argument regarding who should pay the tab, but Casey won out, and they were on their way shortly.

The traffic was heavier than in the morning but Casey was glad that they had stayed for dinner and missed the Saturday evening rush into town. Her SUV was more than comfortable but she hated being trapped between hundreds of cars for any length of time and only gaining inches toward her destination. She turned the radio up to sing along with a favorite song and, surprised, found that Ann also knew all of the words. The tunes made the drive seem quicker than usual.

"You don't have to walk me to my door, Casey. I am a grown woman," Ann said as they both got out of the car at the hotel.

"Yes, well, it is my belief that you always walk a beautiful woman to her door."

They rode the elevator in silence. Ann opened her door, then turned to give Casey a hug.

She squeezed back. "Good night, Ann. Sweet dreams."

Chapter Six

Casey joined Pam and Diane at the table on the patio. The three (and sometimes more) had brunch every Sunday at the Yellow Rose Café on the outskirts of Beverly Hills. The well shaded street was lined with specialty shops including antique stores that the women had wandered through on occasion after breakfast.

Pam broke into a wide grin. "So . . . how was last night?" she asked impatiently.

Confused, Casey frowned at her.

"Last night? With Amy?" Pam asked as if her question was obvious.

Casey looked down at the menu. "I canceled on her."

Pam purposely dropped her glass to the table. "What? You canceled on the woman who has been lusting after you for weeks?"

Casey did not look up from her menu. "Yeah, well, I was with Ann, and I kind of lost track of time."

Pam looked at Diane and pulled out a cigarette. She handed the pack to Casey as she fished for her lighter.

Casey looked at the pack. "No, thanks. I'm trying to quit."

Pam almost burned her hand with the flame. "Okay. Who are you and what have you done with Casey?"

"Ha ha," Casey remarked with sarcasm. "You're just jealous because I have a new friend."

Diane and Pam both rolled their eyes. Pam said dismissively, "Friend. Yeah, right."

"Okay, we're dropping this discussion right now," Casey declared as she took her mimosa from the waitress. She looked up. "Hi, Jenny! I'm so glad you're off pregnancy leave. That other waitress had a stick up her butt."

"Yes, she had a few things to say about you too." Jenny laughed. "Do you want your regular?"

"Please." As soon as Jenny left, Casey leaned in and asked, "Do you guys think I'm a bitch?"

The other two women laughed.

"No, I'm serious. Do I have the reputation of being a bitch?"

Pam thought for a moment, then glanced at Diane. "You can be bitchy at times," Pam began softly, "but . . . you are also a true friend and would give your shirt off your back to help someone."

Casey grimaced. "I never thought I was bitchy . . . a little brash at times . . . I don't ask for outlandish things on the set . . ."

"Yes, but if they're not exactly as you asked, that's when hell breaks loose," Diane said.

Casey sank back in her chair and all she could hear were the conversations at the other tables for several minutes. The waitress brought her plate of Belgium waffles with strawberries and whipped cream, but Casey wasn't that hungry anymore.

"Hey, when did this get to be such a deep conversation?" Pam said as she took a bite of bacon. She was clearly trying to lighten the mood. "Sunday is fun day! What are you doing after this?"

"I'm going to try and do some repairs on my house." Casey pushed her fingers through her hair. "I thought I might try and put up the ceiling fan today."

"That's what you get for buying a fixer-upper." Diane dragged her forkful of French toast through the syrup on her plate.

"So I guess you two won't be helping me this afternoon?" She dabbed her spoon in the whipped cream and licked it off.

"Oh, well, we would, but . . . I have to wash my hair . . . .I'm leaving the country . . . I'm feeling sick . . ." Pam gave the regular excuses.

The three women finished their brunch and went their separate ways.

Ten minutes into her project, Casey realized that the instructions she was reading weren't sinking in. She knew the reason why. Ann was all she could think of. She decided to take a break and phone her.

"Good morning . . . uh . . . afternoon, Ann," Casey said cheerily.

"Hey, Casey. You sound happy."

"Hmm . . . must have been that mimosa." Casey chuckled. "I had to have something to drink to get my courage up to hang up my kitchen ceiling fan this afternoon."

"Have you ever hung a ceiling fan before?" Ann asked hesitantly.

"Nope," Casey admitted. "But how hard could it be? Just putting a couple of wires together, right?"

"Umm . . . yes, there is a little more to it," Ann said.

"So, I guess that you've had experience? 'Cause if you have, I'm swinging by to pick you up right now."

Ann moaned. "I'll be ready."

An hour later, the two of them were standing in Casey's kitchen, the instructions laid out on the kitchen table.

"I know that you don't want any help, but I believe if you connect those two wires you're holding, you will most probably have a very big fire on your hands."

Casey stopped and studied the directions again. Looking down, she sighed as she selected a different set of wires and began twisting. "So you're a writer, a lawyer and now an electrician. Is there anything you're not good at?"

Ann smiled at her teasingly. "I haven't had any complaints."

"I do believe that's a line from the script," Casey commented.

"Well, you asked me the other day if there were any common traits between me and my two women characters, and that's one—I haven't had any complaints."

"Stop teasing me and hand me that Phillips screwdriver!" Casey chuckled.

Ann arrived back at her hotel room as the telephone rang. She tripped twice before grabbing the receiver.

"Hello?" She was panting.

"Ann? What are you doing?" It was Kathy.

"Hi, babe." She took a deep breath. "I was just getting in. I was over at Casey's house."

"Mm-hmm. What were you doing over there? It seems like you two have been spending a lot of time together."

"Oh, Kath, she's just been so nice to me, keeping me company and all. She's fixing up her house a bit. I was helping her with the ceiling fan. She almost put the red and the yellow wires together . . ."

"You're babbling," Kathy said coldly.

"I'm . . . I'm sorry. I . . . you . . . asked me what I was doing," Ann stammered. Several seconds of silence followed. "Are you feeling okay?"

Kathy sniffled. "I'm okay. I'm just so tired."

"Honey, you're just working yourself to death. You need to have some rest. Take some time off. Come down here. You can lie out on the beach, get some sun . . ."

"We both know that I can't do that. I have a whole list of people whose lives are in my hands. I can't just take off, on any whimsy, like you, and fool around—"

"Excuse me," Ann cut in. "I am not just down here fooling around. I'm working ten to twelve hours a day—"

"Okay, okay." Kathy cooled down. "I'm sorry I insinuated that you weren't working." She said calmly, "I'm going to let you go.

We're both tired and irritable. We'll talk tomorrow, okay? I love you."

"I love you too," Ann softly said. "And Casey and I are just friends, okay?"

"I know. She's just some silly actress. I'm not worried."

"You're still coming next weekend, aren't you? I miss you."

"I'm still going to try. Depends on how this week goes. I'll call you tomorrow. 'Bye."

Ann heard the click of the receiver but didn't think of replacing hers. What just went on? She just stood there, receiver in hand, replaying the conversation in her head. It was a nice conversation, then a bad conversation, then an apology, then she blew her off. This job of hers, Ann thought, must be driving her crazy.

Chapter Seven

Ann closed her magazine and shut her eyes. Kathy's plane was a little late and Ann used the time to try and relax in case Kathy was in one of her "moods." It had been a long week, full of casting changes, set reworking and script readings. The only thing that had saved her was the time she spent with Casey. Each evening they had shared dinner, ran lines and watched television. The hotel suite was feeling like home.

Hearing the flight notice, she stood and stretched. Ann caught Kathy's figure as she walked into the baggage claim area. The smile on Kathy's face made Ann feel more at ease, and they hugged as if there had never been a quarrel. Ann picked up Kathy's carry-on and they headed toward the car.

"It's January and it's warm here. It was so cold back home," Kathy commented.

"Yeah, it's been beautiful here," Ann said. *Great*, she thought, *weather talk*.

"Have you had dinner yet?" Kathy asked. "I'm starved."

"No, I was waiting for you. Where do you want to go?"

"If you don't mind, can we just pick something up or order room service?"

"No problem." Ann tried to hide her disappointment. "You must be tired, huh?"

"You have no idea. But you and a good night's sleep is just what the doctor ordered."

Ann smiled, heartened by Kathy's last statement. Tonight was going to be fine.

Kathy had fallen asleep after dinner and had slept most of the next day, but Ann didn't mind. At least they weren't arguing. Ann used the time to catch up on work but her concentration was weak. She tried to call Casey but had only reached her voice mail. Casey had told her that she would be doing yard work all day. At five o'clock, Ann had to wake Kathy. They'd agreed to meet Leslie, Debbie and Casey for dinner to wind down from the long week. Ann assured her it would be an early night.

"So, how are the renovations coming along, Casey?" Leslie asked after their drink and appetizer orders had been taken.

"Slowly." Casey sighed.

"I still wish that you could knock out that one wall." Debbie had mentioned she'd taken a tour of Casey's house when she dropped off the business card of a handyman they used.

"I know, but Ann thinks that it's a supporting wall . . ."

Kathy laughed. "I can't believe she still remembers anything from being with Tyler." As Ann groaned inwardly, Kathy explained, "Tyler was a woman carpenter Ann dated before we met. I could've never competed with her muscles. It's a good thing that my intellect appealed to Ann more than Tyler's brawn." She paused, glancing pointedly at Casey. "You know, the way that your body is toned right now, you remind me a lot of Tyler. If you had a college degree, I'd have to worry about Ann spending so much time with you."

Ann cringed as she saw an argument brewing. She was right. Casey wasn't going to sit there and take Kathy's arrogance.

"I do have a college degree," Casey stated matter-of-factly.

Kathy smiled. "Well, I don't really count a degree in theatrical arts as intellectual."

Casey smiled back. "My degree is in political science."

"You'd better quit while you're still standing, dear." Ann shook her head. Kathy had picked the wrong group for this discussion. She was glad that Casey was holding her own.

"No, Ann, let Kathy explain herself." Leslie raised her voice. "We both have degrees in theatrical arts, Kathy. Are you trying to say that you hold yourself above us?"

Casey gestured for them to stop. "Guys, I think the statement was more of a personal attack on me. I'm sure she didn't mean anything by it."

The drinks arrived and each woman took a gulp as if arming herself for a fight.

"I didn't mean to step on any toes." Kathy tried to backpedal. "I don't think that I'm any better than you. I just was trying to say that someone with, say, a law degree, probably appeals more to someone else with a law degree . . . you know, intellectually."

"Of course, we understand. We have trouble communicating at all with Ann. Casey usually has to translate the conversation into simple English for us," Leslie said sarcastically.

Kathy smirked and returned her attention to Casey. "Ann never mentioned that you had a degree in political science. What school?"

"Berkeley."

Kathy seemed impressed, then glared at Ann. "Maybe I should be a little more worried about you two, huh?" Looking back at Casey, she started in again. "Of course, why would you want to be involved with Ann? You could have anyone."

"I think you've forgotten, Kathy. Ann is a very beautiful, intelligent woman." Casey raised her glass to Ann.

"I haven't forgotten," Kathy said. "But I do think that you better not look any closer at my wife."

"Is that a threat?"

"You bet it is. I'm tired of all this talk. Ann, let's go home." Kathy wiped her mouth with the napkin and pushed back her chair.

"Kathy! We haven't even had the appetizers yet!" Ann argued.

"I'm going now. Are you coming with me or not?" Kathy stalked out of the room.

Ann just shook her head in disbelief and downed the rest of her wine.

Casey grabbed Ann's arm. "Damn it, Ann! Why do you let her treat you like that?"

"Drop it, Casey," Ann replied sternly.

"No. I'm sorry. I can't drop it. I can't stand to see someone that I care about repeatedly slapped in the face like that. Why, Ann? Why do you take it?"

"You wouldn't understand."

"Then try to explain it to me." Casey was clearly frustrated.

"Look, Casey, how long was your longest relationship . . . two weeks? So you wouldn't understand that after ten years with someone, you don't just walk away because one of you has a bad spell."

"Okay. I can understand that. But tell me, Ann, when do you realize that it isn't just a bad spell . . . but just a bad relationship?"

Ann scooted out her chair, stood and threw her napkin on the table. "Maybe it is time for me to leave after all."

Stung, Casey did not lift her gaze but rather concentrated on swirling the wine in her glass. Finally she looked up at Leslie and Debbie still sitting at the table. "Do you think she left because I planted a seed, or because I just totally overstepped my bounds?"

"You didn't say anything that we haven't wanted to say for months now," Debbie answered. "But yes, we felt like it wasn't really our place to say—"

"Ann was right," Leslie broke in. "We don't know that Kathy isn't just going through a bad spell. Kathy may just be incredibly lonely . . . or jealous of Ann."

Casey stared at her glass for a few moments, then made a decision. "Excuse me for a minute, guys."

She dialed Ann's cell number as she made her way out to the lobby. She was just about to give up when she finally heard Ann's voice.

"What?" Ann practically yelled into the phone.

"I'm sorry," Casey said softly. Not receiving a response, she continued, "I stepped over the line."

"Yes, you did," Ann said a little more calmly.

"Forgive me?" Casey asked.

"Only if you promise never to bring up the subject again."

Casey paused, then conceded, "Okay. Scout's honor."

Ann suddenly laughed. "Would that be Boy Scouts or Girl Scouts?"

"So, should I be worried about you and Casey?" Kathy asked as Ann slid in between the sheets.

Ann lay her head down on the pillow right beside Kathy's. She faced her and caressed the soft skin on her cheek. "Babe, I hope you're not serious."

Kathy ran her fingers through Ann's hair. "If you tell me there's nothing to worry about, then I won't worry."

"Don't worry then," Ann whispered into her ear.

Kathy touched the ring on Ann's hand. "Just remember what this symbolizes."

"Our love, promises made . . . I belong to you," Ann said softly.

"I don't like that word *belong*. It sounds like we own each other or something."

"Don't be silly. You know that I didn't mean it like that."

"Well, sometimes I kind of think that you see it that way. But it doesn't, not literally, because then you wouldn't do anything that I didn't want you to do."

Ann cleared her throat. "Excuse me. It's not like I have to ask you for permission. I ask you to consult with me about things, just like I consult with you. It's what couples do."

"The point is, you do things that I don't want you to do," Kathy said sharply.

"I generally try not to. Is there an example you can give me?" Ann remained calm.

"My God, Ann! We're living it right now," Kathy said with irritation. "I didn't want you to come to L.A. I didn't want you living here. I didn't want to fly down here all the time. I didn't want any of it."

"But, Kathy . . . this was a once-in-a-lifetime opportunity for me!" Ann cried out.

"Yeah, well." Kathy turned over abruptly. "It's not keeping my bed warm at night. Maybe you're fine with it because your bed is being kept warm with someone else."

Ann groaned and rolled over to the other side of the bed. She tossed and turned for hours before she finally got up and took a sleeping pill. Funny, she'd been alone in a strange city for weeks now, but she hadn't had to take any kind of sleep aid until tonight.

Ann awoke to the sound of the telephone ringing. Rolling over, she grabbed the receiver before it could make the shrill sound again. She looked at the clock, nine a.m.

"Ann Covington," she said into the receiver. She had learned to identify herself quickly because the hotel was forever ringing the wrong room. The voice she heard on the other end was Suzie, her administrative assistant at her office in San Francisco. She hoped that this wasn't about work; after all it was Sunday.

"Hi, Ann. Look, I've tried to take care of this matter the best that I could, plus I've enlisted some of your associates, but we just can't take care of it. I'm afraid you'll have to." Suzie's words came spilling out like *supercalifragilisticexpialidosis*.

Ann laughed. "Okay, maybe a bit more slowly this time. Now, what is it that only I can take care of?"

Suzie took a deep breath and let her words out slowly this time. "Mr. Garland, from the Internal Revenue Service, will not speak with anyone but you."

"Hmm . . . Mr. Garland . . ." Ann tried to connect the agent with one of her clients. "Ah, the Zinmans' case."

"Yes. He said something about the deadline for the Offer in Compromise being last week."

"And did you look in the Zinmans' file?"

Suzie sighed. "I found the document that you forwarded to him, but he won't talk to anyone else in this office besides you. Only you are listed on the Power of Attorney form. Blah, blah, blah."

Ann raised herself to a sitting position. "Well, I can't talk to him without the file in front of me, and it's too thick to fax. I'll just hop on a plane today. I have some other matters to take care of at the office, so this will just be first on the list."

Kathy awoke around eleven as Ann was packing her suitcase. Rubbing her eyes, she asked, "Why are you packing?" She sighed. "I'm sorry about last night. Don't go home just because I don't want you to be here."

Ann, still upset from last night's conversation, huffed, "Like I would leave for that reason. Suzie called me this morning. She needs me back at the office. I called and got a seat on the flight that you're taking later."

"Oh, yes. Suzie calls and you go running," Kathy muttered.

Ann turned around and placed her hands on her hips. "What, now I'm having an affair with Suzie too?" She ran her fingers through her hair. "Like if your work came calling, you wouldn't run off as fast as you could."

"Yeah, well, I'd rather be there most of the time."

Ann's eyes welled with tears. She turned away, listening while Kathy slammed into the bathroom.

Ann stumbled into the living room and sank down on the couch. Her head in her hands, she wrestled with her situation. She knew that Kathy was just burnt out. And now she knew that Kathy didn't agree with her decision to be in L.A. *Just give her some space*, she said to herself. *Just give her some space.*

Kathy was still in the shower when Ann called Leslie. She left a message on her voice mail. "Hi, Leslie. Hey, I know this is short notice, but I've got to go back home for a few days. Work needs me. So, give me a call when you get this message." She hung up and began dialing again.

"Hello." Casey was gasping.

"Casey, are you okay?"

Casey slowed her breathing. "Yeah, I had to run for the phone. I'm trying to paint the spare room. Wanna help?"

"I'm sorry. I would if I could but—"

"I know, I know. Kathy is there," Casey said bitterly.

"Yes, but it's actually because I need to go back to Frisco for a few days. I need to get some work done."

It was so quiet on the other end of the line, Ann thought that they had been disconnected.

"Casey?"

"Uh . . . I'm sorry . . . When are you leaving?" Casey asked. Ann thought she detected a quiver in her voice.

"This afternoon. I caught a seat on Kathy's flight." Ann waited for a response, but when she received none, she continued, "I just wanted you to know. I didn't want you to think that I just went away on a whim."

"First, I find it hard to believe you do anything on a whim." Casey chuckled. Then in a more somber voice, she added, "Thank you for telling me. What will I do with my nights?"

This time Ann laughed. "I'm sure you'll find something to do. Take a look into your little black book."

"Hey, I resent that. I don't have a little black book!" Casey said. It was probably blue, Ann thought. "So . . . call me when you get back? Or before, if you need to talk or anything."

"You know I will, Case." Ann felt a little twinge of sadness. "Have a great week."

"You too."

Chapter Eight

"Hey, you're in early!" Suzie stuck her head into Ann's office. Ann had come in early, four a.m. to be exact. She and Kathy had gotten home around six p.m. Sunday night but were already fighting when they walked in the door. Kathy went to her office immediately. Ann optimistically waited up for Kathy to come home. At four a.m. Ann gave up and retreated to her office too.

"Good to see you, Suzie." Ann gave her a heartfelt hug. "Thank you so much for keeping things up here. You're doing a great job."

"Well, I wanted to help out." Suzie lay her hand playfully on her own forehead. "Maybe you'll remember me when you make it big."

Ann laughed. "I could never forget you, dahling."

Both were brought back to reality when Suzie's phone rang at her desk. "Can I get you anything?" Suzie asked quickly as she backed out of Ann's office. Ann shook her head as her office door shut.

The day went by quickly. She resolved the matter with "Mr. Cranky," as she thought of him, at the IRS and informed her clients that their offer had been accepted. Before she knew it, the office was shutting down for the day. She dialed Kathy's number, but her voice mail answered.

"Hi, Kath. It's me. I was just wondering if you had time for dinner with me tonight. Give me a call when you get this message."

Ann walked out to Suzie's desk to drop off some paperwork. Suzie was pulling on her jacket, preparing to leave.

"So, is Kathy excited to have you back at home for a few days?" Suzie asked.

"I'm not sure that it really matters to her."

Suzie sighed. "Is she still being moody?"

Ann nodded, then, hearing her direct line ringing, said good night and jogged to the phone.

"Ann Covington."

"Hey, babe." Kathy's voice was soft and calm. "I'd like to go and relax for a while. How about meeting me at The Greenhouse in about half an hour?"

"Sounds great. I'll see you there." Ann was pleasantly surprised. She hung up and actually began humming.

Walking into The Greenhouse, Ann felt all tension drain from her body. She loved this place, the greenery hanging from the lattice-like ceiling and walls. There was a cool breeze . . . was it from open windows, or from the ceiling fans circling slowly? She looked around for Kathy but was seated without her. Sinking back into the plush oversized chair, the waiter took her drink order. She dared not order for Kathy—who knew what she would want—and Ann didn't want it to start an argument.

Ann had just closed her eyes when she heard the familiar voice. Before she opened her eyes, she tried to gauge Kathy's mood: happy, relaxed, tired. Yes, definitely tired. She just about fainted when she felt lips on her face. Soft kisses, one at a time on each eyelid. She slowly opened her eyes. Kathy was placing a final kiss on her lips.

"You are still the most beautiful woman I've ever seen," Kathy whispered.

Ann didn't quite know what to do. She was paralyzed. Who was this woman, and what had they done with Kathy? Kathy sank into the chair opposite Ann and sighed.

"I . . . didn't order . . . anything for you," Ann stuttered. "I . . . wasn't sure . . ."

Kathy smiled. "That's okay. I'm really not sure what I want yet. Are you having your usual?"

Ann nodded as she sipped from her glass of white chardonnay. The waiter approached.

"Martini, dirty, and double the olives," Kathy said decisively.

The waiter nodded in understanding and whisked away. Kathy reached across the table for Ann's hand. Ann clasped her hand, still believing that this was another woman sitting across from her.

"I'm sorry for last night. Your first night at home and we went and screwed it up." Kathy gently rubbed Ann's hand.

"I'm sorry too," Ann said, although she really had no reason to apologize. It was Kathy who had gotten upset over something petty, and Kathy who'd stormed out. It was flat out Kathy's fault.

The waiter came back to the table with Kathy's drink and reeled off the specials in a memorized fashion. He then left to give them a few minutes.

"Have you looked at the menu yet?" Kathy asked as she opened her menu.

Ann shook her head and proceeded to read the listings. Each dish sounded savory, but she selected the broiled salmon with garlic and mushroom glaze and relayed her choice to Kathy.

"Wow, I would've bet that you would have chosen the lobster special," Kathy said, still looking at the menu.

"Casey took me to a place down on the beach that had incredible lobster. I was afraid if it wasn't as good here that I'd be really disappointed." The words left Ann's mouth without her brain being consulted. As soon as they were out she realized that she had brought up Casey. She felt a lump form in her stomach. She just sat there waiting for a backlash and took a deep breath when Kathy spoke.

"Well, you'll have to take me there one of these times, honey. You know I love lobster almost as much as you do."

Ann waited . . . and waited. But that was it. No harsh words. No anger. Kathy was an alien.

The waiter arrived back at their table as soon as the menus were set on the table. Ann ordered her dish and Kathy ordered the grilled scampi with white wine sauce. Dinner was served. The women commented on how delicious each entrée was and tasted forkfuls across the white linen tablecloth. The conversation was light and amusing. Ann felt like she was floating on a cloud.

"Are you going back to work?" Ann asked gingerly.

"No. Tonight is about us. Work will be there tomorrow."

It was eleven o'clock by the time they walked in the door to their apartment. Ann surveyed their home through the dim light as they made their way into the bedroom. They both undressed and began taking their makeup off in front of the bathroom mirror. Ann finished first.

"Go ahead and get into bed. I'll just be a minute," Kathy said to Ann's reflection.

Ann nodded and went into the bedroom. Kathy closed the door to the bathroom behind her. Folding the comforter back, Ann heard the slamming of drawers and cabinets coming from the bathroom. Then the swearing started.

"Shit!"

"What's the matter?" Ann called out.

"Uhhh . . . I'm out of this special lotion for my face!" Kathy answered, followed by more opening and slamming of drawers and cabinet doors. Finally she emerged and slid into bed. Ann nestled up to her.

Kathy rolled over. "You know that I can't stand to have you right next to me."

"I'm sorry." Ann moved away. "So what's this new lotion your using?"

"Just something for my oily skin," Kathy mumbled.

"What's it called?"

"I can't think of the name right now."

"You got so upset over something you can't even remember the name of?"

"Look, I can't remember everything. I've got a full plate right now."

"I was just thinking that I could try and pick some up tomorrow," Ann said softly through the dark.

"Well, then, I'll tell you tomorrow."

"You'll probably leave earlier than me."

"Just drop it, Ann! Jeez!"

"Why are you getting so irritated?" Ann asked.

"God. At least when you're gone I don't have to play twenty questions!" Kathy scooted out of the bed, stood staring down at her and proceeded to drag her hands fiercely through her hair. "I'm going to the office!" she blurted out. She pulled on her clothes while she began muttering, "I didn't have time to lollygag about all evening. What was I thinking?"

"Kathy? Kathy!" Ann tried repeatedly to get her attention. She watched as Kathy dashed around the room getting dressed. It felt unreal.

Finally Kathy looked at her. "I can't just drop everything when you decide to drop into town, you know!" She stomped out of the room, grabbed her keys and slammed the front door.

Ann felt the air whoosh from her lungs. She fell back onto her pillow. The alien was gone.

Finally asleep at one a.m., Ann tossed and turned and dreamed. Her mind took her back to Los Angeles . . . she was lying in Casey's arms, and they were comfortable in their silence. She closed her eyes, but when she opened them, she found herself wrapped in Kathy's arms. And then Kathy spoke, but it wasn't her voice but a voice out of a horror movie, deep and angry. She closed her eyes again, opening them again when she was back with Casey, but then Kathy's monster voice came from Casey's lips. Just as abruptly, Kathy's voice suddenly turned calm and soothing.

Ann awoke to the sound of Kathy's voice on the answering machine. She looked at the clock, three a.m.

"I'm sure you're asleep—"

Grabbing for the phone, Ann interrupted her. "No, I'm not asleep."

Kathy sighed on the other end. "You should be asleep. Asleep and dreaming sweet things."

"Yes, well . . ."

"I know. I upset you and so you haven't been able to relax." Kathy sounded cool and composed. "God, Ann, why do you stay with me? Why do you put up with my shit?"

Ann was silent for a moment. "Because I love you."

"I love you too, but sometimes I don't feel like I know you anymore."

"I don't feel like I know you anymore either. You have these mood swings that come out of nowhere."

"Well, I'm just so overloaded with work . . ." Kathy began to take the defensive.

"We both work hard, Kath . . ."

"I'm sorry, I know we have busy lives." Kathy paused, then continued, "I'm going to try and spend more time on 'us.' Okay?"

Ann felt a sense of relief. "Okay, baby. I would love that." Her body became heavy and she knew that she would be able to sleep well now. "I'm going to try and get some sleep now. Are you coming home?"

"No, I'm not that tired. I have this couch in my office if I need to nap."

"Good night then."

"Sleep well," Kathy whispered, then hung up.

Ann placed the cordless phone on her bedside table, rolled over and slept soundly the rest of the night.

Chapter Nine

"Ann, do you want to take a call from a Casey Duncan?" Suzie's voice came over the intercom.

"Yes, I'll speak with her," Ann replied with a smile. "Ann Covington."

"Hey, girl. Are you whipping the IRS into shape?" Casey's cheery voice came over the line.

Ann laughed. "Not today. Today I'm working on trying to alleviate the capital gains on a sales transaction."

Casey made a sound like she was snoring. "Such exciting work. How's everything else going up there?"

"Oh, okay, I guess."

"So, when are you coming back?" Casey asked her.

"I'm not sure. I can tie up work in a couple of days."

"Great!"

"Yeah, but Kathy and I need to spend some time together." Ann relayed the problems that she and Kathy had been having and that Kathy wanted to spend some time on just the two of them.

"Yes, relationships come first." Casey was obviously trying not to sound disappointed.

"I'll call you as soon as I know when I'm returning, okay?" Ann hung up and immediately dialed Kathy's number. Kathy was in court and so her voice mail would have to do. "Hi, it's me. Just wanted to know what we're doing for dinner tonight. You said you wanted to spend some time on 'us,' so I hoped we'd have some time together. Give me a call, okay? Love ya!"

Ann filled her afternoon with research. Boring research. But it had to be done. She was ready to call it a day at six o'clock. Several calls had come through but none had been from Kathy. Ann dialed her number, just to get her voice mail again.

"Hi, babe. I left a message earlier. Just wondering if we are going to eat together. I'm leaving the office now, so call my cell phone." Ann sang her parting words: "I'm getting pretty hungry!"

It was nine o'clock when she finally heard from Kathy. She had already given up on plans for dinner with Kathy; the Chinese food had been delivered two hours ago.

"Hi, hon." Kathy sounded wired. "I only have about five minutes to talk. I hope you've eaten already."

"Uh-huh. Chinese food. There's leftovers if you're hungry. I can start heating them up for you," Ann offered.

"Well . . . I'm not going to make it home anytime soon. Actually, I may only come home to take a shower and change."

"Kathy, when do you sleep? Did you get any sleep since I spoke with you last night?"

"I took a little nap. But I'm fine right now . . . not tired at all. I have a lot to get done before court tomorrow morning."

"Okay . . . .so . . . will you wake me when you come home?" Ann asked, not really sure of what she wanted the answer to be.

"I don't want to wake you. I'll only be there for a few minutes," Kathy stressed.

"Well, when will I get to see you again?"

"Tomorrow night, for sure. We'll rent a movie, snuggle on the couch . . ."

"Mmm . . . sounds nice. Call me tomorrow and I'll pick up a movie."

Ann heard someone walk into Kathy's office and ask her a question.

"Five minutes are up, babe. Call me tomorrow."

"Wait! You're supposed to call me—" But it was too late. The line was already disconnected. Her disappointment from tonight was overcome with hope for tomorrow night.

The morning came and went with no phone call. Ann left a voice mail for Kathy. The afternoon came and went with no return call. At seven o'clock, Ann tried her line again from home. This time an actual voice answered. Unfortunately, it wasn't Kathy's.

"Can I speak with Kathy, please?" Ann said politely.

"She's awfully busy right now. May I ask who's calling?"

"This is Ann . . . her wife." Ann kept her voice calm.

"Can you call her back later? She hasn't even been able to eat the food we ordered in."

Ann's irritation was beginning to rise. "I'd really like to talk to her now."

"Just a second, I'll ask her."

Ann listened as a hand was placed over the receiver. She only heard mumbling. Finally, the hand was removed and the voice came back.

"I'm sorry. Kathy says she's really busy and can't talk right now. She'll call you back later."

Ann didn't get a chance to say another word. The line went dead. Now she was livid. She poured herself a glass of wine, downed it and poured another. Calming down a bit, Ann began unwrapping the leftovers from the night before. For a minute, she imagined that it was Kathy's head being pushed into the microwave. She pushed the buttons and Kathy's head exploded under the heat. She smiled.

⊸⊱

The next morning, Ann got to the office two hours late and brushed past Suzie's desk without saying a simple "good morning."

Suzie followed her into her office and leaned against the closed door. "What's wrong, Ann?"

Ann sank into her chair and covered her eyes. The office lighting made her head throb more than the sun had. "She didn't call last night."

Suzie frowned. "Who didn't call last night? Kathy?"

Ann nodded slowly, then proceeded to tell Suzie about the past few days, weeks and months. "And now, the whole thing has given me a migraine."

Suzie sat down opposite her. "I'm so sorry, Ann. This should be an incredibly happy time for you right now."

"Yeah, well, it's not." Ann said, angry. There were no more tears; she had cried them all out last night and this morning. "It's just that she keeps setting me up and I keep crashing down. I must be an idiot."

"You are not an idiot. She's the idiot. My husband asks me all the time what you see in Kathy. I tell him that she used to be a different person. When I first started working for you, she called you ten times a day, dropped by just to say hi or to take you to lunch." Suzie sighed. "She's just not the same person anymore."

"Okay, enough about Kathy. Anything pressing for today?" Ann tried to focus.

"You're going to try and work with your migraine?"

"I need to finish up a couple of things."

"Well, there's nothing pressing," Suzie assured her as she stood. "You know, Ann, if at any point you don't have time to come back and work here, I wouldn't mind at all flying to Los Angeles and working out of your hotel room."

Ann smiled. If it had been anyone else making that offer, she might suspect an ulterior motive. But this was Suzie, and although Ann had always thought she was extremely cute, she was also an extremely happy heterosexual woman.

"I'll keep that in mind, Suzie. Thank you," Ann said sincerely.

Several hours went by before Ann took a break. She had just stood up and was wandering from window to window, taking in her view of the grand architecture of the buildings below her and the bay bridge behind them. The silence was interrupted by the intercom.

"Ann, it's Kathy's office." Suzie's voice was gone as quickly as it came.

Ann took a deep breath before picking up the receiver. "Ann Covington."

The voice was not Kathy's, nor was it the voice from the day before. "Yes, Ms. Covington, Kathy requested that I call you. She needs to cancel any plans that you and she may have made tonight. She asked me to express her deepest apologies about the matter."

Ann thought that she should feel angry, furious, even livid. But the feeling that overcame her instead was that of extreme sadness. Kathy couldn't even make the call herself.

"Thank you for the message. Please give a message to Kathy, would you? Please inform her that I will be leaving for Los Angeles this afternoon and that she may call me there if she ever gets a free minute." This time she hung up first.

Suzie stuck her head into Ann's office. "Well?"

Ann shook her head. "One of her associates canceled our plans tonight."

"What plans?"

Ann shrugged. "We didn't have any plans. It was just another way of saying that she wouldn't be around again tonight."

Suzie gave Ann a hug. "So what are you going to do?"

Ann pulled away. "Get me on the next plane to Los Angeles."

Ann sat in her window seat watching the men load the baggage. Luckily, the next flight had been at five o'clock. She had gone home directly from the office to pack and still had time to lie down after taking her migraine pills. Glad to be feeling better, she made conversation with the man in the next seat. It wasn't until he made a comment about calling his wife that Ann remembered she had promised to call Casey. She quickly dialed the number before the plane departed the gate.

"Casey, it's Ann. I'm coming back," she said when Casey picked up.

"Great! When? Tomorrow?" Traffic hummed in the background.

"Well, actually, I'm on the plane right now."

"Thanks for the early notice." Casey laughed. "I guess I'll have to forget about the cake and the balloons."

Ann smiled. It was nice to hear her voice. "No cake?"

"No, but I can cook you dinner if you'd like. Just come to my place from the airport. What do ya say?"

Ann's stomach rumbled. She hadn't eaten anything all day. "You're an angel. That's what I say."

"Okay. See you in about an hour or so?"

Ann agreed and hung up the phone. Before she knew it, the plane was in the air. She adjusted her seat. Laying her head back, she felt a warmth envelop her. Casey was excited about seeing her. It felt nice.

Ann arrived at Casey's feeling oddly refreshed. Casey welcomed her with a big hug and a delicious Italian meal . . . delivered from her favorite Italian restaurant. Casey emptied the cartons of food onto their plates. Ann was handed a dish of ravioli with Alfredo sauce accompanied by warm garlic bread. A mixed green salad was in the middle of the table.

"Hey, I thought you were going to cook dinner for me," Ann joked as Casey filled their glasses with red wine.

"When you see my kitchen, you'll be glad that I didn't." Casey laughed.

Finished with the meal, Ann stood and picked up several plates.

"Well, let's take a look at that kitchen. I'll help you with the dishes."

Casey took the dishes and set them back on the table. "No, don't go in there, you're too clean. I have to move a couple of things just to get to the sink."

Ann wandered over to the kitchen and looked at the disarray. "Don't you need my help to move those things?"

"No. But wait a minute, I don't want to get this shirt dirty." Casey peeled it off to reveal the undershirt beneath. She hefted the large box by the sink.

"Jeez, Casey!" Ann exclaimed as she watched Casey's bulging biceps flex under the weight.

"What?" Casey looked down as if expecting to find something on her shirt.

"These!" Ann said as she reached out and felt the muscles. "Have you been working out more or what?"

Casey blushed as she completed the task at hand. "Yes. Thanks to you I've been assigned a personal trainer five days a week."

"Thanks to me?" Ann was baffled.

Casey nodded. "You had to write about how muscular my character is."

"Well, I thought you were fine before, but now . . ." Ann, impressed, admired the muscles.

Casey flexed in response. "You think that's pretty sexy, huh?"

"Oh, now you're going to be all full of yourself, huh?" Ann smirked. Eyeing the plant water spray bottle, she picked it up and aimed it in Casey's direction. "Here, this should cool you off!" She pumped the lever.

Seeing the revenge in Casey's eyes, she dropped the bottle and ran out of the kitchen.

Casey followed after her with the squirt bottle. Ann darted down the hall with Casey closely behind her. All of a sudden Ann tripped on the area rug, causing her and Casey to tumble to the floor. Ann was laughing so hard that she had a hard time catching her breath. Clearing the tears from her eyes, she found Casey leaning on her elbow smiling at her.

"It's good to see you laugh. You don't smile often enough," Casey said.

"You make me laugh!" Ann was still wiping the tears of laughter from her face.

"Should I consider that a compliment?"

Ann reached out to brush the hair from Casey's face and smiled. "Of course."

Casey placed her hand over Ann's and brought it to rest on her cheek. "God, I missed you!" she whispered. Then, with a look of panic on her face, she sat up and stuttered, "Did I say that out loud?"

Ann nodded and softly smiled. "I'm sure that you meant it in a purely platonic sense, right?"

Casey closed her eyes as she took Ann's thumb and ran it over her own lips. When she opened her eyes, Ann could see her passionate need.

After several minutes of intense gazing at each other, Casey quietly admitted, "This time, I need you to leave."

Ann closed her eyes and sighed. Slowly she stood, grabbed her purse and shut the door behind her.

Chapter Ten

Ann awoke with the sun streaming in her eyes. Slinging her legs over the side of the bed, she stretched. She felt a lot better this morning. Last night she had come back to the hotel and gone straight to bed. The blinking red message button caught her attention. She pressed the button, one message.

Kathy's familiar voice grated in Ann's ear. "I thought that we were going to try and work on 'us.' But you go running off, back to Los Angeles, just because I've been unable to keep you company for the last few days. I can see how important our relationship is to you. Well, it's damn important to me. I love you, Ann. Call me."

If the phone had been cordless, Ann probably would've thrown it across the room. Instead, she just crashed the receiver down. *Again, it's all my fault*, she said to herself.

She began pacing, then caught a glimpse of the blue sky through her window. Brushing the curtains aside, she was overwhelmed with the warmth of the sun flowing through her. It lifted her up, and suddenly she was no longer irritable but eager to enjoy the day. It was Saturday and she was going to make the most of it.

"I am going to the beach today. Would you like to join me?" Ann asked Casey cheerily.

"I don't know. I have so much to do around here." Casey moaned.

"Haven't you been working hard all week?"

"Yes, but—"

"I'm going to ask you again. Would you like to join me at the beach?" Ann said whimsically.

Casey laughed. "How can I say no to you?"

"I'll pick you up in about an hour," Ann responded, excited.

"Are you ready to go?" Ann asked as she closed Casey's front door behind her.

"Yeah, I just need to put my shoes on." Casey replied. Ann followed her into the bedroom. Casey sat on the edge of the bed to pull on her shoes. Ann sniffled and looked around. "Do you have any tissue in here?"

Nodding, Casey motioned with her chin. "On the bedside table."

Ann pulled out a tissue and the box fell to the floor. Leaning over, she spotted an item that made her blush. "Hmm . . . what are these for?" She smiled as she pulled a pair of handcuffs from under the bed.

Casey's face turned bright red. "Please don't tell me that you're really asking. You're just trying to embarrass the hell out of me, right?"

"You must have some sex life!" Ann laughed as she placed the item back on the nightstand.

Casey turned her attention back to her shoelaces. "So, you and Kathy never—"

"Please," Ann cut in. "Kathy's idea of something new and different is to be on the top instead of the bottom."

"And your idea of something new and different?" Casey grinned as she finished her process at hand.

"I'm not going to have this discussion with you!" Ann exclaimed.

Casey whined, "Come on . . ."

"No! I am not going to discuss my sexual fantasies with you."

"I'd love to hear them," Casey teased.

Sauntering over to Casey, she leaned over, making Casey collapse back on the bed. Ann looked down at her. "And I'd love to show them to you, but it's not going to happen. So let's get going."

Ann straightened up and pulled Casey up off the bed.

Casey and Ann spread out the blanket on the sand and stripped down to their bathing suits. Thirsty, Ann opened her soda while Casey unwrapped the sandwiches they had picked up.

"Damn it. I told them no mustard." Casey opened her sandwich and held out the bun for Ann to see. "I told them twice. They probably did it on purpose. If we were closer to the deli . . ."

Ann laughed. "Are you going to throw a fit, or what?"

"Oh, yes. Calm Ann. Don't you ever throw a fit?" Casey said sarcastically.

Ann nodded. "Yes. But I've learned to pick my battles. You see, I've learned that if you overreact all the time, no one takes you seriously when something is really important. Being an attorney, I've come to understand that there is usually some kind of compromise that you'll be happy with. For example . . ." She paused as she took the bun with the mustard off of Casey's sandwich and replaced it with the bun without mustard from her sandwich. "Now, you see? We're both happy."

Casey smiled. "I bet you're pretty good at this compromise thing."

"I haven't had many complaints. Just last week I saved my client from one hundred and forty-five thousand dollars in back taxes." Ann mentally patted herself on the back.

"Gee, when I grow up, I want to be just like you." Casey laughed.

"That's a pretty high aspiration when you only have about three years to go."

"Okay. You know my age. What else do you know about me?"

Ann tried to remember the details. "I know that you're originally from Malibu. You graduated with a degree in political science from Berkeley and intended to work in politics. Then you went to your first audition on a dare and caught the acting bug." She paused. "I know that you have brown eyes that remind me of dark caramel, your hair always smells like vanilla and you have a tiny little scar on your chin." She gently touched Casey's face. Realizing immediately that she was getting too hot, in more places than one, she jumped up and grabbed Casey's hand. "Come on, let's go in the water. I need to cool off."

Casey allowed herself to be pulled up and smiled. "You and me both."

Ann toweled off after a long shower in which she found she was switching the water from hot to cold and back to hot again. Her day in the sun had left her exhausted from playing in the water and sunburned. Collapsing onto the bed, she felt her skin scratching against the rough comforter. She needed the lotion that she had purchased in the hotel gift store. It was cool against her skin and she decided against dressing to avoid agitating the burn. She wrestled whether or not to call Kathy. Did she want to ruin such a nice day? *Stop thinking like that,* she told herself. *You love Kathy and you will work out your problems.* She tried to convince herself. She picked up the phone and dialed.

"Kathy?"

"Were you expecting someone else?" Kathy quipped.

"No, it's just been so long since I haven't gotten your voice mail," Ann explained.

"Yeah, well, I'm working from home and trying to relax just a little."

"Try that wine in the refrigerator. It's wonderful."

"It's already gone, my dear, and yes, it was good," Kathy replied. "So, what's kept you so busy that you're just now returning my call?"

Ann cringed. *Tell the truth.* "Well, last night Casey offered to feed me after my flight in. And then today, we went to the beach. It was a beautiful day—"

"So did you have sex with her?" Kathy burst in.

"What?" Ann was speechless.

"You heard me."

"It's just that I didn't know that word was still in your vocabulary," Ann snapped back. "It's been so long since I've seen you naked that I don't know if I'd even recognize you."

There was silence on the other end of the line. Finally Kathy asked again, "Did you have sex with her?"

"No, Kathy. I didn't." Ann was irritated. "Now, can we talk about something pleasurable for a change?"

The line was silent for a moment. Finally, Kathy began telling her about some of the cases she was presently working on. Ann disagreed with a lot of Kathy's tactics, but she was, after all, a defense attorney. It was her job to defend the suspects until proven guilty. The conversation went on until Ann felt herself falling asleep.

"I'm sorry, babe, my eyelids are closing, I'm going to have to say good night." Ann said delicately.

Kathy said lovingly, "Okay, sweetie. Sleep well." Then her softness turned sour. "Oh, and tell Casey hi for me."

Ann heard the line go dead. Her head hit the pillow and she wished that Kathy hadn't let her sarcasm end the evening.

Suddenly, the phone rang, reawakening Ann with a jolt. Maybe Kathy was calling to apologize. *Yeah, right.* She grabbed the receiver.

"Hey, are you sunburned? Need someone to rub lotion all over over?" Casey chuckled.

Ann smiled. "Yes, I am sunburned. And no, I already took care of the lotion myself."

"Too bad. Lotion is my specialty," Casey said. "Are you naked?"

Laughing, Ann confirmed that she was indeed without clothes. "I was just falling asleep. I am so tired."

"Oh, I'm sorry. I was just calling to say thank you for a great day."

"It was a nice day, wasn't it? But I might be hating you tomorrow morning when I wake up."

"Mmm . . . call me if you need me to rub on some more lotion. Good night." Casey's voice warmed Ann from head to toe. She drifted off to sleep remembering Casey's body in her bikini . . . her teeny tiny bikini . . .

Chapter Eleven

Ann dreamed of doughnuts. She could smell them. Wait a minute. She could smell them. Opening her eyes, she stared into a glazed doughnut being waved in front of her nose.

"Hey, I brought breakfast, sleepyhead!" Casey's face was hovering over her.

Ann rolled over onto her back and rubbed her eyes. "I knew giving you that key would come in handy." As she moved, her skin felt like it was cracking. "Oh . . . ouch." She moaned.

"I brought this too!" Casey pulled some aloe vera lotion out of a paper bag.

Grabbing the bottle, Ann chuckled. "I think I can take care of that for myself."

Ann shooed Casey out of the bedroom, but not before stealing the glazed doughnut out of her hand. Ann washed up, covered herself with lotion, then rifled through her clothing to find something extremely loose-fitting.

Joining Casey in the living area, Ann gently lowered herself into the overstuffed chair. "This room needs another couch," she said as she tried to get comfortable.

"Sorry. I got here first." Casey stretched out. "You snooze, you lose."

A pillow flew through the air and landed on Casey's head. Within minutes, Casey had her wrestled to the ground.

"Ouch, ouch, ouch!" Ann cried out. "I need more lotion!"

"Fine!" Casey let her go. "Oh, you'd better start getting ready anyway."

Ann stood. "Ready for what?"

"Did I forget to tell you? You're going to a baby shower with me tonight," Casey said casually.

"A baby shower?" Ann shook her head. "No, thanks. I won't know anyone."

"You'll know me," Casey whined. "I don't want to go alone."

Ann thought for a moment. She certainly didn't want to sit all night by the phone for Kathy's call . . . if she called. And a baby shower with Casey just might be fun. "What should I wear?"

The party was . . . pink. Not just a slight hint of pink here and there. The afghan covering the sofa was pink. The chair pads were pink, as well as the tablecloth and every single throw pillow in the room. Balloons were everywhere, of course, also pink. If she had been a baby coming into this room, she'd puke.

Casey nudged Ann. "Think it's a girl?"

Ann tried to squelch her giggles as they made their way through the swarm of women making small talk. Casey left her side to find beverages for them. Ann wandered through the crowd to observe the presents being opened. As she watched, she never realized how many baby items there were.

"Unbelievable, huh?" Casey said from behind her. "I bet it's been a long time since you've been to one of these."

Ann nodded. "Do you want kids?" she asked as Casey handed her a glass of wine.

Casey fiddled with her earlobe. "Yes, I think I do. But only if I had a partner to help out. Someone who I knew was going to be around for the long haul."

"Yeah, same here. Plus I wouldn't do it if I was still busy all the time. You really need time for kids."

Casey agreed. Suddenly, a woman interrupted their conversation.

"Casey, there's someone back here that I want you to meet." The woman grabbed her by the arm and led her away. Casey looked back at Ann and shrugged.

Ann felt a twinge of jealousy. *What was that about?* she asked herself. Turning around she was absorbed in the unwrapping of presents.

A while later, Ann casually searched the room for Casey. She was feeling tired and her sunburn was starting to itch. The search ended as she located Casey in the corner, laughing with several young attractive women. Instinctively, Ann met Casey's gaze. She was captivated by the look in those deep brown eyes, then she quickly glanced away. The look sent a warm gentle wash over her entire body. She had seen that look before. Kathy used to look at her that way . . . long ago. The look had said, "*Don't worry, my heart belongs to you.*"

Ann sensed a panicky feeling growing inside. She needed some fresh air, so she wandered out onto the patio. Taking a deep breath, she tried to overcome the emotions inside her. What was happening to her? Was she just lonely, or was she actually falling for this woman? She chided herself. Casey could probably give Wilt Chamberlain a run for his money in the one-night stand department. Yet she couldn't help but feel something was different between her and Casey. The connection was undeniable. It ran deep, she had to admit, deeper than anything that had ever been between her and Kathy.

"You okay?" asked a voice out of the darkness.

Ann turned as Casey approached her. "Yeah. Just needed a breath of fresh air."

They stood in silence, Ann ignoring the growing sounds of the party behind them.

"Missing Kathy?" Casey said hesitantly, as if not really wanting an answer.

"No." Ann ran her fingers through her hair and stared straight ahead. "I think that's the problem. I really don't miss her at all." Realizing what she had just said, she tried to change the subject. "Are you ready to leave? I'm getting tired."

"Hell, I was ready a long time ago," Casey confessed. "I just kept getting pulled from one person to another . . ."

"Yeah, I saw some of the women you were pulled to," Ann said sarcastically.

Casey smiled and that same look was in her eyes from earlier that evening. *Don't worry, my heart belongs to you.*

"Let's go."

Ann opened the door to the dimly lit hotel room. She had been continuously trying to scratch her back during the drive home. Casey followed her in.

"Bring the lotion out to the living room and I'll rub it on your back."

"Excuse me?" Ann stopped in her tracks.

Casey put her hand on her heart. "I promise. I won't try any funny stuff. You just aren't able to reach your entire back area."

Ann stood still for a minute, trying to make a decision. Itchy skin, or nice soothing lotion? Itchy skin or Casey's warm hands rubbing in the soothing lotion? Her heart was racing. Maybe it wasn't such a good idea. It wasn't a good idea at all.

"Okay, I'll get the lotion," Ann blurted, then pointed her finger at Casey. "No funny stuff."

Ann changed into her pajama pants and wrapped a towel around her upper body. While picking up the lotion, she glanced at herself in the mirror. Ann Covington looked back at her. Ann Covington—attorney, writer, wife, woman. *God, help me be a strong woman tonight*, she repeated as she went into what she knew was a risky situation.

"Ahh." Ann moaned. She had removed her towel only after positioning herself on the couch in a safe manner . . . no access to her breasts. Casey caressed her skin with the silky lotion, making her way from Ann's shoulders to her lower back. All Ann could feel were the sensuous hands massaging her, and the wetness forming in between her legs.

"I want to touch you, Ann. Let me touch you," Casey almost begged.

"Oh, God, Casey," Ann said breathlessly.

"Let me touch you, Ann," Casey repeated.

This has gone way too far, Ann said to herself. But it felt so good . . . Casey felt so good . . . It had been so long since anyone had made her feel this way. She felt like she had an angel on one side of her brain, and the devil on the other, just like in the movies. Yes, no, yes, no. *Oh, brother, no. No, no, no, no, no.* The angel had won out. Ann held on to her towel as she rolled over.

"I can't, Casey. I just can't," Ann murmured.

Casey sat up and dragged her fingers through her hair over and over again in frustration. "No one has to know, Ann."

"I'm sorry, Casey, but I'll know." Ann held steadfast to her towel as she tried to sit up.

Casey stood and helped Ann stand. "Well, then, I guess this is my cue to leave."

Ann nodded and walked Casey to the door. She reached out and gave her a hug. Casey hugged her back.

"I'm really sorry, Casey," Ann said as she pulled away.

"You know, many more nights like this and I'll need to go buy a jumbo pack of batteries for my vibrator," Casey said with a gleam in her eye.

"Yeah, well, you may want to pick up a pack of those for me too," Ann replied with her own teasing smile.

❧

When Ann arrived in her trailer late the next morning she found a present on her desk. As she pulled the tissue paper out of the brightly colored bag, she chuckled. Along with the jumbo pack of batteries was a small note: "What do you want to do tonight?"

Chapter Twelve

"Cut! Cut!" Leslie yelled. "Casey, you're supposed to be in love with this woman. Take five."

Ann stopped her modifications to the stage directions in another scene. Watching as Jennifer plopped down in a chair, she found herself thinking how glad she was that they had found her. Jennifer was exactly as Ann had pictured the character of Chris in her mind: thin, medium height and brunette. The actress's crooked smile completed the vision.

Casey came to where Ann was standing. "I don't think I can do this," she whispered.

"Yes, you can," Ann said reassuringly. Then with a teasing smile, she looked into Casey's eyes. "If it helps, pretend it's me."

Casey returned the remark with a grin and went back over to her mark.

"Okay, let's roll!" Leslie called out.

Casey stepped over to Jennifer, the actress playing Chris. She wiped the tears from Jennifer's face, kissed her softly, then played out the remainder of the balcony scene. Ann felt her entire body heat up. Looking around, she saw that it apparently had the same impact on the others.

"Cut! That was excellent. Let's get ready for the next scene, people."

Casey smiled and walked past Ann. "Great advice."

After a few minutes Ann heard the same voice just over her shoulder.

"You know, if I'm going to continue following your advice, it would be helpful if you didn't watch." Casey spoke softly into Ann's ear.

Ann turned to find that Casey was indeed serious. Shrugging, she walked off the set and to her trailer, where she tried to work out some kinks in a later scene. She found that she couldn't concentrate, instead daydreaming about what if Casey had been kissing her. An hour later she was interrupted by Caitlin, one of the production assistants, ranting and raving as she entered the trailer.

"Wow! You left at the best part!" she exclaimed. "After that first take of that balcony scene, I thought Casey was going to be a cold fish. But man, was I wrong. She heated up the entire crew in there."

Ann looked at her, feeling a twinge of jealousy as Caitlin proceeded to give details.

"The way she kissed and caressed . . ." Caitlin shivered. "Well, I don't think I've ever been made love to like that before." She asked, "Do you think that there's something going on between those two?"

Ann shook her head and tried to look as if she was concentrating on her work.

Caitlin grabbed a pile of papers from the table and headed out the door. "In case you wanted to know, they're through for the day."

Ann waited until she heard the door close before she lowered her head into her hands and repeated to herself, "I'm a married woman, I'm a married woman, I'm a married woman."

"So, aren't you going to say anything about the dailies?" Casey asked without looking up from her menu.

Ann thought the dailies were excellent. It was always surreal watching her characters come to life. She always found it odd that she had an upset stomach while the dailies were rolling, but as soon as they were over, she was ravenous. Casey had suggested a little Mexican food place around the corner.

"I'll tell you one thing. You sure made Caitlin's panties wet. She couldn't say enough about your performance," Ann said, scanning her menu.

Casey raised her eyes. "And what did you think?"

Ann glanced up at her. "I'm having a hard time thinking about anything else but begging you to take me right here on this table."

Casey raised an eyebrow. "You wouldn't have to do much begging." Her gaze flicking to the tables around them, she bent forward with a mischievous grin. "I don't think anyone would mind."

Ann leaned toward her with a straight face. "I think there's someone who would mind."

Casey looked around again, clearly confused. "Who?"

Ann sat back in her chair. "Kathy."

Casey's grin was immediately wiped from her face.

"Here, this should cool you ladies down," the waitress said as she placed the margaritas on the table.

"What?" both Ann and Casey exclaimed. Ann wondered if the waitress had overheard their conversation.

The waitress gave them a funny look, then explained, "It's like a hundred degrees out here. Aren't you guys hot?"

Casey mumbled, "Actually, I just felt a sudden chill."

The waitress shrugged slightly. "Well, are you ready to order?"

Ann decided on the fajitas, and Casey opted for the enchilada dinner. The waitress departed , and Ann stirred her drink in silence, watching as the ice circled in the glass.

Casey sighed and fell back into her chair. "God, I'm sorry. It's just that you start putting these ideas in my head—."

Ann broke in. "And I have to do something to bring myself . . . us . . . back to reality."

Casey glanced up at Ann, then focused again on her drink as she nodded. "So is she coming this weekend?"

Ann shook her head. "She's busy." She had spoken with Kathy earlier, and was reminded about a deadline on a case.

"Maybe you should go to San Francisco," Casey said, a glimmer of pain in her eyes.

"Is that what you want?" Ann asked, irritated.

Casey ran her fingers through her hair. "Damn it. It's not about what I want!"

"God. It seems like everyone is having relationship problems," the waitress said as she set the hot plates on the table.

"It's not like that," Casey explained to her.

"Really?" The waitress crouched down next to the table as she propositioned Casey. "Well, I get off in half an hour. I'd love to buy you a drink."

Clearly tongue-tied, Casey looked her, and then at Ann.

"Oh, you don't have to answer right now." The waitress winked as she left the table. "I'll be back."

Watching her as she walked away, Ann mumbled, "She's cute. You should go with her."

Casey looked up. "Now I'll ask you the same ridiculous question. Is that what you want?"

Ann smiled and simply shook her head no.

Ann spooned the fajita fillings into a tortilla. Visions of the scenes she just watched kept flashing through her mind. Between the spices of the food and the excitement from her imagination, the heat was almost unbearable.

"So, how does one manage a steamy love scene like that and not get totally hot and bothered?" Ann asked after a few minutes.

With fork still in hand, Casey explained, "Well, this is the first time I've ever done a scene like that with a woman . . . but I took some advice given to me before my very first love scene. Before we began the scene, the actor took me aside because he had heard that it was my first. He put his arm around me and said, 'Sometimes it's really hard not to get too excited in one of these scenes. I find it helpful if I tell the woman what really gets to me, then ask her politely to refrain from that action. That way, I don't get too aroused.'"

"And what did he ask you to refrain from?"

Casey chuckled. "To tell you the truth, I don't remember." Then, setting her fork down, she continued, "But then he asked me if there was anything that he should hold back on." Laughing, she finished, "I told him he could do anything he wanted because I was a lesbian. I guess I shouldn't have said that because that seemed to excite him even more."

Taking another bite of beans, Ann asked with a teasing smile, "So, what did you ask Jenny to refrain from?"

Blushing, Casey exclaimed, "Are you asking me what my biggest turn-on is?"

"Yes . . . no . . . Oh, I don't know . . ." Ann felt her face getting hotter.

Casey leaned forward and motioned for Ann to join her in a secret. "Doing anything to my neck . . . especially those little teasing bites . . . it drives me crazy." Casey fidgeted in her chair as she felt the wetness forming below as she imagined the feeling.

"And Jenny . . . what did she ask?" Ann asked.

Casey shook her head. "I'm sorry, I don't really feel comfortable about divulging that information. It's a pretty personal thing . . ."

Ann nodded. "You're right. I'm sorry. I really shouldn't have asked."

"And you? What's your biggest turn-on?" Casey asked teasingly as she took a bite of her enchilada.

Ann blushed again. "It's really kind of a personal thing . . ."

Casey huffed. "Oh, I tell you, but now you won't tell me. You are such a tease."

Ann smiled and shrugged. "You didn't have to tell me."

After dinner, Casey drove Ann back to the hotel.

Ann leaned back in the window. "Oh, and Casey . . ." she said with a glimmer in her eye, "the smooth line where your leg meets your hip . . . that's what drives me crazy." She watched as Casey's face flushed with excitement. "Sweet dreams!" she chimed and waved good-bye.

Casey just sat in the car for a moment in a daze. She didn't even think about moving the vehicle. All she could concentrate on was Ann's body and the area that made Ann crazy. Her body was overheating. Suddenly, she heard a car horn behind her. She swiftly placed the gear to drive and was on her way. *Looks like it's going to be another vibrator night!* Casey said to herself.

Back in her suite, Ann noticed the red light blinking on the phone. Great, she thought, *this ruins the perfect ending of a nice night.* She switched on some lights on the way to what seemed like a strobe light through the darkness. Sinking down onto the couch, she called in for her messages. She prepared herself for whatever Kathy had to say. But the voice was not Kathy's. Suzie had received a call from a new client and wanted to schedule a meeting this week.

Ann pushed the delete button, then made the appropriate calls to Suzie, the airline and Casey.

"You're leaving tomorrow morning?" Casey asked. "How long will you be gone?"

"Just a couple of days. I can't leave for very long. We're in the middle of trying to secure the beach house for the shot on location. Then we have to adjust the script for the design of the house."

"Well, it will be good for you to have some time with Kathy, too." Casey's voice was tinged with sadness.

"Yeah, if she's not too busy to see me," Ann said pointedly.

"I'm sure she misses you. She just isn't communicating it very well."

"Whatever," Ann stated. "I'll call you when I'm returning to L.A., okay?"

They said their good-byes, and Ann found that she too was overcome with sadness.

❧

Early the next morning, Ann stepped off the plane into a hazy fog, one of the things that she didn't miss about San Francisco. Leaving the airport she was confronted with a sea of cabs. She looked for the cleanest one, then climbed in. Sighing as they entered the traffic, she pulled out her cell phone. Maybe Kathy would want to know that she was in town. The call went straight to voice mail.

"Hi, babe. Just callin' to let you know that I'm in town for a couple of days. It would be nice to have dinner with you tonight, or just to see you later on. I'm headed toward the office right now. Give me a call, okay?"

Ann hadn't heard from Kathy by mid-morning. She was trying to concentrate on work, but her mind kept going back to the sadness she felt about her connection with Kathy. Their relationship wasn't failing because Ann had decided to go to Los Angeles. It had begun a long time before that. Kathy with her mood swings, her work habits . . . was it all Kathy's fault? Yes, Ann decided. Yes, it was all Kathy's fault. She had just thrown another log in the fire by pursuing her dream. When the movie was over, Ann would come back and work on rebuilding their life together. She knew she could make it work.

The intercom broke into her thoughts. "Ann, your appointment is here."

"Suzie, give me a minute, then show him in." She needed to get herself together. She needed to concentrate on the matter of the Red String Corporation, a company focused on cat toys. Unfortunately, their prior accountant had been a little playful with their tax returns.

The meeting went well, and Ann wandered back into the office about three o'clock. Her client had suggested that they talk over lunch, her favorite kind of business meeting. Suzie followed her in and sat down.

"You got that fax that you've been waiting for. Oh, and you got flowers," Suzie said as she dug in her pocket. "Here's the card."

Ann was confused. "And you had the card in your pocket because . . . ?"

"You wouldn't believe how many people wanted to know what that card said."

"Wow! These are beautiful," Ann exclaimed as she admired the two dozen yellow roses. She hadn't even been aware of the flowers sitting on her credenza. She smiled as she opened the card and read the message:

I miss you. (Platonically, of course.) Casey.

Still admiring the flowers, she glanced over at her assistant. "So why did everyone want to see the card? No one usually cares around here."

Suzie closed the door to the office. "I've always felt like you've been more than a boss to me, kind of a friend, so I'm going to be honest with you." She motioned for Ann to sit back down.

Wary, Ann slowly sank into her chair. "Okay, what?"

"There's a rumor going around the office that you're having an affair with someone on the set." Suzie folded her hands nervously in her lap.

Ann raised her eyebrows with surprise.

Suzie continued, "Now, I've known you long enough to know better, but if my opinion matters at all, if you were having affair, I wouldn't hold it against you. In my opinion, you deserve to be treated better than Kathy treats you."

Ann smiled. "I am not having an affair. I have a new friend there that I spend time with, but no affair. Sorry to disappoint everyone. I still take my marriage vows very seriously."

Suzie sighed in relief. "You know that I'm here if you need me?" It was more of a statement than a question.

Ann nodded. She watched Suzie close the door then glanced over at the roses. She went over and let the aroma fill her lungs, then let the petals caress her face. She felt a small tear flit down her cheek. *At least someone misses me.*

≈≈

That night, Ann tossed and turned in her sleep. Kathy had called her early in the evening, once again to tell her that she couldn't drop everything just because Ann decided to come into town. Around one a.m., Ann gave into her sorrow and confusion and let the tears flow freely. She barely noticed when Kathy came in and turned on the bathroom light. Ann sniffled.

"Ann? Are you crying?" The voice came closer and closer to the bed. Kathy sat down and ran her thumb over Ann's cheek. "You are crying. What's the matter?"

"What's the matter?" Ann whimpered in exasperation. "Do you still love me, Kath?"

Kathy chuckled. "Of course I do. What brought this on?"

"You never want to see me . . . .or talk to me anymore . . ."

"Ann! I have a busy schedule. It was much easier when you were here. Whenever I did have time, you were right here waiting. It doesn't work that way anymore."

"It seems like your work is more important than our relationship." Ann's heart ached.

"Don't you even go there! Your work is more important than 'us' right now. Hell, you left town. I didn't leave town." Kathy's face reddened as her anger grew. "I need to unwind. I'm getting a bowl of cereal and watching some television."

Ann's tears turned to resentment. She popped a couple of sleeping pills and drifted off to sleep. Kathy fell asleep on the couch.

Ann was out of the house early, leaving a note behind for Kathy who was still sleeping. She dropped by her office to go over some files before she flew back. When Suzie arrived, Ann handed her a list of items to follow up on.

"So, you're leaving town right now? You just got here."

"I know, but it's a busy time back in L.A. They need me there," Ann explained.

Suzie examined Ann's face. "You and Kathy had it out again, huh?"

Ann's eyes welled up. "Anyway, if your offer is still good, I'd like you to fly down next week for a few days. It won't be all work—you can play too."

"Okay," Suzie said softly. "Now, do you have everything that you want to take with you?"

"Yes, I think I do." Ann closed her briefcase and headed out the door.

"Um . . . Ann . . . you might need this." Suzie handed her the Red String file.

Ann smiled as she reopened the case, stuffed the file in and closed it again. Suzie rode the elevator down and walked to the enormous glass doors with Ann.

Suzie lay her hand on Ann's shoulder. "Remember, I'm here Ann. If you ever need to talk."

Ann nodded then pushed through the doors and slipped into the waiting cab.

Chapter Thirteen

Ann was still depressed when she spoke with Casey to let her know she was back in town. Saying she wanted to cheer her up, Casey surprised her by taking her to the hottest place in town. Unfortunately, she thought, Casey had forgotten that Ann wasn't impressed with the rich and famous. The lobster, however, certainly made an impact on her.

She'd just finished on one claw when a woman approached their table. Upon further review, she recognized her as Toni Williams, a very young but famous actress best known for her work on an evening legal drama. Ann watched as Toni whispered something in Casey's ear, then with a seductive smile gently touched Casey's shoulder before whisking away. Ann smiled as Casey's face turned red.

"You've worked with her, haven't you?" Ann asked.

Casey did not look up from her honey grilled salmon as she nodded. "Uh-huh."

Ann reached over and pulled Casey's plate away. Casey looked up with a sheepish grin.

"Casey, did you do something else with her?"

Casey's face turned an even deeper shade of red as she once again nodded.

"Really?" Ann looked into her eyes. "What?"

Casey looked as if she was trying desperately to find the word she was looking for.

"Was she kinky or something?" Ann was by now really curious. Her thoughts went back to the handcuffs that she had found at Casey's place.

Casey lowered her eyes. "I think the word that would best describe her was . . . .inexperienced."

Ann gasped. "Casey, were you her first?"

Casey let out a slight laugh. "No, but I wouldn't be surprised if I was her second."

"So what did she whisper to you?"

Casey tucked her hair behind her ear. "She said that she had gotten a little more knowledgeable, if I wanted to give her another try."

"Well, are you going to?"

"What?" Casey asked. "Give her another try?" She shook her head, then looked Ann in the eye. "She isn't the type of woman I want to be around."

Ann blushed and went back to her lobster.

It was still relatively early when they finished dinner, so Ann invited Casey back to her hotel. Ann excused herself to change into something more comfortable while Casey surfed through the television channels. Casey, deciding that she wanted to relax too, pulled off her over-shirt.

"You come out in that little undershirt, and I'm not supposed to get turned on?" Casey asked.

Ann pointed to Casey. "Oh, yeah, and that little 'sports bra' showing off all your muscles isn't supposed to make me hot?"

"What, this?" Casey smiled mischievously as she reviewed her outfit.

Ann laughed as she playfully nudged Casey. Push came to shove and they wrestled until Casey had Ann pinned underneath her on the couch. They once again, in Ann's opinion, made the ultimate error of locking eyes. For some reason this eye contact seemed to hypnotize both of them, practically drawing them into a trance. Ann reached up and drew her finger across Casey's lips.

Casey lowered herself, bringing her face down to Ann's. "I'm warning you, I'm not feeling very strong right now."

"And I'm so tired of fighting this thing between us," Ann admitted.

Casey, just inches away now, whispered, "Maybe just one kiss wouldn't hurt."

Ann reached out to touch Casey's cheek. "Oh, sweetie, I couldn't stop at just one kiss. Not even if it was one kiss on every inch of your body."

"Ann . . ." Casey held her gaze, clearly looking for direction.

"Casey—" Ann began in response, her sentence interrupted by the sound of the telephone ringing.

Casey smiled in surrender as she sat up. "That would probably be your wife."

Ann softly smiled and grappled for the phone. "Hello?"

Casey pulled on her over-shirt and headed to the door.

"Yes, she's right here." Ann put her hand over the phone and motioned to Casey. "It's Pam." Ann remembered meeting her and her partner, Diane, at the bar the other night. Through the stories told that evening, she found out that Pam had been Casey's best friend for years. Ann also got the feeling that night that Pam didn't really care for her at all.

Casey hurried over to the phone. "Pam?" After listening for a few seconds, she spoke again. "Of course, I'll be right there." Casey hung up the receiver and turned to Ann. "Diane's been in an accident." Grabbing her bag, she located and inspected her cell phone. "Damn, I still had it set on silent." She moved again to the door.

"Can I go with you?" Ann asked as she pulled at Casey's arm. Casey nodded and waited while Ann changed into another shirt, then the two headed to the hospital.

Ann followed Casey into the hospital room. As they entered, she heard the police officer questioning.

"So you just turned around and the car was there. Is that what you're saying?"

"Yes, yes, that's what I just said. It's the same thing that I told you an hour ago!" Diane replied in frustration.

"And you hadn't had any alcohol?" he proceeded.

Diane shook her head adamantly. "No! I already told you that!"

Ann watched with irritation. She had seen this happen before during the years she spent prosecuting. Officers questioned a suspect over and over again, hoping that the person would get confused and slip up. Finally Ann could take no more.

"Officer, I believe your interview here is over," she said sternly. "You have your statement."

The officer halted his inquisition. "And you would be?"

Ann reached into her purse and pulled out a business card. She was glad that she had never added the words *tax attorney* to her card. "I'm a friend." Then handing the card to the officer, she continued, "I'm also their attorney."

Clearly confused, Diane looked at Pam. The officer examined the card. Glaring at Ann he proceeded to return the card. Pam grabbed the card out of his hand and reviewed it.

The officer shook his head as he closed his clipboard. "All you dykes stick together," he mumbled.

Ann was relieved that a nurse had entered the room. "Excuse me, nurse?" She turned in Ann's direction. "If you were asked to testify in court, could you repeat what this officer just said?" Ann asked.

The nurse smiled and nodded. "Do you mean what he said about 'you dykes sticking together'?"

"Thank you." Ann smiled as she looked back at the officer, who huffed and stalked out the door.

Casey smiled proudly and put her hand on Ann's arm. "I thought you were a tax attorney."

"I am a tax attorney. That doesn't mean that I haven't had any experience on these matters. I worked as a prosecutor for several years."

Ann waited until the nurse had finished her duties and followed her out the door. "I'll be right back."

Pam looked at Casey and then walked out into the hall to find Ann who was getting the contact information from the nurse. Ann turned to find Pam at her side. She took the piece of paper containing the nurse's information and offered it to Pam. "I know you don't really like me, but I will take on the case if you find that you need my services."

Pam took the information and looked at Ann. "It's not that I don't like you . . ." She paused as she examined the slip paper. "I just don't like you fucking Casey."

Ann looked at her in astonishment. "I'm not fucking Casey!"

Just then Ann felt a hand on her shoulder, and heard Casey's voice from behind her. "Pam, did you think that I was lying to you?"

Pam looked at Casey, then at Ann. "I'm sorry that I misjudged you." She offered her hand.

Ann shook her hand. "No apology necessary. You're a good friend, Pam. Casey's lucky to have you."

"Hey, Casey." Ann had thought about going home alone, but she just couldn't bear it. "Will you stay at my place tonight?"

Ann was pulled back into her seat as she felt the effects of the accelerator being pushed down.

"What do you mean?" Casey choked out.

Ann felt the speed being corrected. She could practically read what Casey was thinking and laughed. "It's not like that!" She slapped Casey lightly on her shoulder. "I just don't feel like staying alone tonight. You would just be there to keep me company."

Casey mopped her brow. "Um . . . sure. I can do that," she said, not sounding sure of herself at all. "Good thing your couch is comfortable."

"I wouldn't make you sleep on the couch, silly!" Ann laughed again. "The bed is king-size, so there's plenty of room for both of us. You just stick to one side, and I'll stick to the other."

Back at the hotel, Casey felt herself getting heated again. How could Ann have offered that they sleep in the same bed so casually? Didn't she know how hard it was already to be near her and not be able to touch her? Hadn't they both almost crossed the forbidden line just hours ago? Even so, Casey crawled into Ann's bed. She fell asleep clinging to the side of the mattress.

Awhile later, in a sleepy haze, Casey suddenly felt a movement behind her. Ann had her arm around her waist and was molded into her backside. A warm feeling of contentment overwhelmed her as Ann pulled her body into hers. Casey lay there for a moment assessing the situation. What would be the consequences of remaining in this position? On the one hand, if Ann awoke she would be angry with Casey for not showing strength and could insist on never seeing her again. On the other hand, Ann could get carried away in the moment of closeness and they would make mad, passionate love, in which case Ann would be overcome with guilt and insist on never seeing her again.

It was a no-win situation, Casey conceded, and slowly rolled away and out of bed. For a minute, she stood there watching the woman she loved lie there dreaming. Part of her wanted to climb back in bed and take her right then and there. The other part of her was willing to wait, hoping that someday she would actually be invited into Ann's bed. Casey turned away, tiptoed from the room and curled up on the couch, falling into a sweet dream.

❧

Casey awoke as the curtains on the windows were swept to their sides. The sun streamed into the room. Raising one hand she tried to block it from her eyes. Ohhh, she was sore. The couch just wasn't quite long enough.

"Wake up sleepyhead!" Ann sang. "What are you doing out here? Wasn't the bed comfortable?"

"Yes, well, you tend to move around a lot when you sleep," Casey answered. "I thought you were going to keep to one side."

Ann gasped. "I am so sorry! I had no idea."

"No problem, the couch was okay," she lied through her teeth.

"Well, time to get up. It's Friday, the end of a very bad week, and we have that beach party with all of the cast tomorrow. Our weekend is looking up."

"Oh, yeah, I have tickets to a play tonight if you'd like to go." Casey said while she rubbed her eyes.

"Okay then. Let's start the day. The beginning of a great weekend."

Casey drove home to change and to pick up her clothes for the evening. At least today would be on location instead of that dreary sound stage. The shoots were going to be at a local country club. She had been there before. The place was elegant but conservative. It had reminded her of the club used in the movie *Dirty Dancing*. Showered and refreshed, she loaded her clothes for the play. She also packed a few extra comfortable clothes to keep at the hotel since it seemed like she was spending a lot of time there.

The day turned out to be somewhat enjoyable, Casey thought as she made her last wardrobe change. The dancing had been fun, and the food delicious. Too bad the liquor hadn't been real. Stepping into her shoes, she felt her excitement growing. This would be the last scene of the day, and then she would spend the rest of the weekend with Ann.

The play was to start at seven o'clock. Casey and Ann had gone straight from the set to the hotel room to get ready. Ann was tapping her foot, trying to get Casey to hurry. It was six-thirty.

"Come on, slowpoke!" Ann called out. "We're going to be late!"

"Okay, okay," Casey said as she put on her shoes on the way to the door. She was still hopping as Ann grabbed her purse and jacket.

Ann opened the door to leave. There stood Kathy.

"Surprise!" Kathy exclaimed, looking first at Ann and then over at Casey. Reaching out, she grabbed Ann to kiss her.

Stunned, Ann turned her head and the lips met her cheek instead of her mouth.

Kathy pulled away. "Not exactly the greeting I had expected."

"I thought you weren't coming," Ann explained. "I've kind of made plans with Casey."

Kathy glanced at Casey and sarcastically smiled. "I'm sure she understands, don't you, Casey?"

Casey nodded and smiled politely. "Sure."

"Please excuse us." Kathy motioned for Casey to leave. "We have a lot of catching up to do, if you know what I mean," she said with a wink.

At the door, Casey turned to look at Ann who felt frozen in place. Kathy closed the door and pulled Ann to her once again.

Ann looked into her eyes and softly pushed away. "Kathy, give me a minute, okay?" She then rushed out the door.

Casey was waiting for the elevator.

"Casey!" she called out.

Casey looked toward her and waited even though the elevator door opened and then closed again. Ann approached her and placed her hand on her arm.

"Casey, I'm sorry. I didn't know what to say."

Casey looked at her with complete understanding. "You don't have to say anything. She's your wife. Go to her."

Ann slightly shook her head. "But I don't want—"

"Don't finish that sentence," Casey interrupted. Then, taking Ann's left hand, she pulled it up so that Ann could examine the ring. "This piece of metal has been between us from the beginning. It represents the woman back in your room, and the vow that you made to her."

Ann concentrated on the ring, but more on the heat that was penetrating from the hand that held it.

Casey touched Ann's cheek with her other hand. "Now, go and keep that vow. You need to get laid anyway, right?"

Ann closed her eyes, feeling Casey's touch through every inch of her body. She met Casey's gaze. "I don't know if I can."

Casey softly smiled and entered the elevator. Ann heard her return some advice that she had given several days ago. "If it helps, pretend it's me."

Ann returned the smile as the elevator doors closed. Turning, she made her way back to Kathy.

Ann's thoughts swirled as she walked back down the hall. How could she be with Kathy, she berated herself, when all she could think about was being with Casey? Maybe she just needed to spend some time with Kathy. Maybe she just needed to remember what she loved about her.

Ann composed herself before entering the room. Shutting the door behind her, she felt a twinge of apprehension as she saw that Kathy was not in the living area. She made her way to the bedroom and tried not to react negatively to the woman sprawled naked on her bed.

"Hi," she said softly as she leaned against the doorway.

"Don't act so excited, darling," Kathy said mockingly.

Ann walked over and sat on the edge of the bed. "I'm sorry. It's just that we have hardly spoken in a couple of weeks, and now you want to jump right into bed."

"Are you sure that's what's bothering you?" Kathy asked as she took Ann's hand and placed in on her breast.

"What do you mean?" Ann asked confused.

"Is something going on between you and Casey?"

Swallowing hard, Ann tried not to act guilty. "I've told you before, we're just friends."

"Then come here and convince me," Kathy said as she pulled Ann to her.

"You've got to be kidding!" Ann backed away.

"What, baby?" Kathy acted innocent as she reached out for her.

"I just saw you a couple of days ago. You wouldn't even sleep in the same bed with me!"

"I know. I'm sorry about that." Kathy sighed. "But what you asked that night really got to me. I mean, you actually asked if I still loved you. I had to come prove it to you. I still love you, Ann."

Kathy took Ann's hand and gently pulled her to the bed. The lovemaking was awkward and dull. Ann remembered how to satisfy Kathy, but it felt like Kathy had forgotten all about Ann's body. Ann faked an orgasm just to end the ordeal.

"You do remember that the beach party is tomorrow, right?" Ann asked just as Kathy was taking a bite of her sandwich. They had ordered room service and were sitting cross-legged on the couch.

Kathy swallowed. "Gee, sounds like fun," she quipped.

"Well, it will be fun. It's all in your attitude."

"So now I have a problem with my attitude?" Kathy snapped, clearly irritated.

Ann sighed not wanting another argument. Putting down her sandwich, she stood and sauntered toward the bedroom. "I'm tired Kath. I'm going to bed."

The next morning, Ann had to drag Kathy out of bed. "Come on, Kathy. It's almost eleven o'clock."

"Do I have to go?" Kathy groaned.

"No, you don't have to go. But I'm going, and I'm leaving in thirty minutes." Ann was at wit's end and left the room. She heard Kathy angrily throw back the sheets, her feet heavy on the floor and finally the bathroom door slamming.

She and Kathy walked out the door at eleven-thirty exactly.

Just as they arrived a half-hour later, a set decorator, Linda, approached. "Hey, Ann!" Glancing at Kathy, she asked, "Where's Casey?"

Ann winced at the question that she knew probably irritated

Kathy. Shrugging, she introduced her to Kathy. "Linda, this is my partner Kathy. Kathy, this is Linda, one of the set decorators."

Linda looked confused as she shook Kathy's hand. "Hi, Kathy. How come I haven't seen you around the set?"

Kathy looked annoyed. "I'm not living here. I needed to stay in San Francisco with my job."

Linda nodded her head in understanding, then turned to Ann. "So you don't know when Casey is coming?"

Ann shook her head. "Sorry. Maybe we'll see you later."

She and Kathy walked in silence for a moment, Ann trying to find the exact words to say. Kathy broke the silence.

"So this Linda person didn't know that you had a partner?"

"I hardly know her," Ann quickly replied. "That's probably only the second time I've even spoken to her."

Kathy smirked. "She seems to know you well enough to think you'd know where Casey is."

Ann didn't know how to respond. Suddenly Kathy, as if sensing Ann's nervousness, grabbed her hand.

"Come on. Let's go see who else doesn't know about me," she said meanly.

The answer became apparent as everyone seemed to stop their conversations as she and Kathy walked by. Ann could tell that Kathy was getting more and more pissed off. She was relieved as Leslie shouted out a greeting.

They chatted with Leslie for about ten minutes until Ann's stomach rumbled from hunger. The aroma of barbequed hamburgers led them to the buffet table. Ann and Kathy set their plates on the table and sat down. Noisy chatter filled the air. Another woman approached the table with her hands full and looked to see if there was room enough for her to sit down. Starting to turn away, someone else motioned for her to sit in the empty space beside Ann.

The woman shook her head. "No, Casey will want to sit there." She wandered over to the next table.

"Funny how they would assume that Casey would be sitting

there," Kathy said dryly as she unrolled her napkin.

Ann turned to her. "Kathy—"

"Just go get us some drinks, okay?"

Just then, Casey sat down in the empty space beside Ann and placed a diet soda in front of her.

Kathy, watching this action, mumbled, "How special."

Ann sighed and rose from the table to retrieve a drink for Kathy.

Casey chided herself. She should have brought a drink, or an assortment of drinks, for Kathy. *Ann will probably pay for that one,* she thought to herself. Opening her own drink, Casey tried to relax. She felt tense, not only because of Kathy's obvious dislike for her, but also not knowing what had happened between Ann and Kathy the night before.

After an uncomfortable silence, someone across the table from Kathy tried to strike up a conversation. "So, Kathy, since Ann's been here all alone, we've really tried to keep her from being lonely."

"Yes, well, it seems some of you have been trying a little harder than others," Kathy quipped, glancing over at Casey.

Casey ignored the comment and politely tried to sway the conversation to another topic. "Kathy, meet Penny and Dawn. They play Sam and Beth in the movie."

Kathy finished her bite, then leaned forward conspiratorially. "To tell you the truth, I can't say that I know much about the characters. I never read the entire book. I'm really too busy do any light reading."

Penny and Dawn looked surprised and didn't respond to the statement. Casey just shook her head and dropped her utensils loudly on her plate. Kathy shrugged and continued eating. Casey stood and carried her plate and soda away.

❧

"So, what are you guys talking about?" Ann said as she set a soda in front of Kathy and sat down. Glancing around, she tried as nonchalantly as possible to find out where Casey had gone.

"We were just talking about how busy Kathy is," Penny replied with a tone of irritation.

"Yes, she is a busy woman," Ann agreed. "She can't just set her clients aside like I can."

"Don't tell us that you're an attorney too?" Dawn asked.

"Yes, but she's a tax attorney," Kathy answered, evidently bored.

"Kathy is a criminal attorney. She probably has, let's see, about ten cases on her plate right now," Ann put in.

Kathy looked surprised. "You actually keep track of my case-load?"

Ann nodded as she took another bite of her hamburger.

"So, you're an attorney, a writer, and you take time to keep track of Kathy's workload. Wow! That's busy." Penny said directly to Kathy. Kathy glared back at her.

Ann shook her head modestly. "Being a defense attorney is a lot of work. I remember when I was a prosecutor, I hated it." She took a breath. "That's actually how we met. I was the prosecutor on the same case that Kathy was defending."

"So who won?" Dawn asked.

Ann looked at Kathy and smiled. "I did." Kathy just rolled her eyes. "After we got together, I became a tax attorney so that we wouldn't be put in that situation again."

"So you changed your whole career?" Dawn proceeded with the subject, as if to further irritate Kathy.

She succeeded. Kathy stood. "Excuse me, I need another drink."

Ann smiled, suspecting exactly what Dawn had done. She then explained, "Really, it was my choice. I hated the courtroom. It turned me into a real bitch."

A while later, Kathy strolled back and sat down next to Ann. "So how long are we supposed to stay here?"

"But we just got here!" Ann wasn't ready to leave. She was just finishing dessert. Dawn and Penny had gone to locate the volley-ball net and volleyball.

"Yeah, and how long do we have to stay? I'm bored already."

"Just wait a few minutes. I think we're going to play volleyball, and we can go into the water if you'd like."

Kathy rolled her eyes. "I'm going to the car to make a call."

Ann stood and headed to the water. All she could hear was laughter and music behind her. In front of her were rolling waves that came in with a roar, but ran gently over Ann's bare toes. Swishing her feet in the cool water, she wished that Kathy was in a better mood to play.

Casey spotted Ann wading in the ocean and strolled over. Leaning forward, she peeked at Ann's face. "Hi."

"Hi," Ann said as she continued to watch the tide. "I would've come over but I didn't want to interrupt your little groupie thing going on."

Casey laughed. "Yeah. They were trying to talk me into a three-some."

Ann's gaze never wavered. "Sounds interesting."

Casey rolled her eyes and admitted, "Like I could keep up with those two young things."

"I see you gave it some thought."

"Sure. I figured if you were getting laid this weekend, why shouldn't I?"

Ann didn't respond.

"Hey, I was just kidding," Casey said as she touched Ann's arm, then immediately pulled away. She'd noticed Kathy in the parking lot not far away.

Ann finally turned to face her. "Why? You should be out there having some fun."

"I do. I have fun with you," Casey explained, looking into Ann's eyes.

"Okay, let me rephrase. You should be out there getting laid," Ann said, turning back toward the water.

"I don't want any meaningless sex," Casey stated. A second later they both looked at each other and laughed.

"I wish I had a tape recorder." Ann chuckled. "Your friends would have loved to hear that."

The two turned somber and looked out at the bluish green water.

"So, how's it going with Kathy?" Casey asked, not really wanting to hear the answer.

"Great!" Ann replied dryly. "I remember all the reasons that I fell in love with her."

"Really?" Casey said, feeling a pain inside.

Ann looked down and sighed. "No."

Just then, Kathy came jogging up behind them, put an arm around each of them and squeezed. "Hey, guys, they're putting up the volleyball nets!" she said excitedly.

Casey had heard Ann speak of Kathy the alien. Was this her, or was this just sarcasm? "Great! Let's go play!" Ann had taken the bait.

"How about you, Casey? You any good at volleyball?" Kathy asked.

Casey looked at Ann, then back at Kathy. "I haven't played since college, but I'll give it a try."

The three women joined the others and amused themselves until they were all drenched with sweat and rolling in sand. Someone threw the volleyball out into the water, and it became a new game in the waves.

Several hours later, as the sun was setting, the party came to an end. Ann and Kathy were almost to the car when Ann remembered that Leslie had requested some additional changes to the script.

"I'll be right back. I forgot something." Ann began jogging back to where several people were still conversing. Grabbing the script from Leslie, she pulled Casey aside.

"Is your birthday party still at the bar tomorrow night?" Ann murmured into her ear.

Casey sighed. "Like Kathy will really let you come."

Ann turned Casey's face toward her to look into her eyes. "I won't miss your birthday."

Casey averted her gaze. "Have a good time tonight."

Ann flipped through the script as she headed back to the car. "Did you tell your girlfriend good-bye?" Kathy asked sarcastically as Ann slid into her seat.

She threw the script onto the dashboard. "The script. See, I went back for the script."

"You still didn't answer my question," Kathy replied.

"It doesn't deserve an answer."

"Hell, she's probably already in your pants," Kathy said disgustedly. "I should have said 'lover.'"

"Look, I'm only going to say this once. I am not now fucking nor have I ever fucked Casey. And if I hear one more word about it, I won't be fucking you either!" Ann shouted.

"Such nice language from a prominent attorney," Kathy quipped.

Ann sighed. The alien was gone again.

Back at the beach, Dawn cornered Casey and asked, "So did you tell Ann what Kathy said?"

"About what?" Casey replied.

"What Kathy said about not really reading her book."

Casey shook her head. "It would only hurt her."

"Yeah, but maybe it would send her straight into your arms."

Casey was appalled. "Look, Ann takes her commitment to Kathy and her marriage very seriously. I really respect her for that."

Sitting down in the sand, after Dawn had walked away in a tizzy, Casey watched the sun sink into the darkening water. She went to her car and drove home, all the while trying to keep Ann out of her mind and yet wondering what she and Kathy would be doing that night.

Chapter Fourteen

Opening the door of the bar, Ann's eyes adjusted to the dim light. She smiled as she saw the big banner, "Happy Birthday, Casey!"

Ann approached the table of rowdy women. Stopping, she placed her hands on Casey's shoulders and leaned over to whisper in her ear, "Happy Birthday, beautiful."

Casey must have been a little tipsy, Ann thought, because there were tears gathering in Casey's eyes as she broke into a wide smile.

"So how come the birthday girl isn't dancing?" Ann asked as she massaged Casey's shoulders.

"Probably because she can't stand!" Somebody chuckled. The rest of the group broke into laughter.

Ann reviewed the various bottles and glasses that cluttered the table. Looking down at Casey she asked, "Is that true?"

Casey shook her head and laughed. "No."

Ann held out her hand. "Then dance with me." Casey took her hand and followed her to the dance floor.

Casey looked into Ann's eyes as she took her in her arms, allowing several inches of space between them. "I wasn't sure you'd be here."

"I told you that I wouldn't miss your birthday party," Ann replied, watching as Casey scanned the room. "Are you looking for someone?"

Casey brought her gaze back to Ann's and said, "Kathy."

Ann grimaced. "She went home tonight."

Casey was evidently confused. "Didn't she realize that tomorrow is a holiday?"

"Well, I may have led her to believe that we were working tomorrow."

Casey raised Ann's chin so that Ann would be forced to look at her. "You lied to her?"

Hearing a trace of anger in Casey's voice, Ann tried to explain. "I wanted to be here and I didn't think you'd feel comfortable with Kathy here."

Casey looked away not knowing quite how to feel. Part of her was indeed angry that Ann had lied to Kathy. But another part of her was overjoyed that she had been chosen over Kathy. And yet another part of her was confused as to where she stood in this relationship. She couldn't help but to pull Ann closer as she pried for further information. "So can I assume that she satisfied you sexually seeing as you allowed her to leave?"

Ann murmured seductively into Casey's ear, "To be totally honest, she hasn't satisfied me in years."

Casey felt her entire body heat up. "You do realize that you're telling me, the woman who dreams every night of a different way to make love to you, that your current lover doesn't satisfy you?"

Ann whispered, "Only at night?"

"You're just teasing me now." The warmth inside her had turned to frustration.

Ann pulled her hand from Casey's and wrapped her arms around Casey's neck, pulling her even closer. "What did you want to hear? That I had an orgasm on every flat surface available?"

Casey decided to tease back. "Only on flat surfaces?"

"Now you're just teasing *me*!"

"I guess you'll never know, will you?"

The song over, the two wandered back to the table. Over the next hour, Ann watched as Casey downed shot after shot with her friends. After the waitress had delivered several trays of drinks, the bartender visited the table.

She leaned into the group. "Okay, can I ask who the designated driver is here?"

Ann immediately raised her hand in response. "That would be me."

The bartender nodded. "I'll bring you a free soda. So, do you have all of their keys?"

Pam threw her keys onto the table and looked at Casey. Casey grinned as she pulled her keys from her pocket and jingled them in front of Ann. But as Ann reached for them, Casey stood up and dropped them down the front of her jeans.

"Come and get them," she dared.

Pam and Diane broke out in laughter, but Ann looked at the bartender, unamused. "I'll have them by the time you get back." The bartender left and Ann, annoyed, said, "Come on Casey, don't be a jerk."

"Hey, this gives you a good excuse to get in my pants," Casey teased.

Ann stared at her, not finding her comment appropriate in this setting. She looked over at Pam and Diane, but neither would offer help. Reluctantly, she stood and stepped behind Casey. She slipped her arm around her waist and under Casey's jeans.

"Gee, no foreplay?" Casey chuckled.

Ann was angry now. She was not about to make this enjoyable for her. "This wasn't the way I pictured this happening!"

With one swift jerk, she reached in, grabbed the keys and pulled them out. Stuffing the keys into her own pocket, she looked sternly at Casey and dragged her onto the dance floor.

"Is this the obligatory snuggle after intimacy?" Casey joked.

Ann was finding no humor in the situation. "Why are you drinking so much?" Ann snapped.

Casey took several moments before answering, tears in her eyes. "I was just trying to numb myself of the pain . . . the confusion . . . the burning sensation in my body. I want you so bad, Ann."

Ann's wall of anger crumbled. Looking into Casey's eyes, she responded with a soft voice. "I'm sorry. I didn't realize how all this was affecting you. Maybe I should leave."

"No!" Casey cried as she clung to Ann's body. Ann lay her head on Casey's shoulder and gently rubbed her back in a soothing motion as they continued to move to the music. They found a comfortable rhythm that seemed to ease the sexual friction. Then Casey slid her hands down onto Ann's butt.

"Casey . . ." she warned her.

Casey whispered in desperation, "Please, Ann, it's my birthday. Let me have a little leeway."

Ann conceded and let Casey's hands remain. She felt her own burning sensation under Casey's caress. Caught up in the moment, Ann let her own hands roam down Casey's back and onto her butt. A moan escaping Casey's throat brought Ann back to reality.

Stopping abruptly, she grabbed Casey's hand. "Come on, it's time to go home."

Ann grabbed the other keys and motioned to Pam and Diane that it was time to leave. Ann helped Casey into the passenger seat and made sure Pam and Diane were buckled up too. "You guys want to sleep in the spare bedroom?" Ann asked Pam and Diane. She didn't really feel like playing taxi service tonight. They said yes, and Casey immediately lay back in her seat and closed her eyes. Ann wasn't sure exactly what was happening in the backseat on the way to Casey's house. At one point she looked into the rearview mirror and, upon passing a bright light on the freeway, caught the sight of a hand on a bare breast. Shaking off the image running through her head, she remained focused on the road ahead.

Turning into the driveway, Ann hesitated to look behind her into the backseat. She was relieved when she heard the doors open. Coming around the car, she opened the passenger door, woke Casey and helped her into the house.

"Where are you going to sleep?" Pam smiled suspiciously.

Ann shrugged. "On the couch, I guess. I'm too tired to drive back to the hotel."

The two nodded and stumbled down the hall toward the spare bedroom.

Ann led Casey down the hall to her room, turned down the bed and sat her down. Sitting next to her, Ann began to help Casey pull her overshirt off. All of a sudden, Casey showed a burst of energy as she grabbed Ann and pushed her down on the sheets. Next thing she knew, Ann's arms had been pinned underneath her and Casey was looking down at her with a teasing smile. Ann was too tired to play this game.

"Casey, please, I'm too tired for this."

"I'll wake you up," Casey said as she slowly unbuttoned Ann's shirt and ran her hand along Ann's bare skin and over her bra. Ann closed her eyes as she felt the sensation, and then Casey's lips as she kissed her neck. This was indeed waking her entire body. Luckily, the next thing she felt was Casey's body falling limp as she passed out on top of her. Ann smiled in relief as she rolled away.

Ann stood and went to turn out the light. Looking back, she watched as Casey lay limp. Smiling to herself, she thought, *revenge is sweet*. She was amazed how easy it was. Within minutes she had undressed Casey and stood back to admire the tan, muscular, completely nude body, before her. She covered Casey with the sheet, shut off the light and closed the door.

Casey was awakened by a noise coming from another room. Rubbing her eyes, she moaned as the light made her eyes burn and her head ache. Attempting to sit up she felt the sheets against her naked body. She lay her head in her hands, trying to remember how she got home last night and how she had gotten undressed. Responding to the sound of clatter from the kitchen, she got up and pulled on her robe. Heck with how she had gotten home. The question was, who had she brought home and would she remember her name upon seeing her face?

Stumbling through the living room, Casey stopped and leaned against the doorjamb with a sigh of relief. The woman standing in the kitchen was Ann.

"God, am I glad it was you," Casey exclaimed.

"Of course it's me," Ann replied. "Wait a minute. You're not going to tell me that you don't remember my birthday present to you last night, are you?"

Casey tried desperately to remember but her mind was blank. "We didn't . . ."

"Why do you think you were naked?"

Casey saw a little glimmer in Ann's eyes but wasn't sure what it represented. Hoping that Ann was just teasing, she asked, "You are kidding, aren't you?"

Ann came toward her, brought her face in close, then tweaked her nose. Smiling, she said, "Gotcha!"

Casey returned the smile but questioned, "So how did I end up naked?"

Ann laughed mischievously. "I told you I'd get to see you naked someday."

"You didn't!" Casey was appalled.

"Not a natural blonde, huh?" Ann laughed again as she left the room.

Casey wobbled over to the cupboard and pulled out some aspirin. Pouring herself a cup of coffee, she swallowed several pills. What else did she smell besides coffee? She checked the oven and found biscuits. Although they weren't quite ready, they looked like something her stomach could take. Hearing voices from the living room, Casey wandered in and found Pam and Diane sprawled out on a couch, both holding their heads as if they were going to fall off. Casey slumped down into the other sofa with a moan.

"There's more orange juice and it looks like some biscuits on the way," she mumbled. "Ann's sure in a cheerful mood this morning."

"We're actually surprised that she's even talking to you after last night." Pam snickered.

Confused, Casey looked at them.

"You don't remember, do you?" Pam asked. Casey shook her head. "You made her go fishing for your keys in your pants!"

Casey almost choked on her coffee. "You mean in my pockets, right?"

Pam and Diane shook their heads. Diane said, "No, we mean in your pants."

Casey's face burned as she hid it in her hands. "Oh, my God."

Ann came in with a fresh pitcher of orange juice. "What's the matter?"

Diane giggled. "We were just telling Casey about the key incident last night."

Casey couldn't bear to face her, but muttered, "I am so sorry."

Ann sat down and leaned back in the chair. "I don't know why they're giving you such a hard time, I think you all embarrassed yourselves a little last night."

Pam looked innocent. "What did we do?"

Ann looked her straight in the eye. "What exactly were you two doing in my backseat on the way home last night?" She asked as she made her way back to the kitchen.

Diane reached over and slapped Pam. "I told you that she could see us. God, that's embarrassing."

Casey moaned at the sound of the telephone ringing. On the second ring, Pam held her head and glared at Casey. "Get the damned phone!"

Casey groaned as she leaned over and hit the speaker button. "Hello?"

"God! You sound terrible," said the voice on the other end.

"Bad hangover from last night," Casey replied, wondering who the hell was calling so early.

"Last night?" the voice asked.

"My birthday party." Confused, she tried to place the voice.

"How's Ann doing?" the voice continued.

"Fine." Casey gave up. "I'm sorry, who is this?"

"Kathy. You remember, her wife?" There was a pause. "No wonder she wasn't home last night. And the funny thing is, no one is working at the studio today. I guess I should've known to call your house first."

Casey winced and tried to sound calm as Pam and Diane looked panicked. "Let me go get Ann, okay, Kathy?" Casey called out to Ann.

Kathy ignored Casey's statement. "I bet I can guess what Ann gave you for your birthday last night."

Casey grabbed the receiver and spoke directly into it. "I'm going to get Ann." This time she yelled louder for Ann.

"Don't bother," Kathy said as she hung up. Casey closed her eyes as she heard the dial tone.

"What?" Ann came rushing in the room.

"Umm . . . you need to call Kathy."

"Why?" Ann drew out the word while looking at her suspiciously.

"She just called . . . and hung up on me."

"Because I wasn't getting to the phone quick enough?" Ann paused to think. "Wait a minute. She called here . . . on your home phone?"

"Yep. I told you that you shouldn't have lied to her about working today." Casey sang the words.

"Shit! What did she say?"

"She knows that you're not working today. She knows it was my birthday yesterday. She knows that you were with me last night and today. She said that she could guess what you gave me as a birthday present." Casey replayed their conversation.

Ann covered her face in horror. "Oh, God, what am I going to do. I bet she's really angry now."

Casey nodded. "I'd say she's furious."

Ann sighed. "Okay. Well, I'm going back to the hotel. Maybe I'll think of something to say on the way there.

Ann called Kathy. No answer. She busied herself with trying to clean up her work area as she was expecting Suzie to arrive soon. Ann called several time more. Still no answer. When the phone finally rang, Ann grabbed the receiver immediately. It was Suzie, down at the hotel desk. She quickly stacked some papers and set them on the desk before she left the room. She would have to try Kathy again later.

Chapter Fifteen

Casey stood at Ann's door as it swung open. Before her was a woman in her twenties in a white hotel robe combing through her wet hair.

"Can I help you?"

Casey looked at the number on the door and then again at the woman. "Is Ann around?"

The woman looked at her curiously then motioned for Casey to come in. "Yeah. I'll go get her."

Casey watched as the young woman went into the bedroom and shut the door. Soon after, Ann emerged.

"What are you doing here?" Ann asked.

"Now I see why you didn't answer your phone last night," Casey quipped.

"You tried to call?"

Casey frowned at her. "Yeah, several times."

"Suzie, my assistant, arrived at the hotel last night and they didn't have her reservation."

Casey nodded, still irritated. "And you weren't answering your phone because . . ."

Ann shrugged. "She hadn't had anything to eat so I sat with her down in the restaurant. Maybe you called while we were out."

"So where'd she stay last night?"

"Here." Ann was clearly getting tired of this line of questioning.

"And where did she sleep?"

"Is there a reason you stopped by, Casey?" Ann snapped. Apparently, she was aggravated by the insinuation.

"Are you going to answer my question?"

"Are you going to answer mine?" Ann responded.

"I thought maybe since Leslie gave us another day off, we could go to lunch. I didn't realize that I needed to call first." Casey's hurt came out as sarcasm.

"Where were you thinking of eating?"

"Dominic's."

"Okay. I need to drop Suzie off at the rent-a-car place. Can I meet you there in, say, half an hour?"

Casey nodded and looked into Ann's eyes. "Are you going to answer my question?"

Headed toward the bedroom, Ann shot back, "It doesn't deserve an answer."

When Ann didn't come out, Casey left the hotel room slamming the door behind her.

Ann met Casey at Dominic's and she had just sat down when a voice came from behind her.

"Casey!"

Casey looked up and politely smiled. "Hello, Karla."

The woman walked over and stood with her back to Ann. "Did you get my letter? I haven't heard anything from you."

Ann looked at Casey for an introduction. Casey complied. "Ann, this is my attorney, Karla Kaufman. Karla, this is—"

Karla had turned toward Ann and interrupted Casey in mid-sentence. "Oh, my God. Ann Covington. Are you trying to steal away my client?" she joked.

Ann broke into a smile. "Karla! God, no. These actors are way too temperamental for me."

Casey looked confused. "Do you two know each other?"

"For . . . what has it been, five years or so?" Karla turned to Ann again. "What are you doing in Los Angeles? I wish I would've known you were in town. Wow, did we have some crazy times, huh?"

Ann laughed and gestured to keep those memories a secret. Casey mentioned business and then shooed Karla away.

"Did you sleep with my attorney?" Casey said looking up from the menu.

"Before I respond to that question, I want you to take a moment and consider when she and I knew each other. Five years ago . . . hmm . . . I've been with Kathy ten years . . ." With that, she expected the question to be dropped.

Instead, Casey asked again, "Did you sleep with my attorney?"

Ann sighed angrily and threw her napkin down on the table. "You know, that's the second time today that you've questioned my integrity."

Casey still had her eyes glued to the menu before her.

Ann scooted her chair back and rose. "Suddenly, I'm not very hungry." She picked up her purse and stalked out of the restaurant.

What nerve, she thought. She was proceeding to back out of her parking space, when suddenly Casey appeared beside her, slapping the card door to stop her.

Ann rolled down her window. "What do you think? That I've slept with other women and that I'm just holding out on you? Playing hard to get? If you have to hear it then I'll say it. No, I have never been unfaithful to Kathy in the ten years that we've been together. And here's another thing that I'll admit. You are the first and only time that I've been seriously tempted to do otherwise. But right now, I'm extremely thankful that I haven't acted on that temptation!"

"Ann . . ." Casey stuttered.

125

"You know what? We need some time apart," Ann said as she backed out and sped out of the parking lot.

Casey checked several places before she found Ann, two hours later, sitting alone on the beach, at the exact spot they had picnicked days before. Ann was shivering as the cool breeze ran across the water. Grabbing a jacket from her car, Casey approached her, gently placed the jacket across her shoulders and sat down beside her. The two of them sat in silence for several moments while Casey organized her thoughts.

"I'm sure that you've heard stories about my reputation of being a cold-hearted bitch." Casey sighed. "Well, all the stories you've heard are probably true. But lately, I've found myself with feelings that I've never allowed myself before. Jealousy, for one." She paused, but Ann still sat staring out at the sea. "You asked me a few weeks ago if our relationship was going to be a problem for me. Never in my wildest dreams would I have imagined what a problem it's become. I'm finding it extremely hard—"

"And you don't think that it's hard for me? To want someone so badly in Los Angeles, and yet have someone back in San Francisco who expects me to be faithful?"

Casey's heart went out to her. Until now, she hadn't realized Ann's agony. "So what's the solution?"

Ann sighed. "I'd say we shouldn't see each other anymore, but I don't know what would be more painful. Seeing you every day, or not seeing you."

"Not seeing you would definitely be more painful for me," Casey said softly. "Please don't ask that of me."

"If we're going to continue seeing each other, I can't guarantee that I can be strong one hundred percent of the time. I'm going to have to ask you to be strong when I'm not." Ann turned to look her in the eye. "It's extremely important to me, Casey."

Casey nodded. "I know it is." After a long moment of self-reflection, Casey said, "All I can do is promise to try."

"That's all that I'm asking."

Chapter Sixteen

Trouble on the set. First day back for shooting. What a day for Leslie to be sick, Ann thought as she approached Casey and Jenny who were practically screaming at the top their lungs.

"So what's going on guys?" Neither of them stopped their rage until Ann turned to Casey and placed her hand on her arm.

Suddenly Casey, and then Jenny, broke for a breath.

"One at a time, please," Ann said, giving Jenny the first opportunity to speak. Casey immediately started ranting and raving again. Ann turned to her. "Shut up!" Turning back to Jenny she noticed Casey beginning to walk away. Ann snapped, "Don't even think about it, Casey."

Before addressing Jenny, she narrowed her eyes at Casey then said with a teasing smile, "God! You can be such a bitch sometimes."

Ann, now facing Jenny, whispered, "Is she smiling?" Jenny peeked over Ann's shoulder. Ann felt relief as she watched Jenny nod and her lips turn up into a smile. Sighing, she walked over to Shelley.

"Has this been going on all day?"

"Just in the last couple of hours."

"Well, if it gets out of control again, just call it a day." Ann placed her hand on her forehead; it was almost the end of the day. "I can't deal with it. I have a migraine and I intend to lay on the couch in my trailer until someone can take me home."

"I'm so sorry you're feeling bad. Are you absolutely sure that there's nothing I can do?"

Casey had given Ann a ride back to the hotel and helped her undress. Ann shook her head and fell into bed. "I've just been under a lot of stress lately."

"I know . . . and you have to feel better by tomorrow. We go on location, remember?"

"Thank you for the added pressure," Ann mumbled.

"It's only one night," Casey said soothingly. Ann didn't seem to mind her presence. "Are you and Kathy back on speaking terms?"

"No. She still hasn't answered my calls."

Casey caressed Ann's cheek. "I'll be right back." She shut the bedroom door and sat on the desk that Suzie was using. Casey extended her hand. "Hi, I'm Casey. I guess we didn't get off to a great start yesterday. Can we start over?"

Suzie smiled. "I'm sorry about the misunderstanding." She laughed. "Me and Ann having an affair . . . my husband and I both laughed about that last night."

"So, when Ann has migraines in San Francisco, what do you do?"

Suzie shrugged. "Sorry, I don't do much. I call Kathy, call her a cab and send her home."

Casey nodded. "Do you have Kathy's number? I'm going to try and give her a call."

Suzie took out a card from her Rolodex and handed it to her. "Good luck."

Casey began calling immediately.

An hour later, the phone rang. It was Kathy.

"Kathy, I'm so glad that you finally called. Ann has a migraine and I don't know what to do." Casey was frantic.

"Oh, how sweet. You want to take care of your girlfriend, or wait . . . is it my wife? I keep forgetting," Kathy replied sarcastically.

"Stop with the sarcasm, Kathy. The only reason that I'm here taking care of your wife is because you're too damn busy to take care of her yourself." Casey willed herself to stay calm. She took a deep breath to soften her mood. "Please, Kathy. I just want to make her feel better."

After several moments of silence, a more rational, gentler voice came over the phone. "You need to make sure that the bedroom is totally dark. Even the slightest bit of light hurts her." Kathy sighed, then continued, "There's some pills in the cabinet in the bathroom. I made sure that they were there. The label says to take one pill every four hours, but you need to give her two because one just doesn't do the trick. She'll fight you on it because she hates them, but it's the only thing that works. The pills will knock her out for a while and then she'll try to get up because she feels better. Don't let her because when she gets up too quickly the migraine just switches sides. So make her take more pills until she sleeps, like, twelve hours straight." Pausing, Kathy added, "and I can't believe that I'm actually saying this, but you need to hold her until the pills take effect, otherwise she won't stay still long enough for them to help."

Hearing silence on the other end of the phone, Casey was unsure if they were still connected. "Kathy?"

Kathy responded quietly, "Just take care of her Casey. You'd better get used to it because it happens all the time, and it looks like she wants to spend more time with you than with me. I can understand it. God knows I haven't been doing a very good job of taking care of her lately."

The next sound Casey heard was the dial tone on the other end of the line. Casey hung up and went into the bedroom to find Ann lying on the bed with a pillow over her head. Immediately she noticed how much light was in the room. Closing all the blinds and drapes, she made her way to the bathroom to locate her medicine.

"Ann?" Casey whispered as she tenderly removed the pillow from Ann's head. "You need to take these," she said, holding out two pills and a glass of water.

Ann objected just as Kathy had said but finally conceded and swallowed the medicine. Casey wrapped her arms around Ann and held her as she was told. As they both drifted off to sleep she remembered Kathy's gentle voice on the phone. For the first time she realized that maybe Kathy really did care about Ann. And for the first time Casey felt guilty for wanting to take Ann away.

Casey opened her eyes upon hearing Ann's voice. "Hey, you need to get up and get in the shower if we're going to make it on time."

Casey looked at her, fresh out of the shower. "How are you feeling?"

Ann shrugged. "Okay, I guess. I always have this blurriness the next morning. But I'll feel better as the day goes on." She sat down on the bed. "How did you know about my medicine last night?"

Casey wasn't sure if Ann would be angry about her phone call. "I . . . called Kathy."

Evidently shocked, Ann stood up. "Oh, so she would talk to you but not to me?" She shook her head.

"It's not like that. I called about every five minutes begging for suggestions on helping you to feel better."

"And she actually told you?" Ann asked in disbelief. "I would have thought that she would want me to be in pain."

"No, actually she was very helpful. She cares about you, Ann," Casey admitted.

"Uh-huh." Ann stared into the mirror on the wall. "Get in the shower."

Chapter Seventeen

It was a long drive to Coronado Island in San Diego where they would be on location for the next two days. But once they arrived in the area, they both agreed it was well worth it. The grassy knolls stretched out forever. This is where the various outdoor competitions written about in the fictional 'Sun and Fun' day in her book would be shot. Losing track of time, they were the last to make it to the hotel to get their room assignments.

"And here's the room key for Casey and Ann," the production assistant said as she handed the key to Casey.

Ann looked confused. "Why does everyone else get separate rooms and we have to share?" she asked.

The assistant seemed embarrassed. "I'm sorry. I was told that you would want a room together."

Ann looked at Casey, who raised her hands in defense. "Don't look at me. I didn't have anything to do with this."

"She didn't," the assistant admitted. "It was Shelley who told me how many rooms to get."

Shelley came over to the group after hearing her name. "Did I hear my name?"

"Yes," said the assistant. "You told me to only get one room for these two."

Shelley's face turned red with embarrassment. "I am so sorry, you guys," she apologized. "I was being sarcastic. I said that a lot of your problems would be solved if you two would just get a room together." She laughed nervously.

The two women did not smile back.

"Just get another room, okay?" Shelley told the assistant.

"There are no more rooms." The assistant grimaced. "And this one only has one king-size bed."

Casey shrugged and looked at Ann. "We're two adults. We can sleep in the same bed."

Later, after midnight, Casey felt Ann stir and watched her get up and close the window. She rubbed her arms as she shivered.

"Cold?" Casey asked out of the darkness.

Ann's voice shook. "I'm freezing."

"Come here." Casey raised the covers and reached for her. Ann climbed back into bed, where Casey tried to rub the goosebumps from Ann's arms. Then, pulling her down into her arms, Ann's backside molding into Casey's stomach, she held her close. Side by side, they both drifted off to sleep.

Ann was rudely awaked by the buzz of the alarm. With Casey still half asleep, Ann reached over to stop the noise.

Casey murmured, "Are you still cold?"

Ann smiled and placed Casey's fingers on her nose. "Just my nose." Then she added, "You know what they say. 'Cold nose'"— she brought Casey's hand from her nose down to her chest,— "'warm heart.'"

Casey clasped Ann's shirt, pulled her forward and kissed her nose. Their gazes met, their lips just inches away. Casey slowly shifted her thigh in between Ann's legs.

"Mmm . . . you don't fight fair." Ann smiled as she felt the gentle pressure between her legs.

"All's fair in love and war." Casey smiled back.

"Oh, and which is this?"

"I'd say a little of both," Casey replied.

Ann's memory of the tan, firm body below her flashed through her mind. She felt Casey's fingers comb through her hair. She felt Casey's grasp of her T-shirt pulling her closer. Something in her made her surrender. Their lips just a breath away, fate struck again.

"I swear the telephone company must be conspiring against us!" Ann smiled as the phone rang beside her.

Moving away, Ann picked up the phone and set it back down. "Our wake up-call." She explained to Casey. Rising from the warmth, Ann asked teasingly, "Do you want the first cold shower, or should I?" Then, knowing Casey so well, she answered what she thought would be Casey's next question. "And, no, we can't take one together." Ann chuckled as Casey tried to look innocent.

"You go first." Casey crossed her arms and grinned. "And Ann, make sure you lock the bathroom door behind you huh?"

Ann smiled, grabbed her robe and shut the door. She heard Casey's laughter as she turned the lock on the door.

"Hey, today was a great day! We got want we wanted on location, it was a beautiful day for the beach scenes . . ." Casey paused. "So . . . why the long face, cowboy?" She said in her best John Wayne imitation.

Ann looked at her and laughed. "Don't quit your day job!" Then, sobering, she said, "Kathy just canceled on me this weekend. It wouldn't be such a big deal but we have the LAC dinner this Friday night."

Casey looked confused. "LAC?"

"Lesbian Attorneys of California," Ann explained. "I hate going to those things alone."

"I'm sorry," Casey replied.

"Hey, what are you doing Saturday night?" Ann smiled.

"Oh, no. It sounds like a thrilling evening . . ." Casey said, her sarcasm sneaking out. "But I think I'm going to be out of the country."

"Come on. It won't be that bad," Ann whined.

"What's it worth to you?" Casey teased.

Ann blushed. "What do you have in mind?"

"Wipe that smirk off your face. My intentions are honorable," Casey replied. "If I go to the LAC dinner with you, you have to go to that premiere with me next week."

"Are you sure that you want to show up with a 'nobody' at that premiere?" Ann kidded.

"Are you sure that you want to show up with a temperamental actress at your dinner?" Casey kidded back.

"Hmm . . . I'll be the talk of the evening." Ann smiled.

"Hmm . . . so will I." Casey smiled back.

Ann walked out of the bedroom still fidgeting with her dress.

"Wow," Casey exclaimed as she stood. "Do all attorneys clean up this well? Because if they do, I'm calling mine right now."

Ann smiled as she modeled her periwinkle-colored dress. "So I look okay?"

Casey could not keep the smile off of her face. "Yeah, but I don't know if I'll be able to drive."

Clearly confused, Ann looked at her.

Casey could not take her eyes off of Ann, but clarified her statement. "I won't be able to keep my eyes off you."

Ann walked over to Casey and lifted her chin so that their eyes met. "That's okay. It's not your eyes that I'm worried about!"

"Don't tell me that you didn't do this on purpose. You wore this dress to drive me wild all night."

Ann said with a devilish smile, "Maybe."

❧

Casey was overwhelmed by the crowd at the LAC dinner. There must have been five-hundred women in attendance. The dinner had been delicious. She had been afraid that some kind of puny salad would be served. However, when the tri-tip and garlic mashed potatoes were set in front of her, she squelched a joyous scream inside. And the chocolate mousse dessert had been superb. Now that all the dinnerware had been removed from the table, Casey found it difficult to stay awake. All of the women at the table had been pleasant, but their banter was dull. As Ann and the woman beside her engaged in a legal conversation, Donna, the woman across the table, rose and approached Casey.

"Wanna dance?" she asked over Casey's shoulder. Casey glanced at Ann, who clearly had her full concentration on the subject at hand. "They'll be at it for an hour," Donna explained as she offered her hand.

Casey allowed herself to be led to the dance floor.

"I have a feeling that you're used to leading," the woman said to Casey as she stepped into her.

Casey nodded and took the lead.

Donna immediately began a conversation. "So I was little surprised to see Ann here tonight without Kathy. I notice that she's still wearing her ring. Why is it that you're here with her?"

"Kathy couldn't make it tonight. And Ann isn't here 'with' me. It's not like that," Casey replied.

Donna smiled. "Who do you think you're kidding? She may not be here 'with' you, but you, my dear, are most definitely here 'with' her."

Baffled, Casey looked her.

Donna began again, "I've been watching you all night. You can't take your eyes off of her." Donna paused to look Casey straight in the eye. "Look, you're barking up the wrong tree. I know Ann. She's straight as an arrow. She won't cheat in business and she won't cheat on Kathy."

Just then, Ann appeared and tapped Donna's shoulder.

"May I cut in?" she asked Donna.

Donna stepped aside and smirked at Casey. "Hmm . . . I stand corrected."

Casey beamed as she took Ann in her arms.

"So, was Donna trying to pick you up?" Ann asked with a smile.

Casey laughed and shook her head in disbelief.

"What? You *are* the sexiest woman here," Ann teased.

Casey blushed. "Actually, she was warning me away from you."

"Really? What brought that on?"

Casey shrugged. "Something about my not being able to keep my eyes off you all night."

Ann met Casey's gaze. Casey, caught up in the moment, let her hand slide down from the small of Ann's back onto her butt. Ann closed her eyes, obviously taking in the sensation. Suddenly, Ann reached back and moved Casey's hand back to its proper place. She caught Casey's gaze again, relaying an unspoken message. Casey returned the look with complete understanding.

The evening winding down, Casey followed Ann as she made her way through the crowd relaying her good-byes and promises to stay in touch. It was almost midnight when they climbed into Casey's car.

"God, I feel like I embarrassed myself in there. I could hardly carry on a conversation with those people. I hope I didn't embarrass you. Maybe you should've taken someone else."

Ann laughed and brushed the hair away from Casey's face. "I think you held your own in there. I had a great time. There's no one I would have rather been with."

Casey looked into Ann's eyes. "Not even Kathy?"

Ann lowered her eyes then raised them again to meet Casey's. "Don't make me admit it out loud."

Casey softly smiled. She did not need to hear it out loud. She saw everything she needed in the green eyes before her.

Chapter Eighteen

A quiet evening sounds wonderful, Ann told herself. She and Casey would just relax and watch movie rentals. She needed some peace in her life right now. The shoot had dragged on that afternoon, and so Ann left early. Casey was off that day. She wouldn't mind, Ann felt sure.

Knocking on Casey's door helped her unwind. That was, until the door opened.

There stood an attractive woman inside Casey's doorway. Ann heard the voice but was too frozen to move.

Clearing her throat, the woman asked again, "May I help you?"

"Umm . . . I'm Ann . . . I'm a little early . . ." she stuttered.

"Oh, Ann! I'm Carol, Casey's sister. I've heard so much about you." She ushered Ann into the doorway. "Casey's in the kitchen. I'm just here to give her some decorating advice." Carol pulled her into the kitchen where Casey was holding up paint samples to her wall. "Hey, sis, look who I found on your doorstep."

Casey turned around and smiled broadly. "Ann!" Her eyes gave away her happiness at seeing Ann. Ann couldn't help but smile too. Carol stood and watched.

"Sorry, I'm a little early."

"It's okay. I need to leave anyway," Carol said. "But first, Casey, let's show her what colors you're thinking about."

The next hour was a blur. Casey's sister ushered them from room to room showing Ann colors and fabric. It was so fast, Ann couldn't remember afterward if the master bedroom was going to be brown and the spare bedroom would be gold, or the other way around.

"I thought you said Ann was just a friend," Carol said slipping her arm around Casey as they walked out to Carol's car. She turned to Casey. "I saw the look in her eyes when she didn't know I was your sister. I saw the look in your eyes when she walked into the kitchen." Raising Casey's chin so that she could look in Casey's eyes, she continued, "I also saw the ring on her finger."

Casey didn't know what to say. She just looked into her sister's eyes.

Her sister shook her head. "I hope you know what you're doing."

Casey broke away from the eye contact and lowered her gaze. "I don't have a clue. I just know how I feel about her."

Her sister turned and opened the car door. "Well, I'm sure you'll figure it out, you always do. But if you need to talk to anyone, I'm here."

"Thanks."

Ann waited on the couch, watching TV, while Casey walked her sister to her car. She reprimanded herself as she thought about the way she had reacted when an unfamiliar face opened Casey's door. It was jealousy, and it was wrong, she knew it. She was lucky this time, but next time it could very well be one of Casey's lovers. What then? She pondered the question until she lost herself in the murder mystery on the screen.

"What are you watching?" She heard Casey call out from the kitchen. Ann could smell popcorn and could hear the popping of the kernels against the bag in the microwave.

Soon, Casey came into the living room balancing a full bowl, a soda and a bag of M&Ms.

"You're my kind of woman," Ann said as she reached for the candy. "I'm not sure, but I think that man may have killed the woman in that picture." Ann tilted her head to the side, confused. "Or he was the husband of the woman, and the other woman is her sister."

"I think the uncle of the husband's mistress did it," Casey joked.

"What?" Ann turned to find Casey smirking and threw the remote control at her. "Here, you find something else to watch."

Settling on an old black and white movie, they stretched their legs out and relaxed to the soothing voice of Kathryn Hepburn. Several hours later, Casey awoke to the sounds of slicing and dicing on an infomercial. Ann had curled up on the other side of the couch and was clearly in a deep sleep. She covered Ann with a blanket, kissed her gently on the check and whispered good-night.

The next afternoon, Ann sat with Casey as a fire blazed in the fireplace. The weather outside was eighty degrees, but Casey had wanted a cozy atmosphere. She had turned on the air-conditioner to offset the heat in the room. Casey was curled up on the couch reading a biography of Sandra Day O'Connor. Right near her Ann sat cross-legged on the floor working on her laptop. The mood was warm and relaxed. They were each lost in their own worlds but comfortable with their closeness.

"Damn it!" Ann cursed loudly as her screen went black before her eyes. She fell back against the couch in exasperation.

Casey looked up from her book. "What's the matter?"

"I think my computer just crashed," Ann said, frustrated. "Now what I am going to do?"

Casey patted her shoulder. "Can't you work on my computer?"

"All my notes are on mine." Ann sighed, hoping they hadn't been lost. "Plus, your computer is ancient."

"Yeah, I keep trying to get my brother to update it." Casey smiled "Hey, I've got an idea." She picked up the phone and dialed. "You forget. I have connections. I bet he'd love to help out."

Ann watched as Casey tried to convince her brother to make the trip to her house. "What do you mean, 'What's it worth to me?' I seem to remember pulling some strings to get you into—yeah, that's what I thought." Casey turned to Ann. "Now he's changing his tune . . ."

Within minutes, Casey answered the door and led her brother into the room. Ann smiled as Casey introduced him, still holding his hand. What would it be like to be this close to your family?

"Ann, this is Tony." Casey grinned with pride. "My baby brother."

Tony rolled his eyes. "Not exactly a baby anymore . . ." Then, extending his hand, he approached Ann. "I heard Casey had a . . . special friend."

Ann tried not to laugh at his expression, 'special friend.' "Nice to meet you, Tony. How are you at working miracles?" She gestured to her lifeless laptop.

"Hmm . . . I'm not sure I can work miracles . . . but I'll give it a try."

An hour later, the laptop was working again.

"Thanks so much for coming all the way over. I really appreciate it," Ann said sincerely.

"No problem. Any friend of Casey's is a friend of mine," Tony replied. "I was going to come over anyway . . . I have some good news." He turned to Casey. "I finally popped the question to Rebecca last night . . . I guess I'm getting married."

Casey yelled with happiness and grabbed her brother. "It's about time!"

"Congratulations," Ann offered.

"Thanks," Tony said. "Now, Casey, walk your baby brother to his car."

Ann made herself a glass of soda, glad that her laptop had been restored, no data lost.

"What was that all about?" Ann asked when Casey returned.

"He wanted to know what was going on with us. I guess Carol talked to him," Casey said hesitantly as if expecting Ann's wrath.

Ann just smiled and kept reviewing her paper notes.

"Aren't you going to go on some tangent about what people think?" Casey said in astonishment.

Ann gazed warmly at Casey. "Neither you nor I can deny that there's something between us. Everyone we encounter sees it. Even Kathy . . . but as long as we don't act on our feelings . . ."

"You say it like it's so easy," Casey mumbled.

"You know that's not true." Ann looked into Casey's eyes.

The next several minutes were spent in silence.

Ann finally spoke. "Kathy's coming next weekend . . . or so she says."

Casey nodded then chuckled. "I have a date this evening."

"What?" This caught Ann off-guard. Why did it hurt so much?

"I've been postponing this date since I first met you."

"Oh." Ann didn't know what to say. "What time?"

"I'm supposed to meet her at the restaurant at six o'clock."

Ann looked at her watch. "Well, it's three o'clock. You'd better start getting ready." She started picking up her paperwork.

"Wait, Ann," Casey put her hand on Ann's shoulder. "It doesn't take me three hours to get ready. Don't leave yet."

Ann stayed for a while and tried to relax. Turmoil consumed her entire body. How would she occupy her time tonight while Casey was on her date? She didn't want to just sit around and think about it. *Stop it!* she said to herself. *Casey is just a friend. She should be out dating and having fun.* All the way home, she repeated to herself, *I am a married woman, I am a married woman, I am a married woman.*

Ann swung open the door and laughed as she saw Casey standing in front of her. She looked at her watch. The date had only lasted two hours. "Well, I guess it wasn't such a good date, huh?"

Casey shrugged as she brushed past Ann. "It was okay."

"Just okay?" Ann poked her in the ribs. "What was wrong with this one? Too fat? Too thin? Too tall? Too short? Too medium?" She was kidding.

"She was fine," Casey snapped. "Just drop it."

"Oh, come on. Tell me." Ann prodded her, chuckling.

Casey tucked her hair behind her ear and looked at Ann but did not respond.

"What? She wasn't easy enough for you?" Ann teased.

Casey's face turned red as she finally responded. "She wasn't you, okay?" Then, lowering her eyes, she crossed her arms and leaned back on the counter. She finally met Ann's gaze again, this time with tears in her own, and softly admitted, "She just wasn't you."

Chapter Nineteen

Casey grabbed Ann's hand and guided her through the rain as they ran to the limousine. The driver was waiting with an open door. Casey helped Ann into the car, for which Ann was grateful, and slid in beside her. The driver shut the door and ran around to his side of the car. In back, Ann was still laughing when the car began to move.

The premiere had been grand, she thought, just as she had seen on television a time or two. Casey had bought them both new outfits just for the occasion. No one had even cared that they came, two women, together. Of course, when the paparazzi had wanted pictures, they all ushered Ann out of the way. But she had expected that, and Casey only stayed with the cameras for a few seconds. Casey was not in this movie, so when Ann asked why they had bothered to come, Casey said that it was just out of professional courtesy.

She settled back in the seat for the ride. Glad to be in dry surroundings, she looked over at Casey, then down at her hand, which was still being held by Casey's.

Casey began to pull her hand away. "Sorry," she apologized.

Ann held Casey's hand tightly in hers, not allowing it to escape. Instead, she intertwined her fingers further. She stared into the dark brown eyes before her. She and Casey sat in silence, content with the longing, knowing that their hand clasp was crossing the forbidden line. Ann took her other hand and placed it over their intertwined fingers. Softly she caressed the skin on Casey's hand, feeling the heat rise in her from even this simple action.

Casey took her other hand and traced along the line of Ann's fingers. Slowly she ran her fingers around Ann's thumb, along her index finger. A shiver ran through Casey's body as she imagined what these fingers would feel like as they entered her. Continuing, she let her fingers slide along Ann's middle finger feeling the soft skin on her fingertips. Moving to Ann's ring finger, she was suddenly knocked back into reality as she stumbled onto the ring that had been placed on Ann's finger by another. She lowered her eyes and examined the ring as she twisted it around Ann's finger. She concentrated on the significance of the piece of metal that she was touching. Slowly she pulled her other hand away from its embrace and slid her body away, creating distance between them. Running her fingers through her hair, Casey turned toward the window trying hard to stop the tears welling in her eyes from the pain she felt inside.

"Casey . . ." Ann said softly, wanting to sooth her. But Casey held her hand up in response, signifying that there would be no further conversation. Ann sank back against the soft leather seat, her mind racing, her body flooding with emotions. The feeling of want conflicted with her feeling of betrayal. Leaning back, she closed her eyes, surrendering to the tears that began flowing down her cheeks.

The middle window of the limo rolled down. "Am I still taking you to Hillside Road?" He specified the exact address.

Casey verified the address, then touched Ann's knee and offered her a tissue. "Are you okay? Do you still want to go to Pam's house?"

Ann nodded, took the tissue and began blotting at her tears. "I'll be okay."

The car pulled up to the house as Pam was opening the front door. Diane ran out with umbrellas. They all made it inside before getting too wet. Pam led Ann to their sunroom, which Ann really thought of as a screened in porch. She stepped into the room and immediately loosened up. Pam had dimmed the lights, candles were lit, and soft music floated through the air. You could, she thought, still here the pitter patter of the rain as it fell.

"Diane is coming with dessert." Casey came out with steaming cups of coffee. "Wow. It looks really nice out here."

"Hey, we're our own little 'after-party' here." Pam smiled.

Casey placed the coffee on the table and sank back into a chair. She watched as Ann took a sip and made a sour face.

Casey jumped up immediately. "I'm sorry, Ann, I'll bring more cream and sugar out." She said as she jogged from the room.

"You have her wrapped around your little finger, don't you?" Pam kidded.

"Yeah," Ann replied as she watched Casey close the glass door. Trying to decide how to approach the subject with Pam, she pretended to tear at a string on the tablecloth. Finally, raising her eyes, she found Pam staring at her.

"What's on your mind?" Pam asked.

Ann looked her straight in the eye and asked, "From one married woman to another, do you think lusting after another woman is considered cheating?"

Pam grinned. "I hope not. Otherwise I've been unfaithful a million times."

"You? But Diane is an intelligent, beautiful woman."

"From what I hear, so is Kathy," Pam replied. "Unfortunately, so is Casey."

"But Casey is also fun, impulsive, witty . . ."

Pam nodded in agreement. "You've brought a lot of things out in Casey that we've never seen before. I think this may be the first time she's been in love."

The word *love* pierced through Ann. Love? Pausing for a moment, she sat up in her chair and tried to assemble her thoughts. "I can't do this to her. I've got to walk away."

Pam sat up and placed her hands over Ann's. "Look, Casey isn't stupid. She knows exactly what she's gotten herself into." Then, looking into Ann's eyes, she asked, "Has she ever said anything to you about leaving Kathy? I don't think so. Which leads us to the bigger problem."

Ann looked at her in confusion.

Pam posed the obvious question. "What? Do you think that if you don't say it out loud that it isn't real?" She waited for a response, but when there was none continued, "Casey's not the only one in love here. You're just as in love with her. I can see it in your eyes every time you see her. I bet Kathy can see it too."

"Here's dessert!" Diane sang as she headed into the room with Casey in tow carrying cream and sugar.

Ann quickly looked away and tried to calm down. She did not want to have to explain the certain redness in her face. Pam lightly squeezed Ann's hand while she put her cup down.

"Okay, Casey, let's hear all the details."

Chapter Twenty

"Hi, Casey, it's Kathy. Let me talk to Ann."

Kathy had flown in Saturday morning, and she and Ann were fighting already? Casey wondered.

"Kathy? Ann isn't here," Casey replied.

"Casey, please, I know I was a jerk, just let me apologize to her, okay?"

"Kathy . . . she really isn't here."

"Fine."

Casey heard the phone slam down. Forty-five minutes later, there was a loud knock on her door. She looked through the peephole and sighed before swinging it open.

"Kathy, I told you that she's not here."

Kathy stalked into the entryway and surveyed the room. Casey watched as her forceful shoulders suddenly sagged in disappointment. Kathy skulked over to the couch, plopped down, then covered her face with her hands. As Casey shut the door, an uncomfortable silence ensued.

"I don't know what to do." Kathy lifted her face toward Casey. "Ann always ends up running away from an argument. In San Francisco, I know exactly where to find her." She ran her fingers through her hair and smiled. "There's this little bench in Ghiradelli Square . . . she always ends up there, watching the tourists, the street entertainers . . . ." She rose and walked over to the mantle, then shrugged. "I don't even know where to look around here. I don't suppose you have any ideas."

Casey struggled with the decision. Should she take Kathy's word that she wanted to apologize? Or should she let Ann cool off and come back when she was ready? She thought back over the arguments that the two of them had had. Sighing, she realized that Ann rarely made the first move to end a fight.

"I may know a place," Casey admitted.

"Would you take me there?" Kathy asked softly. "Ann took the car. I had to take a cab here."

Casey nodded, grabbed her keys and headed out the door.

"So what was your fight about?" Kathy asked as she stared out the windshield.

Casey swallowed hard. "Excuse me?"

"Well, you know where to find her . . ." Kathy said, "so you must have found her there after a fight, right?"

Casey looked over at Kathy who was still gazing out the window. "I had gone to her hotel room to see if she wanted to have lunch . . . A young woman in a robe answered the door. I made some accusations that I shouldn't have made." She tried her best to skirt around the real reason for the fight; she had been jealous because Ann wouldn't have an affair with her. Running her fingers through her hair, she explained further, "I had never met Suzie before. The hotel lost her reservation. She had to stay in Ann's room . . . In short, I made a fool of myself."

"Mmm..I see." Kathy looked at Casey. "How nice of you to look out for our marriage." Casey just met her stare. Suddenly Kathy laughed. "Ann and Suzie, that would be funny."

Casey smiled as she got a glimpse of the side of Kathy that Ann loved. The glimpse was short-lived.

"Yeah, I'm apologizing for some accusations that I made too." Kathy looked out the window once again. "But I don't think my accusations were unwarranted." Turning back toward Casey, she asked, "Do you think my accusations were unwarranted?"

Casey felt her voice quiver. "What accusations?"

Kathy shook her head in disgust. "Don't treat me like I'm stupid, Casey."

"You know"—Casey tried to steady her voice—"I don't really like to get in the middle of people's arguments."

"Sounds pretty cowardly to me." Kathy turned away.

Casey tried to turn the subject around. "So, if you think there's merit to your accusations, why are you apologizing?"

Kathy shrugged. "Because that's what Ann wants to hear. She always chills after an apology. So, that's what I give her."

"Whether you really mean it or not?" Casey's tone hardened.

"You're right. Maybe you should stay out of people's arguments," Kathy snapped back.

Pulling into the parking lot, Casey spotted the rental car before Kathy did. She swung into a space and shifted into park. She and Kathy followed the path to the area that Casey knew all too well. Stopping, she pointed to a bench looking out over the cliff. Ann sat alone staring out at the ocean.

Kathy squeezed Casey's shoulder. "Thanks."

Casey watched as Kathy walked over to the bench, then eased down beside Ann. Ann suddenly swung around to meet Casey's gaze. Casey backed away, she couldn't stay any longer. No one wanted to watch the person she loved reconcile with someone else. Especially when the person was a version of Dr. Jekyl and Mr. Hyde. She didn't feel the first tear roll down her cheek until she slid behind the steering wheel. By the time she pulled back out onto the highway, her quivering breaths had turned to sobs.

Casey took a sip of beer and set the bottle down to join in the argument over a movie that she and her friends had just seen that evening.

"No, I don't agree," she said. " This was a sexy, intelligent woman. Why would she want to be someone's mistress?"

All of a sudden the entire group fell silent. Casey looked around at the women who seemed to be extremely focused on anything else but meeting Casey's eyes. Pam was the only one who dared to speak.

"Doesn't that sound familiar at all?" she asked Casey.

Casey tucked her hair behind her ear. "What are you talking about?"

"Oh, I don't know. You wait around for Ann to call. Drop everything and everyone when she's around . . ." Pam tried to explain.

"Pam!" Casey was surprised. The thought had never crossed her mind. "You guys!" All eyes were now focused on her. "God. The major point of being someone's mistress is the sex, right? We're not having sex. So there, I've proved my point, so let's just drop it."

Pam looked at Casey and shook her head as if to imply that Casey was obviously in denial. Casey glared at her then put her full concentration into peeling the label from her beer bottle.

Ann had dropped Kathy off at the airport that afternoon and then had a business dinner with an old client. Pulling into Casey's driveway, she sighed in relief. She had looked forward to having some time with her all day. Ann used her key to let herself in. Hearing voices coming from the patio, she wandered outside.

"Oh, sure, just let yourself in. Heaven forbid I have a date here with me!" Casey exclaimed.

Ann stopped in her tracks. "Am I intruding on something?"

Casey raised her arms in exasperation. "No. Of course not. I was just sitting around waiting for you."

Ann looked over at Pam and Diane who were sitting at the patio table. Neither would raise their eyes. "What's going on?" she asked.

"Why don't you guys tell her?" Casey said sarcastically. "Tell her that you called me her mistress tonight. Tell her that you said that I just sit around waiting for her."

Both Pam and Diane stared at Casey. She was a lousy drunk, Ann thought.

"Well they're right, aren't they? You expected me to be here alone, waiting for you, didn't you?" Casey asked loudly.

Ann looked at her. "I didn't expect anything."

"You know what I told them?" Casey said as she balanced herself on the back of a patio chair. "I told them that only a fool would be someone's mistress without getting any sex out of it." Laughing, she said, "I guess that makes me a fool, huh?"

Ann turned toward the sliding glass door. "You know, I think that I'll just go in and change my clothes . . ." She was glad that she had brought a pair of jeans and a T-shirt, if only to escape the awkward situation.

"Yes. Please go change your clothes. How dare you show up in that business suit. I hate seeing you like that. You know why? Because it's just another reminder that your life isn't here with me. You belong at another job, in another city, with another woman."

"Maybe I should just leave. Is that what you want?" Ann asked, feeling hurt.

"Since when is it about what I want? It's never about what I want," Casey said.

The words stung as Ann remembered Kathy's complaints about the same thing. She turned back toward the women sitting at the table. "I'm just going to leave. I'll see you guys later."

"Yes!" Casey shouted. "Just go ahead and leave. You're so good at that. Don't deal with anything . . ."

Ann looked Casey in the eye. "Good-bye then." She watched Casey raise her bottle, signifying her dismissal, then walked through the glass doorway and out the front door. Climbing in her car, she drove directly back to the airport and took the next flight back home. Back to San Francisco.

❧

Ann heard a knock on her office door just as she had ended her conversation with a client. Suzie must have been watching the light on the phone signifying that Ann had ended her call, Ann thought. Suzie waited until Ann finished writing her notes.

"Leslie just called." Suzie stated.

"Okay," Ann said as she picked up the phone to return the call.

"No." Suzie stopped her. "She left a message."

Ann looked up waiting for the message.

"She told me to tell you that she was trying to be as polite as possible with the following statement. 'You'd better get your ass down to L.A. as soon as possible to deal with Casey, before she does.'"

Ann closed her eyes and leaned back in her chair. "When—"

Suzie was already answering her question. "The next flight leaves in an hour. After that, you'd have to wait until six o'clock."

Ann looked at her watch. One-thirty. If she took the next flight she could deal with the situation at the set instead of having to find Casey after they shut down for the day.

"Get me on the next flight and call me a cab."

Suzie nodded and left to handle the details.

Two hours later, Ann called Leslie as soon as she got off of the plane to tell her she was on her way. "I'll be there in about forty-five minutes. What's going on anyway?"

"What's going on? I'll tell you what's going on. Casey's mind is obviously somewhere else because it's certainly not here. She won't talk to me—she's like a brick wall. We've wasted so much time in the last three days that we may have well just stayed home!" Leslie vented. "I'll call for a break in forty-five minutes. You'd better be here by then."

Ann got to the set before the break was called. She went directly to Casey's trailer, let herself inside and spent the next few minutes pacing. She still hadn't arranged her thoughts when Casey came in the door.

"What are you doing here?" Casey said angrily.

"Don't worry. I'm here in a purely professional capacity," Ann explained, reminding herself to stay calm. "Leslie told me to get my ass back here and deal with you before she did something drastic."

"Of course, in a professional capacity. You wouldn't be here otherwise," Casey snapped.

"Excuse me, but you're the one that pretty much told me to leave you alone," Ann snapped back. So much for staying calm.

"I had a little too much to drink. I didn't know what I was saying."

Ann shook her head. "Those words came from thoughts that you obviously had somewhere. They wouldn't just come from out of the blue."

Casey raised her hands in exasperation, then placed them on her hips. "Well, sometimes I do feel like your mistress."

"So what do you want me to do? Leave Kathy?" Ann waited for a response, then continued, "Never once have you expressed a desire for permanency in our relationship. A desire to sleep with me, yes, but never permanency."

Casey just looked at her so Ann went on.

"But before you ask me to leave Kathy, you'd better look deep down in your soul and make sure it's what you want. You'd better make sure that after this movie is over and you go off to New York or Canada or Europe for your next project that you're not going to become infatuated with someone else who just happens to be there at the time. I know all about your exploits. You've been with and thrown away more women than you can probably remember. I'm not willing to throw away my marriage just because I'm your latest conquest."

Just then Leslie came through the door. "Jeez, you guys, can you keep it down a little? I can hear you all the way outside!" She looked at Casey, then at Ann. "Look, I don't know what's going on between you two, and frankly, I don't want to know. But you've got fifteen more minutes to settle whatever it is." With that she left, slamming the door behind her.

❧

153

Clearly exhausted, Ann sat down. Casey came to kneel before her and stared into Ann's eyes. "I'm truly sorry about what I said the other night. And yes, I want to sleep with you. But more than that, I want the bigger picture. I want us to be together. But if you leave Kathy it will be of your own accord. I will never, ever ask you to leave Kathy." Brushing the hair away from Ann's face, she continued to look deep into her eyes. "Do you understand? Those words will never leave my mouth."

Ann nodded in understanding as she caressed Casey's cheek.

"Now, can we make up?" Casey asked. "Because I can't seem to remember my lines, I can't hit my marks, and Leslie's about at the end of her rope."

Ann smiled softly and reached for Casey. "I know."

Casey slid onto the couch next to her and the two embraced. Casey squeezed tightly and thought to herself, if it hurt this much just having a disagreement, how was it going to feel when Ann left for good?

Leslie opened the door. "That's it. Time's up."

Standing, Casey grinned at Ann. "Dinner tonight?"

"At the hotel, okay? I'm pretty worn out."

Casey nodded and followed Leslie back to the set.

That evening, at the hotel restaurant, Ann sat with Casey at a table scanning the menu. She heard Casey's voice but her face was hidden behind her menu.

"So if you heard all about my exploits, why did you get involved with me?"

Ann smiled, moved Casey's menu aside and teased, "Probably the same reasons all of the other women got sucked in. Your deep brown eyes, your beautiful smile, your inexplicable charm."

Casey did not smile back. "Ann. I'm serious. Why did you get involved with me?"

Ann examined the serious face before her. "That night when you volunteered us to babysit for Leslie and Debbie . . . I saw something in your eyes. I can't really explain it . . . almost like . . . I was seeing something, someone, no one ever saw before."

Casey broke eye contact so that Ann couldn't see the fear that had crept inside. The fear that someone actually had seen inside of all the coldness, had broken into the wall that she had kept up for so many years. Amidst all of the thoughts racing in her mind, she kept coming back to the words that she had just sworn she would never say out loud, 'please leave Kathy'.

Chapter Twenty-one

"Well, well. Why am I not surprised to see you two together?" Kathy said sarcastically as she sidled up to the table.

Casey was stunned. Even with her acting ability, she was speechless. Ann was trying to hide the look of shock on her face, but only ended up looking guilty.

"Kathy?" Ann stammered. "You didn't tell me you were coming."

"I needed to talk to you, wherever you were." Then Kathy mumbled, "I had to call your assistant to find you."

"What's wrong?" Ann motioned for her to take a seat.

Kathy sat down and immediately blurted out, "I couldn't wait any longer to tell you. I'm sleeping with someone else."

Uncomfortable with this conversation, Casey fidgeted in her chair. "I think that this is a private conversation." She started to get up, but Kathy held her down by grabbing her arm.

"You might as well hear this too," Kathy said. Then, turning to

Ann, she continued, "It's been going on for a couple of weeks now. I just wanted to come and tell you in person."

Ann looked at Kathy with a fiery gaze, then stood and stalked away.

Kathy looked at Casey. "I don't know what the big deal is. You can't tell me that you two haven't been having an affair."

Casey tried to calm the anger rising inside her as she looked Kathy in the eye and shook her head. "We haven't been having an affair." Lowering her gaze, she said, "Not that I haven't tried." Then, looking back up, she confessed, "She hasn't even let me kiss her."

Casey saw the shock in Kathy's eyes, then the tears.

"What have I done?" Kathy put her head in her hands. "I just threw away ten years of marriage!"

It took all Casey had in her but she put her hand on Kathy's shoulder. "Go after her. Talk to her. I know you two can work it out."

Kathy bowed her head. "I did the one thing that she'll never forgive me for."

"So you're not even going to try and talk to her?" Casey said, confused.

Kathy just shook her head, stood and stumbled away.

Collapsing back into her chair, Casey watched Kathy leave the restaurant. She was still in shock when the waitress brought the drinks that she and Ann had ordered. Running her fingers through her hair, she wondered if she should go up to see Ann or if she should leave her alone. After downing both drinks, she decided to make an attempt to comfort her.

Casey let herself into Ann's hotel room. Leaning on the railing watching the lights that were evidently captivating Ann, she asked, "I wasn't sure if you wanted me to go home."

Ann did not turn but stared straight ahead. "I don't want you to leave." After several moments of silence, she asked, "Did she say anything after I left?"

"She said that she didn't understand why you were so upset since we had been having an affair." Casey grimaced.

Ann shook her head. "She never believed me."

157

"I told her that you'd never even let me kiss you." Casey quickly added, "She was surprised, to say the least. I told her to go after you. She said that she had done the one thing that you'd never forgive her for."

Ann sighed, and nodded still keeping her gaze forward. Only the sounds of the street below were heard for what seemed like an eternity.

Finally, Casey decided to break the silence on the balcony. "So what are you feeling? Are you angry?"

Ann shook her head. "No, not angry. How can I be angry at her for doing something that I've fantasized about for weeks now?"

"I thought you said you could look just not touch," she said. "We never touched."

Ann chuckled. "No, not physically, just emotionally. Honestly, looking back now, I really don't know if there's a difference."

"So what are you feeling?" Casey asked again, truly curious.

Ann ran her fingers through her hair. "Truthfully, I don't know. Hurt, I guess, although I have no right to be. But mostly"—finally she turned toward Casey—"relief."

Casey looked at the woman before her. "You're not going to try and work things out?"

Ann shook her head. "What I'm going to do right now is take a hot shower." Stopping at the balcony door, she turned to Casey. "Please stay."

An hour later, Ann, still in her bathrobe, lay down next to Casey on the couch. The shower had done her good. Casey combed her fingers through Ann's still wet hair. Looking into her dark brown eyes, Ann traced Casey's lips with her finger. The room was dark, the only light flickering from the television danced across the smooth tan skin before her. She slowly moved toward the lips she had dreamed of.

Casey pulled back slightly. "I don't think—"

Ann placed her finger over Casey's lips. "We've both been doing too much thinking. I don't really want to think anymore, do you?" She ran her fingers through Casey's blond hair. Searching Casey's eyes, she still found hesitation. "What's wrong? I know that you've wanted this as much as I have. Don't you see? There's nothing in the way now."

Casey lowered her gaze and gently touched the skin exposed between the lapels of Ann's robe. She whispered, "I don't want this to be 'rebound sex' that you regret and end up asking me to leave. Don't you understand? I'm in love with you. It may sound corny, but I want to stay the night, eat breakfast with you. I want the whole package."

Fine, Ann thought. She picked up the phone and dialed. "Room service? Yes, I'd like to order two breakfasts for, say, nine o'clock. Eggs and bacon, and some of those waffles with the strawberries and whipped cream." Pausing, she turned to Casey and asked, "Would you like me to order lunch and dinner too?"

Casey smiled and shook her head.

Ann said into the receiver, "That will be all. Thank you." Rolling back toward Casey, she placed her hand on Casey's cheek. "As for the 'rebound sex' thing, I believe we would be making love."

"It takes two people in love to make love," Casey replied softly.

Ann was confused. "You know how I feel about you."

"Humor me," Casey replied, looking into Ann's eyes.

"I love you," Ann said, stroking Casey's hair.

Casey closed her eyes. "Say it again."

Ann whispered, "I love you, Casey."

She brushed away the single tear that had escaped Casey's eye. Casey placed her hand on Ann's, fingering the ring that still remained. Ann twisted the ring in place, tears now streaming down her face. Casey gently took Ann's hands and pulled her close.

"You don't have to do that right now. You've been through enough tonight. I'm in no hurry. I'm content just holding you in my arms."

Ann let herself relax as the strong arms wrapped around her. She nuzzled her face against the soft skin of Casey's neck. Within minutes both women had drifted off to sleep.

Chapter Twenty-two

Ann awoke to the pounding on the suite door. It was then that she noticed that she was in her bed, but still in Casey's arms. Funny, she didn't remember moving to the bed in the middle of the night. Looking at the clock, she realized that their breakfast must be a little early. She caressed Casey's cheek lightly. "I think our breakfast is here." She lightly kissed her cheek before getting up.

She swung open the door expecting to find the room service attendant with their breakfast. Instead she found Kathy.

"Hi." Kathy smiled shyly. "Don't you look sexy all bundled up in that robe." She seductively ran her finger along the open neckline of the robe.

Suddenly Ann heard Casey's voice. "I'm hungry."

Kathy was clearly stunned as Casey wandered out of the bedroom.

Casey stopped dead in her tracks and pulled at her robe. "I'm sorry. I thought it was breakfast."

Kathy stormed past Ann. "Well, you certainly didn't waste any time, did you?" she growled at Casey.

Ann recognized Kathy's fury, but clearly Casey wasn't going to let herself feel guilty. "Hey, you're the one that closed the door. I just opened the window."

Kathy stared coldly at Casey then turned to Ann. "So are we even now? I slept with someone, you slept with someone?" She scowled. "You know, I decided to stay last night, decided to try and work things out between us. But I guess you didn't give it another thought, huh?"

Ann looked down, fixating on the floor, knowing nothing she said would make a difference.

Turning to Casey, Kathy started in again. "And you. You were just waiting around until you saw your chance."

"It wasn't like that," Casey said angrily. She turned to look at Ann and admitted, "I just fell in love. I just wanted to be near her."

Ann raised her eyes to meet Casey's and softly smiled in complete understanding. "You know, Kathy, this isn't all of our fault. You left me here alone for way too long. I haven't seen you in weeks. Your voice was so cold in our telephone calls—"

Kathy cut in, "Yeah, lonely and cold, that's why I cheated too."

Ann shook her head. "You're right. Our relationship has been failing for a long time now. Let's just end it now before we end up hating each other."

Knowing that the two women needed time alone, Casey slowly backed out of the room and closed the bedroom door. She reemerged ten minutes later, fully dressed. It wasn't even nine a.m.

Ann got up from the couch where she and Kathy had been sitting and approached her. "Where are you going?"

"I'm just going to give you two some time to sort things out," Casey replied.

Ann touched her arm. "She and I are through. I haven't changed my mind."

Casey sofly smiled at the words. "I'm just going home. Call me when she leaves."

As soon as she climbed in her car, Casey dialed Pam's number.

"Hey Casey, we haven't heard from you in a while."

"Yeah, sorry. But I really need to talk to you now." She relayed what had transpired in the last twenty-four hours. "Ann told me she loved me, Pam."

"Haven't we all known that for quite some time?"

"Well . . . I had hoped. But now it's for sure, she actually said the words," Casey said, nervous.

"Casey, isn't this what you've wanted? Why are you so nervous?" Pam asked softly.

"I don't know . . . it's all so real now. What if I disappoint her?"

"She loves you. She's spent practically every night and day with you. How could you possibly disappoint her?"

"You know . . ." Casey mumbled.

"Oh, God, you can't be serious." Pam chuckled. "She loves you. Nothing else matters."

The two talked a few minutes more then said their good-byes. Immediately after hanging up, the phone rang again. Casey answered quickly.

"Sorry, it's just me, Pam, reminding you about the anniversary party tonight. Don't miss it."

Casey heard the dial tone as soon as Pam had finished.

Back home, Casey paced back and forth in her living room waiting for Ann's call. She had heard Ann's words, but how could she compete with all of those years of marriage? And, if it was over, why was it taking so long for a phone call? Maybe Ann had decided to give Kathy another chance; maybe she decided that she needed some time apart from both her and Kathy. The phone finally rang, this time giving Casey the answer that she had longed to hear in Ann's voice.

"I love you Casey Duncan."

ᐸᖇᕊᐳ

That evening Casey picked up Ann for the drive to the party in Malibu. Once there, Casey rang the doorbell, and as they stood on the porch, Ann placed her hand in Casey's.

"Is this okay?" Ann asked.

Casey pulled their intertwined fingers up and gently kissed the back of Ann's hand. "It's more than okay," she said softly.

Just then, the door swung open.

"Oh, my God! Hell must have frozen over!" Jenna squealed.

At that moment Judy approached and placed her hands on Jenna's hips. "Look, honey, Casey actually brought a date."

Casey gave out a sarcastic laugh before making introductions. "Guys, this is Ann. Ann, the comedian here is Judy, and this is Jenna."

Ann smiled. "Happy Anniversary!"

Judy showed the couple in. "Yeah, can you believe it? Ten years. Not many couples make it that long anymore."

Casey cringed. She knew that Judy had no idea what significance her comment just had. She glanced at Ann, who shot her a smile to show her that all was okay.

Jenna pulled at her partner's arm. "Honey, you're needed in the kitchen."

Judy nodded then motioned toward the patio. "Come on in and enjoy yourselves. I believe Pam and Diane are outside."

Casey led Ann through the crowd, clasping Ann's hand. After stopping several times to greet friends, the two finally made it outside. She and Ann called out greetings to Pam and Diane as Casey scooted two more chairs to the table. Casey motioned for Ann to take a seat, then asked her if she wanted something to drink.

Ann nodded and motioned for Casey to come closer. "Why don't you just get us a couple of sodas? I don't want our senses to be dulled tonight," she whispered into Casey's ear.

Casey flushed, nodded and left to find their drinks.

ᐸᖇᕊᐳ

Pam leaned forward and placed her hand on Ann's arm. "Casey called and told me about the events of the last day or so. How are you doing?"

Ann smiled. "Good. A lot better than I thought." Pausing, she confided, "But I am a little worried about Casey. She doesn't seem herself, kind of withdrawn and—"

"Nervous." Pam finished her sentence.

"Nervous?" She hadn't pegged it as nervousness, but something was making her fidget.

Pam nodded. "She's worried that you'll be disappointed." Ann frowned, and she continued, "I guess you told her at one time that Kathy didn't satisfy you? She's worried that she won't either and you'll question your decision about Kathy."

Ann closed her eyes and shook her head. "That's ridiculous."

Pam shrugged and lifted her chin, signifying Casey's return. "Well, that's why you're here tonight and not spending the evening alone."

Casey and Ann swayed slowly to the music.

"I hope you don't mind being here tonight," Casey said into Ann's ear.

"You know, last week at this time, I was happy just to be in the same room with you. Tonight I'll be totally satisfied if all we do is hold hands. Just being with you, freely touching you without any feeling of guilt, it's all I need." Ann replied as she brushed the hair away from Casey's face.

Casey looked deeply into Ann's eyes. "God, I love you."

"I love you, Casey."

Casey moved in for their first kiss. Ann grinned and slightly pulled away. "I can't believe our first kiss is going to be in front of all of these people."

"Do you want me to stop?" Casey teased.

"God, no!" Ann whispered. Her excitement was visible.

Casey's lips touched Ann's gently at first, the pressure increasing as the heat grew between the two women.

Casey pulled away. "Let's get out of here."

They said their good-byes. Their friends argued that they had just arrived, but Pam rushed Ann and Casey along with a glimmer in her eyes. By the time they got back to Casey's car, the two were kissing passionately.

Casey pulled away as she started the ignition. "If you keep kissing me like that, I'm going to take you right there in the backseat." She looked at Ann. "I don't want our first time together to be in this car, do you?"

Ann shook her head and let Casey drive. Just Ann's hand on her knee made Casey delirious. Her kisses at the stoplights almost drove Casey over the edge.

The two barely got into Ann's suite before Casey pinned her to the wall. Her hands explored Ann's body and her lips and tongue were on every area of exposed skin. Ann moaned in delight.

Suddenly, Casey pulled away and took a deep breath. She needed to put on the brakes.

"What's wrong?" Ann choked out.

Casey leaned against the wall with an arm on each side of Ann. "I need to slow down . . . I wanted to make love to you tonight . . . not pounce on you like some hungry animal."

Ann's breath was ragged as she raised Casey's chin with her fingertip to meet her gaze. "Oh, Casey . . . don't you understand? Whatever . . . however we do this tonight . . . we'll be making love."

"But . . ." Casey stammered, unsure how to proceed.

Ann took Casey's face in the palms of her hands. "God, Casey, I don't care how you do it . . . just take me . . . now!" She sounded frustrated.

Casey gave into her longing and took her hand. "Well, let's at least go into the bedroom . . . I don't want our first time to be against a wall either."

"You're right, the wall can wait till tomorrow," Ann said with a teasing smile.

Casey led her into the bedroom where they began kissing hungrily, their tongues exploring new territories. Ann pulled Casey's shirt over her head with ease, but Casey fumbled with the buttons on Ann's blouse. Ann took Casey's shaking hands and slowly assisted in the task, finally letting the blouse fall to the floor.

Ann's lips found Casey's neck, and Casey let out a deep moan. Ann smiled at the sweet sound as she nipped at the silky skin with her teeth. She got the reaction that she wanted . . . needed. Apparently, Casey couldn't take it anymore. She turned Ann swiftly and pressed her down to the bed.

Bras were unhooked and thrown to the floor. Jeans unzipped and pulled off. Wet panties peeled off and lost somewhere in the struggle. Casey found Ann's hardened nipples with her tongue and made them swell with excitement. Ann clutched Casey's butt and straddled her thigh. The action did not go unnoticed. Casey pressed into Ann's wetness and rubbed her thigh against the heat, creating even more friction. Ann slightly adjusted her own thigh to press into Casey, who moaned again with delight.

Finally Ann could take no more. "Casey . . . please . . ."

Casey kissed her roughly as she slid her fingers into Ann's awaiting body. Ann gasped and fell back against the bed, twisting and grinding with desire. Casey felt lightheaded with passion as she thrust herself deeper and deeper inside Ann. She pressed hard against Ann's thigh to relieve some of her own anguish. The two rocked back and forth as one. She felt Ann's fingers dig into her back, then that wonderful sensation, pure rapture just as Ann came in her arms.

Ann flipped Casey over on her back. Keeping her fingers inside Ann, Casey felt Ann thrust her own into the body now underneath her. Casey soared. Beads of sweat served as a further source of friction between them. Seconds later, Casey screamed out in ecstasy.

Collapsing against her, Ann gasped. "Oh, my God!" she said breathlessly as she gazed at Casey.

Casey smiled, unable to speak just yet. She felt Ann's hair on her breasts. The two women chuckled as they both clearly tried to ease their breathing patterns.

"I feel like I've waited an eternity for that!" Ann groaned.

Casey laughed. "I thought I was never going to get your blouse off. I'm sorry, I'm usually a bit more coordinated than that."

"I know," Ann said. "It only took you a few seconds on the night of your birthday!"

Frowning, Casey raised Ann's face to hers. "I thought nothing happened on the night of my birthday."

Ann smiled. "Nothing did happen. You passed out."

Casey's face burned. "But you were going to let me—"

"I didn't say anything about my letting you. You had my arms pinned down underneath me . . . I can't match your strength. You unbuttoned my shirt, caressed my breast . . . then passed out as you were kissing my neck."

"I passed out," Casey said, mortified. She covered her face in embarrassment.

"Hey." Ann stroked Casey's cheek. "I'm glad you passed out. It wasn't the right time . . . or the right place . . ." She circled the still erect nipple with her fingertips.

"But now . . . now's the right time . . ." Casey said, feeling the heat rise again. She turned Ann onto her back and began kissing her way down her body.

"Mmm . . . .now is definitely the right time . . ." Ann whispered.

Casey felt the excitement build as she reached her intended destination—the soft smooth line between hip and leg . . . the place where she had spent most of her wet dreams. Her tongue softly drew the invisible line as Ann moaned. She then kissed all along the line, softly sucking as she withdrew her lips. Ann writhed with pleasure. Casey moved to the opposite side, this time kissing hungrily and nipping at the tight skin, the motion much like what she had enjoyed on her own neck. Ann grabbed hold of Casey's hair and guided her mouth to the area in great need, the moist spot where the invisible lines both led.

Casey felt intoxicated at Ann's sweet scent. She drank in the juice as she probed expertly with her tongue. Her hands grasped Ann's hips and brought the soft folds closer still. She felt Ann moving in time with her gentle strokes. The movement quickened, Casey felt Ann's tight muscles constrict then relax as they rolled into a deep wave, finally crashing into the awaiting shore.

She and Ann made love until the early morning hours, until their bodies could take no more. They drifted off to sleep wrapped in each others' arms.

The next morning, Casey awoke first. She was in heaven as she found Ann in her arms. It was not a dream. Caressing Ann's cheek, she felt the body next to her stir. Ann's eyes fluttered open and she smiled. Casey kissed her lightly, but the flame ignited almost at once. They were soaring at new heights within minutes.

Hours later, Ann finally had to get up to go to the bathroom. When she emerged, she found Casey staring at her. Wondering what Casey had up her sleeve, she stopped for a moment. "What?" She smiled at her.

Casey smiled back. "Is it too early to ask you to move in with me?"

Ann opened the closet door and pulled out her suitcase.

"What are you doing?" Casey asked.

Ann laughed as she pounced on the bed. "I'm packing! I'll move in today."

Casey grabbed her and squeezed her tight. "We can start, but there's a family dinner at four o'clock."

"A family dinner?" Ann gulped.

"Yes, a family dinner," Casey confirmed. "And you're coming too. You're part of my family now."

❦

"So, how do you feel about displays of affection in front of your family?" Ann asked, as they drove across town.

"Are you asking me if you can hold my hand in front of them?" Casey answered her question with another question. Receiving a nod from Ann, she said, "I'm sure they won't have a problem with it."

Getting a feeling of hesitation from Casey, Ann said, "you act like you're guessing . . ."

Casey shrugged, then turned to Ann with a sheepish grin. "There's something I've been meaning to tell you . . . but I thought that it might make you even more nervous, so I've waited."

Curious, Ann waved her hand for Casey to continue.

"You're the first woman I've ever brought to a family dinner," Casey admitted.

"Excuse me?" Ann was astonished. "Oh, my God! I can't believe you didn't tell me before."

"You see? I was right. Now you're even more nervous." Casey smiled. "But it's too late to back out now, because we're here," she said as she pulled into the driveway.

"Casey . . . what if they don't like me?" Ann said anxiously.

Casey leaned over and took her chin in her fingers. "They're going to love you. They're going to love you . . . because I love you." With that said, Casey gently kissed the lips before her.

"Hey! Stop making out in the driveway and get your ass inside," Tony shouted in the car window then laughed.

Casey turned to Ann and smiled. "I don't think they're going to have a problem with it at all."

"Cassandra!" Casey's dad, Ted, hurried toward his daughter as she came through the door.

Ann looked at Casey. "Cassandra?"

Casey shrugged and embraced him. She made introductions as her niece and nephew pulled on her arms. Ann felt at home immediately as she was welcomed with a parade of hugs. The family accepted Ann with open arms that night and every other family dinner that followed.

Ann moved into Casey's house and they began the renovations and decorating together. Soon the movie shoot was completed and it was time for Casey to begin her next project. The two were in bliss for the weeks leading up to her departure. When the time came, Casey flew out to Arizona and Ann went back to working out of an office in Los Angeles. After much bribery, Suzie joined her at her new location.

Chapter Twenty-three

Casey slid out of the car and entered the Phoenix hotel. She was in a foul mood. The script had been changing daily and her character had taken a turn for the worse. Due to the script changes their days had been getting longer and longer. Now, here she was on a Thursday night at nine o'clock just getting back to her hotel. Stopping in the bar, she had intended to eat and throw back a few drinks. Unfortunately, the kitchen was already closed, which meant she dined on peanuts and several beers. She had never felt so alone. Casey grabbed her cell phone; she needed to hear Ann's voice. Ann was attending a seminar in Palm Springs for the week. After several attempts, she finally got something besides Ann's cell phone voice mail.

"Where have you been?" Casey asked irritated.

"I had dinner with an old friend that I ran into," Ann replied. "We went to law school together."

"Want something to drink, Annie?" the friend asked in the background.

"Yes, please," Ann said.

"Annie?" Casey repeated, never having heard Ann referred to by that name.

Ann chuckled. "Like I said. I knew her a long time ago."

Casey wasn't amused. It sounded like a term of endearment to her. "So, did you ever sleep with this woman?"

Ann sighed. "Yes, Casey. But again, it was a long time ago. She's with someone now, I'm with someone now . . ."

The friend in the background said, "I hope you don't mind. I opened the wine in the refrigerator."

Casey kept silent as she listened, fuming.

"Just give me a minute, okay Rini?"

"Rini? What kind of name is that?" Casey snapped.

Ann sighed again. "It's not her real name—"

"Kind of a pet name, huh?"

"Casey, what's going on, honey?" Ann asked softly.

"Obviously not as much as in your room."

"Casey, come on . . ." Ann was trying to appease her, which didn't make her any happier.

"What? I shouldn't be upset that you're alone in your room, drinking with a 'supposed' ex-lover?"

"What's that supposed to mean? Are you actually asking me if I'm going to sleep with her tonight?" Ann's voice rose.

"Well, are you?" Casey asked.

"That doesn't even dignify an answer!" Ann said angrily and immediately hung up.

Ann couldn't believe what Casey was thinking. She opened the bedroom door and practically threw the phone back on the base.

Rini laughed. "Trouble in paradise?"

Ann shrugged. "Casey seems to overdramatize everything. I'm sure it stems from her line of work."

Her friend seemed confused. "What does she do?"

"She's an actress." Ann sighed.

Rini nodded in understanding. "What's her last name? Have I seen her in anything?"

Ann paused. She really didn't like to advertise her relationship. Oh, well, Rini was an old and dear friend. "Duncan. Casey Duncan."

"Your Casey is Casey Duncan? Oh my God! I can't believe it!" Rini looked shocked.

Blushing, Ann replied. "Yeah. And right now, believe it or not, she's jealous of you. Don't you feel special?"

"Yeah. I do." Rini laughed, then asked sincerely, "So, do you need me to leave?"

"No. She's probably just lonely. We haven't seen each other for two weeks. She's on location in Arizona and I just haven't been able to get away from work, and then I had this seminar—"

"What a minute. You're at this seminar instead of being with her?" Rini interrupted. "You're crazy. I'd catch the next flight out."

Ann thought about Rini's words. "I don't know. Maybe you're right. I'll check when the next flight leaves."

At ten o'clock, Casey struggled back to her room. Sticking her room card in the door, she staggered into the dimly lit area.

"Well, hello there, stranger," came a sexy voice from the living area.

Casey tried to focus her eyes in the soft lighting. Finally, she saw the woman lying on the couch wearing only a black lace bra and panties. She looked familiar, but Casey could not place a name.

"How did you . . ." Casey started to ask.

"Baby, where there's a will there's a way!" The woman seductively rose and approached her.

At first Casey backed away, but the woman grabbed at her belt loops, pulled her close and hungrily kissed her.

"You don't remember me, do you?" she asked as she searched Casey's face. "Well, I thought that last time was pretty memorable, but I guess this time I'll have to try harder."

Casey started to object but the woman again covered her mouth with her own. Suddenly, the woman's hands were everywhere. Trying to maintain control, Casey pushed her away. "I can't do this . . ." she stammered. "I have someone—"

The woman brought her finger to Casey's lips. "Don't worry. She doesn't have to know."

Casey looked at her. She felt her heart racing, her body heating up at the sight of the lace, which barely covered the woman's breasts.

She took Casey's hand and placed it inside her panties and into her wetness. "Oh, God, Casey. Feel how wet you make me."

Casey found it difficult to restrain herself. She did not have to be alone. No one would have to know. Her fingertips explored the moisture and the woman moaned with pleasure.

Stepping toward Casey, the woman whispered, "I remember what you like," then softly bit at her neck and slid her hand into Casey's jeans. Casey gasped and lost all control.

Within seconds the woman had stripped off all of Casey's clothes. Casey expertly unhooked the woman's bra and let it fall to the floor, then shot her panties like a slingshot across the room. Casey first found herself pinned against the wall where the woman bit at her neck so hard that she wondered if the woman was part vampire. She writhed with pain and pleasure as the woman brought the same biting motion down to her now hardened nipples. Before she knew it Casey had been flipped around onto the marble column in the entryway, her bare breasts against the cold stone. Casey had never really liked being taken from behind, but she didn't really have a choice. The woman entered her like a hammer. The woman's nipples raked against Casey's back as she thrust deeper and deeper. Casey hung onto the column for dear life as she felt herself rise higher and higher. The woman plunged so hard into her that several times she swore that she felt her feet leave the floor. With an explosion inside, her knees buckled and she felt herself losing her grasp on the stone. The woman slid to the floor alongside her. Casey collapsed, her back against the woman's breasts, her buttocks resting against the wetness of the woman's coarse hair. Legs wrapped around her, pulling her legs apart, and another sensation began as the woman reached around and stroked her. A deep moan escaped from Casey as the wave came to sweep over her body. The woman's teeth found her neck again and the wave crashed to the shore, ripples running through her body over and over again.

Casey awoke still sprawled on the living room carpet, the bedspread covering her tired aching body. She slowly moved her leg from where it was entwined with the beastmaster and moaned within. Her muscles reminded her of the previous hours' activities. She couldn't remember it all, just that she had been entered from the front and the back on almost every surface of the room. Her stomach muscles ached as she sat up; even her nipples screamed for help as they rubbed against the coarse fabric covering them. She rubbed her face, stood and made her way to the shower, praying that the warm water would help soothe her pain.

Stepping into the hot water, she turned to let the moisture soothe her backside and winced. She knew the sensation immediately, carpet burn. She smiled as she remembered her last encounter with the sensation. She and Ann had spent an entire day making love in front of a roaring fire on a dark and stormy weekend. Suddenly, she felt weak and braced herself against the shower wall as she realized the inevitable. She had cheated on Ann last night—well, all the way into the morning. She tried to convince herself that Ann may have succumbed to temptation last night as well. Somewhere deep within she knew Ann hadn't followed her hormones. Under no circumstances could Ann find out what had happened with Cherie. Casey had the name embedded in her memory now. She would never forget the name that she was forced to chant repeatedly as she teetered on the edge of orgasm. Only after this chant was she allowed the free fall into the cloud of ecstasy.

175

Chapter Twenty-four

Ann took the first flight out and found herself in front of Casey's door early in the morning. She felt the excitement as she watched the door swing open. There stood Casey clad in a white robe. God she was beautiful. But what was the activity within the room? She peered over Casey's shoulder to find another woman in another white robe frantically searching for something. Then the words came.

"God, Casey. Where did you throw my panties last night?"

Ann looked at Casey. All of the air left her lungs; her knees felt weak; she was stunned. She did not say a word. She just turned and started what felt like a mile-long walk to the elevator.

"Were you here to check up on me?" Casey angrily cried out.

Ann turned around and walked backward down the hall. "I skipped out on my seminar. I was here to surprise you. I guess I'm the one that's surprised."

"Ann . . ." Casey pleaded for her to stop.

Ann stopped. "What? Are going to try and tell me that this isn't what it looks like? Please, Casey, don't lie to me. Give me at least that much respect." Turning toward the elevator, Ann had one more thing to say. "You're going to need some makeup on that neck of yours."

Casey brought her hand to her neck and felt some tender areas. Great, not only caught cheating but also with evidence.

She immediately went over to the phone and dialed Ann's cell phone number. Of course, Ann had it on voice mail. She tried to sound calm as she left her message. "Hi. I know we need to talk. Maybe you can come by my room tonight about seven o'clock—oh. You probably don't want to come by my room . . . we can meet anywhere . . . just leave me a message . . . when and where . . . please . . ."

An hour later, Casey went into the makeup trailer and sank down in the chair in front of the mirror. She reviewed all of the various makeup items sitting on the counter before her, wondering if any of this could actually cover up the way she was feeling.

"Hey, have you been crying?" Tracy asked as she approached and met Casey's gaze in the reflection of the mirror. She examined Casey's face. "God! You look awful. I've really got my job cut out for me today."

"You haven't seen the worst of it," Casey mumbled as she pulled away her collar to reveal the bruising on her neck and shoulders.

"Jeez, you must have had some night," Tracy joked. "When did Ann arrive?"

Casey averted her gaze. "This morning. Unfortunately, just as Cherie was trying to locate her panties." As she finished the sentence, she glanced up and grimaced when she saw Tracy's reaction.

Frowning, she just shook her head, then immediately picked up a bottle of cover-up from the counter. "Let's see what we can do. Of course, this is only going to improve your exterior. I don't know what to do about your interior." Once again she caught Casey's reflection in the mirror. "I really thought Ann was the real thing for you. I guess I was wrong."

Casey's eyes began filling with tears for the umpteenth time that morning.

"Oh, no. Don't start that again. We've only got a few minutes. We need a little professionalism here," Tracy said sternly.

Casey wiped the tears from her eyes and straightened up. Tracy was right. She was a professional. She pushed all of her feelings deep inside and took several deep breaths. She emerged as the cool bitch that everyone expected.

Casey checked her messages as soon as the first break was called. She hated that electronic voice saying "no messages at this time". Where did they get that awful voice? Pausing, she looked at the phone. Should she call Ann again? Should she leave another message? Surely Ann had checked her messages already. Giving in, she dialed and spoke into the phone again. "I know you've checked your messages, you're such a fanatic about it . . . Ann, honey, I know you're mad . . . please just call me, okay?"

Casey left her third message at two o'clock. By this time, she was feeling panicked. "Ann, please don't take this so seriously, it's really not that big of a deal . . . it was just sex . . . she didn't mean anything . . . you know I still love you . . . just call me and tell me that you're okay. Please!"

Ann listened to Casey's messages at the airport, and they echoed in her thoughts over the red desert of Arizona . . . over the Sierra Mountains . . . all the way back to Los Angeles. By the time the plane landed, Ann had the beginning of a migraine. Picking up her car from long-term parking, she drove straight to their . . . no . . . Casey's house. Ann let herself in, headed to the bedroom and instantly began packing. She wanted to lie down so badly, but she wanted out of this house as soon as possible even more. Suddenly, she heard keys in the front door. Casey couldn't possibly have made it back already. Cringing, she looked out of the bedroom to see who had arrived. It was Pam. She spotted Ann immediately and strolled into the bedroom.

"Ann . . . why are you packing? What's going on?" Pam asked, a note of frustration in her voice. "I was just coming over to water the plants."

Ann pulled her cell phone from her purse, pushed a few buttons, then threw it to her. "Here. Listen to my messages. That should give you a clue."

Frowning, Pam put the phone up to her ear. Hearing the first message didn't clear her confusion. She looked at Ann and shrugged.

"Keep listening," Ann instructed.

Pam's face turned white and Ann knew she was hearing Casey's third message. "Just sex . . . didn't mean anything . . ." Pam sighed. "I don't know what to say, Ann."

She shook her head. "Anything but 'I told you so.'"

Ann suddenly raised her hand to her mouth and ran into the bathroom. The toilet flushed and Ann emerged wiping her mouth with a tissue.

Pam's curiosity was evidently killing her. "So what exactly happened?"

Ann continued packing frantically. "I went to surprise her this morning . . . left my seminar early . . . only I was the one who was surprised."

Ann glanced at Pam and answered what she knew was the next question. "Casey in a robe with a neck full of little bite marks, a woman wrapped in a bedspread searching for her panties."

When Casey hadn't heard from Ann by five o'clock, she thought her heart would stop beating. Barely able to choke out the words, she left yet another message. "Okay, you're scaring me now. We aren't finishing until late tonight, but I'll be on the first plane out in the morning. Please meet me at home. I know we can work through this. God, Ann, please meet me at home . . ."

Chapter Twenty-five

Casey stepped into the airport swinging her carry on bag over her shoulder. She'd asked Pam to pick her up, and the flight was on time, arriving at eight a.m. on the nose.

"Is that all you brought?" Pam asked, starting toward the baggage claim area, then stopping.

"Yeah. I have to fly back tomorrow," Casey answered.

The two walked to Pam's car in silence and had a strained conversation all the way to the house. Thankfully, Pam spent the entire time keeping the subject matter light. Casey sighed when Pam pulled into the driveway and she didn't see Ann's car. Pam followed her in the house as Casey set down her bag inside the front door. She tried to casually walk through the house. When she came out of the bedroom, she felt as if her face was white as a sheet.

"She's gone. Her makeup, her clothes . . . it's all gone," she said to Pam, feeling as if she was in a trance.

"I know," Pam said softly.

"You know?" Casey asked, shocked. "How do you know?"

"I helped her pack," Pam answered, then backed away from her as if afraid of an attack.

Casey looked at her and ran her fingers through her hair. "So you know . . ."

Pam nodded.

"Why didn't you say anything?"

Pam looked her straight in the eye. "Because I thought if you saw for yourself that it would smack you upside the head."

"And you think that I need to be smacked?"

"Honestly, I think you need to be smacked all the way to hell and back," Pam admitted.

Casey glared at her. "Gee. Whose side are you on?"

Pam placed her hands on her hips. "This time I'm on Ann's side, Casey. You know, usually I find your antics amusing. I've kind of liked living vicariously through you. But this time . . . you made me sick . . . sick to think that you'd throw away the best thing that's ever happened to you."

Casey walked over to the couch and sank down on the cushions. Certain she looked pathetic, she asked, "Where is she?"

Pam shrugged. "I don't know. She wouldn't trust me enough to tell me. Frankly, I'm so disgusted with you at this point that I don't know if I'd tell you even if I knew."

"You can't be more disgusted with me than I already am with myself," Casey admitted as she held her head in her hands.

Pam sat down on the couch next to her. "So who was she?"

Casey shrugged. "Nobody."

Pam pulled back Casey's collar from her neck. "Sure looks like somebody to me."

Casey looked up. "So Ann told you about my neck. What else did she say? She must have called me every name in the book."

Pam sighed. "No. No names. She was just terribly, terribly sick." After no response, Pam continued, "At first I thought that she was just really upset, but after she started throwing up every ten minutes, and the way she kept shielding her eyes from the light, I realized that it must be one of her migraines."

Casey collapsed against the back of the couch, knowing that she was the cause of Ann's illness. She just sat and listened.

"I tried to get her to stop and lie down, but she said that she just wanted to get packed and get out of this house. That's one reason I helped her pack. To tell you the truth, I don't know how she even drove anywhere. I asked if I could take her somewhere. That's when she politely told me that she didn't want you to know where she was and knew that I wouldn't be able to keep it from you." Pam shifted in her seat, then dug something out of her pocket. "She gave me these to give to you. She said that these would signify something to you."

Casey cringed as she felt the sharp metal edges dig into the palm of her hand. The house keys. Casey knew exactly what these keys represented. Both Ann's book and movie contained this event. The leaving of keys signified permanency.

Pam just sighed, stood and headed to the door. Casey silently begged her to stay.

But apparently Pam had one last thing to say. "You know, Ann pointed out something interesting about all of the messages that you left on her cell phone."

Casey looked at her blankly.

Pam shook her head in disbelief. "You never once said that you were sorry."

With that, Pam shut the door behind her.

Casey collapsed on the couch, burying her face in a pillow, and cried.

Casey kept trying Ann's phone all weekend. At first she received her voice mail, but late Saturday, she received the message that her calls had now been blocked. Returning to Arizona, late Sunday afternoon, she could hardly wait for Monday morning to try another call. It might be her last chance.

"Hi, Suzie. Is Ann free?" Casey asked softly into the phone, the next morning at eight o'clock sharp.

"Casey? Wait a minute. I thought Ann was with you. She left a message that she was surprising you . . . then another message that the partners approved a leave of absence . . ." Suzie was clearly confused.

"Yes, well, she surprised me all right," Casey mumbled.

"Oh, no. Casey . . ."

"Look. I know I screwed up. I just need to talk to her. Do you have any idea where she might be?" Casey was frantic.

Suzie sighed on the other end. "I have a few places that I can try, but Casey . . . if she doesn't want to be found . . . I won't be able to—"

"Please, Suzie, just do what you can. I've got to get to the set. If you find out anything, leave a message at my hotel."

Casey hung up the receiver after Suzie agreed, then ran her fingers through her hair in frustration and walked out the door.

Later that night, Casey tiredly stumbled to the hotel desk and asked for her messages. Tears formed in her eyes when she read the slip of paper handed to her, *Sorry, no luck. Suzie.*

Chapter Twenty-six

Two months passed before Ann felt strong enough to enter the world again. Lying out in the sun and sipping assorted flavors of margaritas every day had worn thin. No one knew where she was; that was something that she would stick to. She began reading the want ads for major cities and calling head hunters for a position she could sink her teeth into. Work. She missed it. She wanted to fill her hours and days with work. Work could not hurt you.

Soon Ann found herself on a plane to Boston to interview for a prosecutor position. She was tired of being a tax attorney. She still had a lot of anger inside and wanted a position where she could channel it into a good legal fight. Ann was offered, and she accepted, the position.

Casey felt herself gasp as she unfolded the sheet faxed to her earlier that day. It was an article from the *Boston Herald* announcing Boston's new lead prosecutor . . . Ann Covington. On the bottom was written, *Just in case you're still interested. Suzie.*

Casey arranged with her agent to have the next few days off, and took the first plane to Boston. After checking into her hotel she planned her first step. She made a call to the Boston City Courthouse—more specifically, to Ann's office. Informed that Ann was in court for the remainder of the day, she made an appointment for the following morning. Knowing that Ann would not agree to an appointment with Casey Duncan, she used an assumed name. Having nothing else to occupy her time, she decided to visit the courthouse and, with any luck, catch her as she finished for the day.

Casey settled in the back corner of the courtroom and focused on the case in session. She watched as Ann, dressed in a light gray suit with a pale pink blouse, approached the witness on the stand. Her love for this woman overwhelmed her. Finding it hard to catch her breath, she melted into her chair. She had missed Ann so much. Suddenly, she heard Ann's voice.

"Mr. Johnson. You testified that Mr. Smith was—" Ann looked down at her notes—"an all-around good guy."

Mr. Johnson, a man in his late thirties with a comb-over, leaned forward. "Yes."

Ann paced in front of the prosecution desk. "Mr. Johnson, would you lend money to Mr. Smith?"

"Objection!" the defense attorney cried out. "Relevance?"

Ann looked at the judge and explained, "Mr. Johnson called Mr. Smith a 'good guy.' I'm just trying to determine how the witness defines this term."

The judge nodded. "Overruled." Then, turning to the witness, he instructed, "You may answer the question."

Mr. Johnson swallowed hard then admitted, "No."

Ann continued with her line of questioning. "Mr. Johnson, you own a business. Would you hire this gentleman?"

The witness squirmed in his seat, then again answered no.

"Would you trust him to babysit your children?"

He sat back in the stand, averted his gaze, and shook his head. "No."

Ann looked at her notes then crossed her arms. "Isn't it true,

Mr. Johnson, that Mr. Smith did look after your children one night? Isn't it also true that Mrs. Johnson told you 'never again'?"

Mr. Johnson shifted in his seat. "Yes, but that was because Dan had had a little too much too drink."

Casey winced at the phrase. She thought she saw a sadistic glimmer in Ann's eyes, but the glimmer suddenly turned cold. Mr. Johnson had walked right down the wrong path.

Ann leaned on the stand. "A little too much to drink? Does that happen very often?"

The witness looked down. "Well, it used to. I wouldn't know anymore."

"Why is that?"

"My wife asked me not to hang out with him anymore," he admitted.

"Your wife asked you not to hang out with Mr. Smith anymore." Ann turned theatrically toward the jury. "Any particular reason, Mr. Johnson?"

The witness looked at Mr. Smith as if to apologize for his next statement. "She said that he got too belligerent."

"Belligerent? What kind of things would he do?" Ann asked.

"He'd get really loud. Call people names. Provoke fights."

Ann paused and scratched her head. "So, you don't trust the man with money, your business or your children. And you say he drinks too much and becomes belligerent. Sounds like he's not such a 'good guy' after all."

She stared into the witness's eyes until he finally shrugged and admitted, "I guess not."

Ann walked over and sat down behind the table. "No more questions."

You could hear the defense attorney's pen slam down on the table in frustration as the judge excused the witness.

After sitting in the back row of the courtroom, watching as Ann humiliated witness after witness, Casey chickened out and decided to wait until the next day.

Chapter Twenty-seven

"Ann, there's a Lynn Gregory here to see you," came the voice over the intercom.

"Okay . . ." Ann said, not recognizing the name. "Send her in."

Ann's assistant opened her office door, came in and handed her a file. The woman followed her in but Ann was concentrating on the file that had just been handed to her. When Ann finally raised her eyes, she chuckled.

"Cute. Lynn Gregory. I didn't even make the connection until now," Ann said bitterly, throwing the file in her briefcase. She watched as Casey's gaze followed the assistant's butt out of the room. "Nice butt, huh?"

Casey snapped her head back, her face red.

Ann stepped to the front of her desk and crossed her arms. "She's good in bed too. Oh, let me put it in terms you might understand. She's a good fuck."

Casey's face turned a deeper shade of red.

"You know, I decided to try your lifestyle out for a while. A different woman every night . . . it's really quite therapeutic. You get laid, you can leave in the middle of the night, you don't really even have to remember their names. It's a nice diversion from my stressful days."

"But it's not you," Casey said softly as she stood before her.

"How do you know? I mean, how well did we really know each other? I obviously didn't know you as well as I thought I did," Ann said sternly.

Several moments of silence followed until Casey said. "Ann, I didn't mean to hurt you. I just had a little—"

"Oh, wait, I know this line. 'I just had a little too much to drink.' God, Casey! Can't you come up with something new?"

"Ann . . . I was scared. I'd never felt so lonely before. I'll have to live with what I did for the rest of my life."

"And you think I wasn't scared? I left my friends, my home, my marriage—all to try and make a life with a well-known whore! I wasn't only scared. I was stupid. That's what I have to live with for the rest of my life," Ann cried. She snapped her briefcase closed. "And now if you'll excuse me, I'm going to court, where I'm prosecuting someone for spousal abuse. The defense thinks they have it all sown up because he never hit her. I'm contending that emotional abuse is just as bad. And they're going to lose, because I've got a lot of experience to feed from." With that, she pulled her briefcase from the desk and briskly walked to the door.

Casey reached out and grabbed her arm. "Don't write our relationship off yet, Ann."

Ann pulled her arm away. "You're the one that wrote it off. You not only wrote it. You wrote it, signed it and sealed it with a kiss."

She waited for a moment for a response, and receiving none, swung open the door and left.

Floored, Casey stood there. Ann had called her a whore.

Ann's assistant poked her head through the door. "Excuse me. Do you need your parking validated or something?"

Casey stood facing the large windows overlooking the city and shook her head.

"Umm . . . then I need to ask you to leave."

Casey nodded. She understood. As she headed to the door she stopped. She went over to Ann's desk and scrawled a note on a legal pad. *What I really came here to say was that I'm sorry. I hope someday you'll forgive me. Casey.* Tearing the sheet from the pad, she folded it once and set it on the center of the desk blotter. She wrote Ann's name on it, and slowly left.

After stopping for a cup of coffee, Casey sat in the anteroom of the courthouse re-playing the conversation in her mind. Ann was clearly still very angry and hurt inside. And Casey still ached for their companionship. She had to try again. Sneaking around the corner just as Ann left the courtroom, Casey watched as she made her way down the hall. *Great, now I've become a stalker,* she said to herself.

Ann stopped as her assistant rushed toward her. "Ann, here's that note that Ms. Gregory left for you."

Ann took the piece of paper, thanked the woman for bringing it to her and dismissed her. Setting down her briefcase on a wooden bench, she slowly unfolded the note, read it and began rubbing her temples almost immediately.

Casey watched the reaction, not knowing how to read Ann's body language. Was she so tense because she was angry? Or maybe she was trying to force back feelings of joy at the long overdue apology? Casey let herself fantasize for a moment. Maybe Ann was thinking of taking her in her arms and—.

Suddenly a voice called from the opposite end of the hall, interrupting her fantasy. "Ms. Covington!"

Casey peeked around the corner. The voice came from a beautiful woman wearing a dark burgundy suit, her blond hair falling upon the squared shoulders, her breasts bouncing with each step.

Ann turned around and smiled at the woman. "Dr. Williams. What brings you to our humble courthouse?" Ann joked as she placed her hand on the woman's arm.

The woman smiled back. "I had to testify on the Terrance case. How about you? Done for the day?"

Ann nodded. Casey felt a sense of sadness as Ann stuffed the apology into her pocket.

189

"Wow, you look like you've been through the wringer," the woman said as she touched Ann's cheek. "Nothing that a nice warm bath wouldn't cure? I'll wash your back if you wash mine?" she asked seductively.

"Hmm . . . only if it's followed by one of your great massages, Lauren," Ann replied in the same seductive tone.

The woman blushed and put her arm through Ann's. "I think that can be arranged. Maybe this time I can talk you out of sneaking out in the middle of the night."

Casey felt as if a stake had been driven through her heart. Is this how Ann felt when she'd opened the door that fateful morning? Up until now, it hadn't really sunk through that Ann was sleeping with other women. All she had heard were Ann's words, but now as she saw the teasing glimmer in Ann's eyes, the touch of Ann's hand on this woman's arm, it was all becoming a painful reality. Casey's knees almost collapsed as a sharp pain enveloped her. She leaned against the wall for support. Unable to move or speak, she watched as the two women strode arm-in-arm down the corridor and out of view.

"Hey, it's me," Casey mumbled into the phone. She had gone back to her hotel room after picking up Chinese carryout. The food smelled delicious, but she found she had no appetite.

"What's wrong?" She sounded bothered.

"What do you mean?"

"Well, let's see . . . you're calling in the middle of my class . . ."

"Oh shit. I'm sorry. I forgot about the time difference." Casey apologized, realizing that Pam was in the middle of teaching her night school session.

"Time difference? Where are you?" Pam asked.

"Boston."

"Boston? Is something wrong with Ann?"

Casey paused. "How did you know Ann was in Boston?"

There was nothing but silence on the other end of the line. Casey finally put two and two together. "Oh, my God! You've known where she was all this time! Why didn't you tell me?"

Pam sighed. "She asked me not to. She just wanted me to know in case of some kind of emergency. Plus, you haven't asked about her lately. I figured that you'd lost interest," she explained. "So you didn't answer me. Is there something wrong with Ann?"

"No. She's fine. Just fine," Casey answered sarcastically.

"So . . . she just called you out of the blue?" Pam asked, confusion in her voice.

"No. I found her," Casey replied, then admitted, "with a little help."

"Casey." Pam sighed again. "Why can't you just let it go? She's finally getting on with her life—"

"Yeah, I could tell."

"Did you see her?" Pam asked softly. "It sounds like you're sad."

"Yeah."

"I gather that it didn't go too well if you're there sitting talking to me instead of being with her."

"No. It didn't go so well."

"You sound awfully sober for someone who has obviously had a bad day." Pam commented.

"I thought I might try and cut down for a while. Ann pointed it out as another one of my bad habits." Casey paused, then knew exactly why she hadn't received a response. She knew her friend too well. "Wipe that smirk off of your face!"

Pam laughed.

"You seem a little preoccupied tonight Ann," Lauren said as she leaned against the doorjamb, after Ann had ignored her open robe exposing her sleek naked body.

"Do I? I'm sorry," Ann apologized as she looked up.

191

The doctor sat on the edge of the bed next to her and brushed a strand of hair from her face. "Does this have anything to do with Casey?"

Ann's face immediately flushed. "What? How do you know about Casey?"

"I don't," Lauren admitted, then took Ann's hand. "I'm sorry. The note fell out of your pocket when I was moving your clothes."

Ann just stared, not knowing what to say.

"Do you still have some issues with this woman? Is this why you insist on all of these relationships with no strings attached?"

Ann looked at her, took her hand and placed it inside her robe. "Do you want to analyze me doctor? Or do you want to fuck me?" she asked seductively.

The doctor's lips slowly turned into a wicked smile. "I want to fuck you."

"Then stop talking and put your mouth to good use." Ann offered her breast.

The doctor did not have to be asked twice. Ann felt the doctor's tongue circle her nipple. She let out a hungry moan as Lauren began sucking, clearly inviting her to the rest of the body before her.

Ann slipped from the sheets as the clock beside the bed turned to two fifteen a.m. Rubbing her hands over her face, she tried to adjust her eyes to the dim moonlight streaming in the bedroom window. Where had Lauren put her clothes?

"Your clothes are on the chair in the corner," Lauren said as if Ann had asked the question aloud.

She startled Ann. "I'm sorry. I didn't mean to wake you," she whispered as she made her way over to the chair where her suit had been draped with care. Pulling on her panties and bra, then slipping on her blouse, she cringed as she heard the question from out of the darkness.

"Are you just going to leave without talking about it?"

Ann turned around to face the bed and saw the outline of the doctor as she leaned up on her elbow. "What?" She played dumb.

Lauren sighed as if being a psychologist sometimes got in the way of her personal life. "Ann. You didn't come all evening."

Ann laughed nervously. "I don't think you should be complaining . . ."

Lauren's voice was gentle. "I'm not complaining. I'm totally and completely satisfied. I'm just worried—"

"Lauren, it's not your fault . . ." Ann finished buttoning her blouse and pulled on her skirt.

"I know. Talk to me, Ann."

The zipper of the skirt sounded like a shriek in the silence. Ann pulled out her brush from her purse and whipped it through her hair. "Just drop it, *doctor*." In her opinion, Lauren was walking a thin line between lover and analyst.

"This woman—Casey—are you in love with her?"

Ann placed her brush back in her purse and leaned against the wall. Lauren refused to quit. "Yes . . . no . . . it doesn't matter . . . it's over."

"So, her apology . . ." She was provoking her into an explanation.

"Her apology came too late," Ann answered, angry.

"How late?"

"About two months." Pausing, Ann shook her head. "I don't know if it would've mattered if it came any earlier . . ."

"Does she still love you?" The doctor kept prodding her.

"I don't think she knows what love is. I believe she loves in the present moment." Ann stopped for a minute, trying to clarify what she meant. "If you're there with her, she loves you. As soon as you're out of sight, it kind of slips her mind . . . she succumbs to temptation a little too easily."

"It seems that you were on her mind for the past two months . . ."

Ann stepped into her pumps. "Look. It just doesn't matter anymore. I've gone on with my life!" she yelled as she grabbed her purse and stalked from the room.

"Like hell you have." Lauren called out as Ann slammed the door.

A half-hour later, Ann was pacing back and forth across her east side apartment. Why did Casey have to appear out of nowhere? She was doing fine on her own. She hadn't thought about the woman in . . . okay, she thought about her all the time. God, Casey was beautiful . . . Why did she have to look so good? Why, why, why . . . . .why did she have to cheat on her? Flashbacks of Casey and that woman filled her mind. Damn it!

The mail she had thrown on the table caught her eye. She picked it up and began shuffling through it. Advertisements, credit card offers . . . hmm . . . what was this envelope?

Anthony Duncan and Rebecca Johnson
Request your presence at their holy union

Ann rubbed her temples as she read the remainder of the invitation. Pam must have given them her address. Tears filled her eyes. She would just send some money . . . or a gift card. She did not need this, not after everything that had happened today . . . or yesterday . . . well, in the last twenty-four hours. She propped the invitation up on the mantle. Pulling her gaze away from it seemed impossible until she was jolted back into reality by the shrill sound of her alarm coming from her bedroom.

Chapter Twenty-eight

The next few days were extremely hard on Ann. She could not get Casey out of her mind. Of course, the flowers that arrived from Casey with the message, *'I still love you'*, did not help matters. She needed a distraction. A distraction, and maybe a nice massage . . . hmm . . . she picked up the phone and dialed Lauren's number.

Ten minutes later, Ann was standing in the doorway of Lauren's office. Leaning on the doorjamb, she looked down at the doctor, who was sprawled out on her stereotypical leather couch. Her shoes off, she appeared relaxed as she watched an entertainment news program on the television.

Ann smiled. "Are you ready to go?"

Lauren glanced up at Ann and returned the smile as she raised herself to sitting position. Just as she reached for the remote to turn off the television, Ann heard a familiar voice that made her jaw drop.

"Wait!" She turned quickly toward the TV. With her hand over her mouth, she made her way to a chair to avoid her collapse. There before her on the television screen was Casey, being interviewed by a well-known entertainment reporter. The subject was a new movie opening this coming weekend. Ann guessed it was the movie that Casey had completed before they met.

Ann could feel Lauren watching her and her reaction to the screen, but obviously Lauren didn't understand the situation.

"And the movie opens nationwide this weekend?" the woman interviewer asked.

Casey smiled and nodded politely.

"So, what's this I've heard about your personal life? You've had someone special occupying your time?" she prodded.

Casey's face turned red as she tried to recover from the shock of the personal, usually "off-limits" question. "You know that I won't answer personal questions."

"Oh, come on, Casey. There are a lot of ladies out there sitting on the edge of their seats right now . . ."

Casey's smile disappeared. "Well, let's just say that the keyword in your question is 'had.' I pretty much screwed up that relationship."

The woman tried to look sympathetic. "She must have been someone pretty special."

The statement hung in the air until Casey could compose herself enough to reply. Finally, she let out a deep breath. "You could say that she was the best thing that ever happened to me."

Ann wondered when Casey had done this interview. Probably a week or so ago, for the advance promotion of the film, before she came to Boston.

"Any hope of reconciliation?"

Casey tucked her hair behind her ear. "There's always hope."

The interview ended with that statement, and the show went to commercial.

Ann's eyes were filled with tears. She missed her so much.

Lauren suddenly gasped. "Ann? This is the Casey from the note?"

Ann ran her hand through her hair, met Lauren's gaze and nodded. Lauren just stared back for several seconds, as if trying to decide if she dare try to cross the line that Ann had so clearly drawn on several occasions.

She drew a deep breath. "You know, I thought that maybe you didn't want to discuss your past because you believed that I'd be bored with a story that I had probably heard a million times before. But believe me, Ann, I think I'd be interested in your story."

Ann just sat still staring at her hands, which were clasped tightly in her lap. Did she want to confide in her? Would it change their relationship?

Lauren made another attempt. "How did you two meet and what exactly happened to your relationship? I mean, she looks like she's in just as much pain as you are."

Ann glared at her. "Don't you dare feel sorry for Casey! She's the one that threw it all away. You heard her. She screwed up."

"So tell me what happened, Ann," Lauren said gently.

"I caught her with another woman," Ann blurted out. She crossed her arms. "She tried to tell me that it was just sex. Just some woman who appeared in her hotel room one night." The memory was still appalling.

"I hear that happens all the time. Strangers throwing themselves at famous people."

"Oh. So that makes what she did okay?" Ann threw her arms in the air. "Is that what you're saying, doctor?"

Lauren slowly leaned back on the couch. Ann knew she had vast experience with anger. She stretched her arm out on the back of the couch, no doubt to show Ann she was being open and relaxed. "No, of course I'm not saying that. Why don't you tell me the whole story?"

"Shouldn't I be on the couch if you're going to analyze me?" Ann said sarcastically.

Lauren sighed. "Why don't you just come sit beside me and treat me like a friend who cares about you?"

Ann didn't move but glanced back to another commercial on the screen. Evidently irritated, Lauren took the remote and clicked the television off. Several moments of silence passed before Ann gave in and quietly sat down on the couch next to Lauren. Trying to lighten the mood, Ann began, "Once upon a time . . ."

An hour later, Ann had finished the story. She had explained about Kathy, her series of books, the movie deal and finally about Casey. Lauren had remained quiet the entire time. Well, Ann thought, Lauren's specialty was the art of listening. When Ann finished, Lauren leaned forward and gently kissed her lips.

"You are truly an amazing woman," she said, looking into Ann's eyes. Then, taking her hand in hers, she smiled. "I knew you were a brilliant prosecutor, but now I learn you're an author, a screenwriter, a tax attorney . . ." Then her smile faded. "Unfortunately, you are also the most stubborn, pigheaded woman I've ever known."

Ann's eyes widened as she tried to pull her hand away. "Frankly, doctor, I'm surprised that your patients return each week."

Lauren held on tightly to Ann's hand. "All I'm saying is . . . your professional life is so full of gray areas. Plea bargains, settlements—it's all about compromise. But your personal life is so black and white, cut and dried." Pausing for a moment to collect her thoughts, she said, "Like when we got together. You made it very clear that it was going to be a fuck-and-run relationship. No compromise. Anytime I tried to make it more, a little more meaningful, you left. No discussion. You just left. I'm sure you've recently dealt with a lot of other women that way. No involvement, no commitment. Black and white."

Ann looked coldly out into space.

Lauren, however, apparently believed that she was listening, so she continued. "You know, it's been my experience that everyone deserves a second chance."

Ann finally turned to her. "Doctor, have you been guilty of an indiscretion in your past?"

"If you had ever gotten to know me a little better, you'd know that I'm incapable of cheating." Lauren now looked into Ann's eyes. "No, I'm afraid that I was in your position. She spent the rest of her life trying to make it up to me."

Ann was confused.

Lauren elaborated, "She died two years ago in a car accident."

"Any regrets?"

"Two. That somehow I made her feel that she needed to spend the rest of her life making it up to me. But mostly I regret the year that we wasted separated because I couldn't see past my pride and forgive her." Sighing, Lauren admitted, "I'd give anything to have that year back again."

Chapter Twenty-nine

Ann's mind wandered as she rode in the taxi from the Los Angeles Airport to her destination. Was she doing the right thing? Had she made the right choice? She was going to the wedding, but just the wedding. She would slip out before Casey could see her.

Ann spotted Tony pacing outside the church. He looked up and smiled as she approached. As she expected, he was wearing the traditional black and white tuxedo.

"Ann! I'm so glad that you came . . . Casey will be glad too."

Ann hugged the groom, then straightened the rose bud on his lapel. "I'm here for you and Rebecca, not for Casey."

Tony released her and held her at arm's length. "Thanks. I know being here is hard for you."

Ann softly smiled and tried to change the subject. "So, are you nervous?"

Tony smoothed back his hair. "Isn't it noticeable? I'm scared to death. Not of marrying Rebecca . . . but she insisted that we write our own vows, and I just know that I'm going to make a fool of myself."

"I'm sure that you'll do fine."

"I'll bet you a dance that I flub up," Tony kidded.

Embarrassed, she looked at him. "I'm sorry, Tony. I wasn't planning on attending the reception . . ."

"What? You've got to stick around for the reception. Rebecca will be upset if she doesn't get to see you." He paused. "It's because you don't want to have to deal with Casey, isn't it?"

"Would you stop worrying about your sister? This day is about you and Rebecca, not me and Casey."

"Then I'll see you at the reception?"

Ann tried to stall but noticed the pastor coming to pull Tony away. Tony followed her gaze and waved to the man approaching.

"Well?" Tony prodded.

Ann looked into his brown eyes. For a second she was stunned by the resemblance she had never noticed before. Before she could catch herself she conceded with a nod. "I'll be there. Don't make me take you up on that dance." She smiled.

Tony laughed and turned to follow the pastor, then suddenly turned back and took her in his arms once again. "She's truly miserable without you, you know," he whispered into her ear.

Ann sighed. *This was probably a big mistake*, she said to herself. Running her fingers through her hair, she made her way up the concrete stairs to the chapel.

The service was lovely. Rebecca looked stunning, her traditional white dress had a plunging back, but she had covered the space with lace. Casey, as maid of honor, was gorgeous in cobalt blue.

Ann wandered into the reception hall adjacent to the church, searching for a seat in the back so she could make a quick exit if she needed to. She took a glass of wine and was lulled into staying for the meal after eyeing the prime rib on the plates served around her. Tony and Rebecca weaved in and out of the tables, obviously on a mission to find someone. Tony stopped and pointed at Ann. Rebecca waved and proceeded to drag Tony over to her table. Ann stood to receive the couple.

"Ann, I'm so glad that you came! We miss you so much," Rebecca said, excitement in her voice.

"You look beautiful," Ann remarked. "I wouldn't have missed this for the world." A little white lie couldn't hurt.

After talking with Ann for a while, Rebecca was whisked away to another table. Ann sat back down with Tony still standing beside her.

"Dance with me, Ann." He pulled her up to her feet and led her to the dance floor. He took her in his arms, then chuckled. "Are you used to leading?"

Ann smiled and laughed. "No, I've always been led or, in some cases, mislead."

A dozen other couples joined them on the dance floor.

"Can I cut in?"

Ann heard the voice and closed her eyes as she recognized it immediately. She suddenly felt her body heating up as Tony pulled away to let Casey take the lead. Ann looked at him as he shrugged and walked away. Casey took Ann into her arms and swayed to the music.

"I think I've been ambushed," Ann said, not looking directly into Casey's eyes.

"Don't be mad at him. He didn't think his sister had enough nerve to cut in," Casey explained.

"Well, at least I'm not in bad company," Ann replied, finally looking at Casey.

Casey looked at her as if confused by the comment.

"If your own brother underestimated your nerve, I guess I'm not as big of a fool as I thought." Ann said to clarify her previous statement.

Casey looked into Ann's eyes. "You're not the fool here. I'm the fool, Ann."

"Well, I don't really have time to debate over who's the biggest fool. I have a plane to catch." Ann pulled away from Casey.

Casey looked hurt. "Already?"

Ann nodded. "My cab is probably sitting outside the hall right now. I really need to go."

Casey followed her out of the hall and leaned on the doorway as Ann made her way to the awaiting car. "I wish you would have let me drive you to the airport."

Looking back as she opened the car door, Ann smiled. "I can't imagine you driving anywhere in that dress."

Casey's heart took a leap at Ann's attempt at lightening the mood. Maybe it was Ann's way of telling her that the tension between them was subsiding. Looking down at the tight-fitting dress, she tried to rub the creases out. "I knew it. I thought it was too tight! Rebecca told me it looked fine. It's too tight, isn't it?"

Ann looked away, then slowly eyed her up and down. "It's perfect."

Casey felt warm from the comment. She watched the door of the cab shut and suddenly felt desperate. She didn't want Ann to leave. "Ann?" she called out.

Ann rolled down the window, her look questioning Casey's intentions.

Casey approached the cab, but stopped at a short distance, still giving Ann the space that she knew she needed. What could she say? Her mind went blank. Finally she stammered the first thing that came to her mind, "Thanks for coming."

Ann ran her hand along the door ledge as if it needed dusting, then nodded as she glanced quickly at Casey, then just as quickly away. As the window rolled up, the cab slowly crept away. Casey watched until the car was just a yellow spot on the horizon. Feeling her eyes welling up with tears, she went back into the hall and directly into the restroom.

Ann walked into her apartment after the long red-eye flight home. The silence affected her as it never had before. She was overwhelmed with loneliness. Opening the refrigerator, she grabbed a bottle of water, unscrewed the top and took a swig while she played her messages on her answering machine.

The first call was Kathy. They had been able to remain friends, although the friendship had really become one-sided. Ann just couldn't take Kathy's mood swings, which had gone from bad to worse. And as she saw it, she didn't have to take it anymore. So, Ann was friendly and polite but kept the calls short.

She had mixed emotions about the second message as she heard Casey's voice.

"Hi . . . it's Casey . . . I hope you don't mind me calling you. I just wanted to say thanks again. It really meant a lot to Tony and Rebecca . . . and me. I promise I won't bug you all the time now that I have your home number. Anyway, I hope your flight was all right. Well, you know how to get in touch with me . . . .same cell number and all. I still love you, Ann."

Ann deleted the message. Great, Casey had her home number now. *She better not call me all the time*, she thought.

Weeks went by and Casey was true to her word, not one phone call. No phone calls, but flowers every week and cards every other day. All signed, "I still love you, Ann." She didn't respond. Inside she still felt hurt, anger, humiliation . . . .and it was all tangled up with love.

On one dreary Wednesday, in the midst of preparing for an upcoming case, Ann's thoughts were interrupted by her assistant's voice on the intercom. "Ann, it's Kathy."

She sighed as she picked up the phone. "Hi, Kathy!"

Listening to the voice on the end of the line, Ann's hand began quivering. Her voice began quivering also. "I'm sorry, when was this? And where? Okay, what time is the—yes, I know the location. Thanks so much for calling."

Ann's assistant had come into her office to put some files on her desk. "Are you okay?" she asked as the first tear rolled down Ann's cheek.

Ann looked up at her. "Kathy's gone . . . I mean . . . Kathy is dead."

Chapter Thirty

Ann wandered through her old San Francisco apartment as she surveyed its contents. The place felt cold and empty. Picking up a picture off the mantle, she lightly traced the photo of her and Kathy. It had been taken a few years into their relationship . . . when they were both happy. A tear rolled down her cheek. She jerked when she heard a knock on the door.

She opened the door to find Casey. Throwing her arms up in exasperation, she exclaimed, "Oh, God! Why the hell not? Let's just make this the week from hell!" She turned and stalked back into the apartment.

Casey waited for a minute, then followed her as if not exactly sure if she had been invited in. "I came as soon as I heard. I wasn't sure if you had anyone to—"

Ann shook her head. "It's pretty pathetic if you're the only one that I have to console me."

"Ouch!" Casey said. "Do you want me to leave?"

"I don't care. I'm just too tired to fight," Ann admitted while running her fingers through her hair. "You might as well come in and help me drink this wine. There's so much of it. It's not like I'm going to ship it back to Boston with me."

Casey followed her out of the entryway and into the living room. She was taken aback by the size of the apartment. For some reason she had always pictured it as small, dark and cramped. But this was nothing like that. The ceilings were high, and several large plate glass windows let in filtered sunlight, which obviously made the numerous plants flourish. The polished oak floors looked as if they were brand new. A large area rug covered the center of the living room, where several pieces of plush dark green furniture were arranged in a seating area. In front of the couch was a coffee table that held a bottle of wine, a single wineglass and what looked like a photograph album. She was drawn to the large brick fireplace where dozens of framed photographs sat on the mantle. The largest frame contained a picture of Ann and Kathy leaning against a tree with their arms around each other. Casey was concentrating so hard on her new surroundings that she barely even noticed Ann leave the room and return with another wineglass. Casey continued to look at the pictures on the mantle as Ann filled another glass with wine.

"She overdosed. I wasn't sure if you knew," Ann said, interrupting Casey's thoughts.

Casey turned around and took the wineglass offered her. "I heard. What exactly happened?" She asked gently.

"She had a drug problem. Cocaine," Ann said as if she was still having a hard time comprehending it.

Casey sat down across form her. "Did you know?"

Ann shook her head. "That's what everyone keeps asking me. No. I didn't know. We had separate checking accounts so I had no idea how much money she had or what she spent it on." She paused to take a sip of wine. "We spent so much time apart during the last few months . . . years . . . I guess it explained her mood swings."

Casey didn't know what to say. What she wanted was to hold her in her arms and take the pain away. Instead she just patiently listened.

Ann looked at her, then stood and went over to the window. "You should've seen her family at the funeral." She watched the wine in her glass as she swirled it. "They wouldn't even look at me," she said solemnly.

"Her family didn't say anything to you?" Casey asked in disbelief.

Ann shook her head, then sighed. "Oh, yeah, her sister asked me where my new lover was. The lover that I left her sister for." She glanced at Casey, then closed them tight. Casey thought that she was trying to hold back tears. "What could I say? I felt like a knife went through my heart when I had to admit that it didn't work out."

Ann's pain was obvious, and Casey was overwhelmed by her sadness.

Now standing by the mantle, Ann drew her finger across the picture of her and Kathy. "They blame me, you know."

Casey stood and approached her. "Ann, you didn't do anything wrong."

"I'm sorry, but I can't really rely on your sense of right and wrong," Ann shot back.

Casey stopped and dug her hands in her jeans pockets. "I guess I deserved that."

"I should've known. About the drugs, about her state of mind . . ." Her sentence trailed off. "I'm wracking my brain for clues that she gave, but there's nothing. I didn't see it coming."

Casey reached out to touch her on the arm.

Flinching, Ann backed away, emptied the rest of the wine in her glass and poured herself a refill. "Odd how things change in such a short amount of time. I never could've imagined last year at this time how screwed up my life would be right now. No home, no family, no companion . . . It's like I'm having this extremely long nightmare." She ran her hand over her face. "I just wish someone would wake me up."

Casey sat down and put her head in her hands. "It's all my fault, don't you see? If I hadn't pressured you . . . then fucked up so badly . . ."

"You didn't make me do anything I didn't want to do. I'm not sure that eventually Kathy and I wouldn't have gone our separate ways, especially with her drug problem. But yes, you did royally fuck up. You fucked up good."

Abashed, she said, "I succumbed to temptation. It won't happen again."

"Everyone encounters temptations every day, Casey."

She was right of course. Casey thought of the dozens of come-ons she faced on practically a daily basis. Casey crossed her arms. "You just don't know the difference between everyone else's temptations and mine."

"Maybe not. But I do know the difference between strength and weakness."

"So you think that I'm weak?" Casey said, surprised. "How about in L.A., Ann? There were a few times that I was strong enough to help you with temptation. You didn't think I was so weak back there."

"You're right." Ann sighed and nodded. "So what happened in Arizona? Out of sight, out of mind?"

"Ann, you were definitely not out of my mind."

"Oh, now you're going to tell me that when you were fucking her you were pretending she was me?"

Casey laughed. "No, I could have never pretended that was you."

Ann took offense. "Oh, excuse me. I guess she was better than me in bed, huh?"

"No!" Casey tried to explain. "It wasn't enjoyable at all!"

"That's too bad," Ann said, her face blank. "You would think that if you were going to throw our relationship away, it would at least have been for something enjoyable."

"If there was any way that I could ever make it up to you, I would." Casey was unable to look her in the eye.

Ann sat down on the couch across from her. "Will you just answer one question for me? And will you please answer it truthfully?" She drained her glass.

Casey finally brought her eyes up to meet Ann's. "I've always tried to be honest with you."

Ann nodded, then reached down to fill her glass yet again. "Do you think that you ever really loved me? I mean, I know that we're friends—you wouldn't be here right now otherwise—but did you ever really love me?"

Casey's eyes filled with tears. She felt the droplets running down her cheeks and was only able to choke out, "I still do."

Ann was sitting on the couch flipping through the photo album when Casey reemerged from the bathroom. She had spent the last twenty minutes splashing water on her face and trying to recover from her admission. Ann had remained unemotional through the entire conversation, although Casey was unsure if it was because she didn't care or if it was because of all of the alcohol in her bloodstream.

Casey sat next to her on the couch and looked over her shoulder at the photographs. Occasionally Ann would smile at a picture and explain the circumstances under which it was taken. One bottle of wine was replaced with another as Ann reminisced. After the second bottle was emptied, Casey suggested they order Chinese food. When it arrived, they sat at the dining room table, which was already fully set as if Kathy had expected company.

Ann surveyed the table and sighed. "I don't know why we kept this table set. We always had these grand ideas about throwing big dinner parties. The truth is, our jobs controlled our lives so much that we were lucky if the two of us ate together once a week."

"Speaking of jobs, how's it going in Boston? Your office sure impressed the hell out of me." Casey remembered the fabulous views from each and every window.

Ann laughed nervously and shrugged. "I don't know. I guess I'll see when I get back."

Confused, Casey looked at her. "What do you mean?"

Ann wound the noodles around her chopsticks. "Well, they weren't really receptive about my leaving right now. Basically, they said don't go, and I left anyway. So, I may not have a job when I get back."

"What are you going to do if they fire you?"

"I'll live. There are plenty of people out there who'll hire me," Ann replied.

"Well, if you need help financially . . ." Casey offered.

Ann gestured for Casey to stop. "Don't worry about me. I could live for years on what I have in savings alone." She cast an eye around the room. "Then there's the sale of this place. I should get a pretty penny for it."

"You own this place? I just assumed that you rented, like most people in San Francisco."

"No, it's mine. Free and clear. I bought it before Kathy and I got together," Ann explained. "I let her stay here rent-free. How could I not?"

"You don't want to keep it?"

Ann grimaced. "No, too many memories. Besides, who knows where I'll end up."

Casey gathered her nerve to ask the next question. "Would you consider coming back to Los Angeles?"

Ann laughed and shook her head. "Not too many good memories there either."

Casey, a bit hurt by the statement, shrugged. "I don't know. I think we have a few good memories."

Ann looked at her and smiled. "Yeah, I guess I can think of a few."

Casey swallowed the last bit of wine in her glass, then braced herself for her next statement. "Ann, I know that you have no reason to believe me, but I've changed. I haven't slept with anyone since our little confrontation in Boston. Your words hit me like a brick."

Ann picked up the bottle of wine and tipped it toward Casey's glass. Casey immediately put her hand over the rim. "I'm trying to tone down on my drinking these days. I've come to the conclusion that I do some pretty stupid things when I drink too much."

Withdrawing the bottle, she set it back down.

"I want to try and prove myself to you, Ann," Casey said sincerely.

Ann rolled her eyes. "Casey, you are who you are. I've come to accept that in the last few months. I wish that it hadn't cost me my entire life before I figured it out, but I guess that's what it took."

Casey's eyes began filling with tears for the second time that day. "I miss you," she whispered.

Reaching over, she placed her hand over Casey's. "I miss you too. But a relationship without trust is no relationship at all." Ann studied her for a moment. "Tell me the truth. If I hadn't surprised you that morning, would you have ever told me about it?"

Casey lowered her eyes. She had thought about that question many times. Should she tell her what she wanted to hear, or should she tell her the truth? She decided Ann deserved the truth. "No . . . at least not until maybe our fiftieth anniversary or something."

Ann gave an exasperated sigh. "When you would confess all of your indiscretions?"

"No," Casey said flatly. "You see, that's the point, Ann. There wouldn't have been any others to confess. What you don't understand is that morning . . . I finally realized that I didn't want any part of that life anymore. All I wanted was you." Her voice cracked as she looked up into Ann's eyes. "All I want is you."

That night around two a.m., Casey got up to get a glass of water, her mouth dry from the alcohol she had consumed. As she went through the living room she found Ann sitting alone in the dark. Stopping, she looked closer to make sure that Ann hadn't started drinking again, then got her glass of water from the kitchen. Sitting on the edge of the couch, Casey took a sip then offered the glass to Ann, who drank the rest. Moving closer, Casey began massaging Ann's shoulders, kneading the tense muscles through the material of Ann's robe. She did not want to cross the line by tucking her hands underneath the robe and stroking Ann's bare skin. Casey continued the massaging motion down Ann's arms. Ann let a moan escape as Casey kneaded the small muscles in her hands.

"I would know these hands anywhere," Ann whispered as she caressed and inspected Casey's fingers. Then, their fingers intertwined, she pulled Casey's arms tightly around her.

After a moment, Ann looked up at her. "Can we just have some meaningless sex?"

Casey shook her head. "I don't have meaningless sex anymore. But we could make love."

Ann looked away, ignoring the suggestion.

Casey tried again. "Okay, you're so big on compromise, how about I make love to you and you can just consider it meaningless sex?"

Ann's face lit up and she pulled Casey down to the plush fabric.

Casey touched her lips gently to Ann's, then with the insistence of Ann's hand on the back of Casey's neck, she kissed her harder. Ann urged Casey closer still, and Casey was tempted to thrust her knee between Ann's bare legs. But she held back. If this was the last time that she would ever make love to Ann, she would not be rushed, she was going to relish every minute. She wanted to touch, wanted to kiss every inch of her. Her lips left Ann's and traveled downward, tasting the salt left from the tears on Ann's cheeks, the remnants of the perfume on her neck, and finally back to taste her wine-soaked tongue. She heard a soft moan escape from Ann as her fingertips gently grazed Ann's nipples.

Casey then pulled Ann up and led her to the spare bedroom. Beside the bed, she stopped and helped Ann out of her T-shirt and underwear before tenderly pushing her back onto the comforter.

213

For several moments, Casey just stood there. She wanted to memorize Ann's body. Everything she had taken for granted for those several months they had been together rushed through her mind. Ann didn't seem to mind, stretching her arms out to fully expose her firm breasts and flat tummy, then separated her legs for further view.

Casey removed her clothing and lay down next to Ann, then ran her fingertips along the smooth skin before her, tracing each muscle as Ann breathed, evenly at first, then in shorter spurts. Casey moved on top of her, relishing her touch, as she kissed her deeply, and the kiss was just as deeply returned. Casey's lips and tongue began their search—Ann's neck, Ann's nipples, Ann's tummy, Ann's belly button, down to the coarse hair, her fingertips caressing each area that her lips had just left. Ann's body was writhing as she continued, placing soft kisses down Ann's thighs, knees, calves, then pausing to suck on each toe. She heard Ann's moans graduate, getting louder and louder. Casey brought her mouth back up to Ann's wetness, breathing in the heavenly scent, then lightly blowing her own warm breath onto the velvety folds before her. Ann was practically wimpering now, and Casey knew exactly what to do to bring her further toward the edge. She began with soft kisses along Ann's hip, then nipped the skin, afterward caressing her with her tongue.

Casey smiled as Ann began pleading. She then ran her tongue down to taste the pleasure she had brought from Ann's body. Slow strokes brought convulsions below her, and as her fingers entered the moistness, the wave of orgasm ushered in a cry of ecstasy. Casey pulled herself up to kiss her while increasing the pressure, producing several more surges before Ann fell limp with exhaustion.

Ann's body was throbbing. Every inch of her was tingling. She felt Casey's fingers inside her and clenched them as they began sliding from her. She grasped them and stopped them from leaving her, and at the same time she rolled Casey onto her back and brought her lips to Casey's nipples.

"Please . . . .just touch me," Casey mumbled. "I'm ready. Just touch me, please," Casey begged.

Ann looked into her eyes as she slid her fingers into Casey. God, it felt so good . . . she was so wet. She had barely begun stroking her when Casey's body tightened and released a spurt of moisture. Sliding her fingers into her, Ann gripped Casey's fingers still inside her. Rocking back and forth, the two came simultaneously. Ann finally collapsing onto Casey, they lay in that position for what seemed like an eternity, until Casey's caresses on Ann's back led them to begin all over again. Only after the minutes turned into hours did they collapse in exhaustion, falling into a deep sleep in each other's arms.

Ann lay in Casey's arms, Casey gently stroked Ann's arm and stared at the ceiling.

"Do I dare ask what you're thinking about?" Ann asked, still sleepy.

Casey sighed. "I just thought that at some point in our love-making—er, meaningless sex—that you would admit that you still love me."

Ann propped herself on one elbow and brought her other hand to Casey's cheek. "I didn't think there was ever any doubt about that. Of course I still love you. But it doesn't matter because so do half of the other women you're sleeping with."

"Slept with," Casey corrected. "Let's change that verb to past tense."

"Uh-huh," Ann responded sarcastically.

Casey rolled over and propped herself up on her elbow to face Ann. "Ann, just give me another chance," she pleaded. "We can go back to L.A. and start over."

Frustrated, Ann looked at her. "Casey, it's not L.A. that's the problem. The problem is that everytime you go on location I'll be wondering—"

"Then come with me," Casey said. "You can work by computer everywhere I go."

Ann laughed. "Oh, yeah, a roving attorney. Every employer's dream."

"I know there's a compromise here. How about if you go out on your own? That way you won't have to answer to anyone," Casey suggested.

"Casey, I'm an attorney. I have to meet with clients, go to court. I can't just follow you around like some groupie," Ann said, her frustration growing.

"Okay, counselor. I didn't think it would come to this, but I'll throw my last offer out on the table." Casey paused. "After I finish with this movie, I'll announce my retirement. It's about time I put that college degree to work."

Ann was stunned. "You'd make that kind of sacrifice for me?"

Casey looked her in the eye. "You sacrificed everything in your life for me and I screwed up. Now it's my turn." After taking a deep breath she added, "There's only three conditions to my offer."

Ann chuckled. "I knew that there would be a catch." She motioned for Casey to proceed.

Casey raised one finger. "Number one: we settle in L.A. so that I can be near my family." Raising her second finger, she continued, "Number two: you go back to being a tax attorney, because you're a real bitch when you're a prosecutor."

Ann smiled, knowing the truth in the statement.

Casey raised her third finger. "And the third condition is"—she placed her hand on Ann's cheek—"that you'll marry me."

Taken aback, Ann felt her smile fade. "You're serious?"

Casey swallowed hard. "I've never been so serious about anything in my life."

"Casey, I can't bury my former lover one day and accept a proposal from you the next. It's just too much."

"I can understand that," Casey replied. "In fact, I don't want you to say yes right now. I want you to wait until I'm done with this project. Until I've proved myself. Then you can give me your answer."

Ann closed her eyes. Suddenly, she felt at peace with herself. "I'll think about it."

Casey lay back down and held Ann in her arms. "That's all I ask, baby, that's all I ask."

It was late morning when the two awoke. They ate breakfast in bed then retreated to different rooms. Ann needed time alone to go through some of Kathy's belongings. Casey retreated to the living room into a good book she found on Kathy's shelf. The apartment was peaceful with soft music playing throughout. About three, she was interrupted with a loud knock on the door. Ann called out for her to answer it.

Casey opened the door to find an older woman, probably in her early sixties, waiting. She appeared rather nervous as she said, "I'm looking for Ann Covington."

Casey motioned for her to enter. The woman stepped inside as if she was afraid the floor on the other side of the threshold would collapse under her weight.

"May I ask who's here to see her?" Casey asked as she closed the door quietly behind her.

The woman twisted her hands over and over again as if having trouble assembling the next sentence. Slowly she raised her eyes. "I'm her mother."

Casey left the woman in the entryway and walked down the hall in a daze. Quietly she approached Ann, who was reviewing a box of papers, in what used to be her and Kathy's bedroom.

"Who was at the door?" Ann glanced up at her.

Casey, still stunned, didn't know exactly know how to answer. Finally, she murmured, "She says she's . . . your mother."

"Sure." Ann looked at her with irritation. "First Kathy dies, then your proposal, now my mother reappears after twelve . . . thirteen years. What a cruel joke that would be."

"I haven't seen any pictures, but she looks an awful lot like you."

Ann sighed, put down the papers and stalked down the hallway, Casey closely behind her.

At the end of the hall, Ann stopped dead in her tracks and gasped. "Mother?" she asked in disbelief.

The woman's eyes immediately filled with tears. Wiping them from her cheeks, she smiled. "I'm sorry. You just turned out so beautiful."

Casey watched as the two of them stood in silence, then offered, "Would you like to sit down?"

The woman smiled and nodded. "Yes, before my knees weaken any more. Thank you . . ."

"Casey Duncan." Casey offered her hand.

"Maggie." She shook her hand. "Maggie Covington."

Following Casey over to the sofa, she sat down on one end. Ann sat on the other end of the couch from her mother. Casey settled into the chair across from the two women. Ann just sat and stared at the woman for several minutes. She's changed, Ann thought to herself. Her mother, who had been a little stocky, now was trim and toned. Her tan complexion, highlighted hair, even her clothes were stylish. Her mother was a changed woman.

Ann was still in shock. "I wasn't aware that you knew where I lived."

Maggie fidgeted with her hands again. "I've always known where you lived, what you were doing." Meeting Ann's eyes she continued, "I've followed your career through the legal publishings, through the paper . . . then I lost track of you about a year ago . . ."

"I lived in Los Angeles for a while. Now I'm in Boston."

"Boston? Oh my. No wonder you were never here. I've stopped by several times now," she admitted. "I guess you're here now because . . . Ann . . . I'm so sorry about Kathy."

Ann kept staring at the woman before her. Frustrated, she ran her hand over her face. "Wait a minute . . . I'm just a little confused here. All this time, you knew everything about my career, about my life, where I lived?"

Maggie nodded. "Until about a year ago, like I said before. What happened? I know Kathy was still in San Francisco . . ."

Ann looked at Casey, then shook her head. "It's a long story . . . And frankly *mom*," she said bitterly. "I don't know if you really deserve . . ."

Maggie looked down at her hands once again. "You're right. Of course you're right. I'm sorry. I knew that it wouldn't be easy . . ."

"Mom, why are you here? After all this time? Why now?"

"Ann, it was always your father. He was just so damned stubborn . . ."

"Hmm . . ." Casey mumbled. "Must run in the family."

Ann gave her a wry smile. Her mother seemed confused, but went on. "I know that I shouldn't have listened to him all those years . . ."

"Did something happen to Dad?" Ann asked, not knowing why she felt so alarmed.

"Oh, Ann . . . your dad and I have separated. I found him with another woman."

"That sounds familiar, doesn't it?" Ann looked at Casey again. "That must run in the family too, huh?"

Casey's face turned bright red. "Would anyone like some coffee?" she said as she stood.

Ann looked at her mother. "Maybe you could open a bottle of wine."

Her mother nodded in agreement, watching Casey as she left the room. "She looks so familiar to me. Are you two close?"

Ann smiled, knowing what was being asked. "Kathy and I . . . we hadn't been together for quite some time. Casey and I . . . well, we're still defining our relationship."

Casey reentered the room with a nice burgundy and glasses. She poured the wine, then sank back into a chair and watched mother and daughter get reacquainted. Ann was a bit standoffish at first but finally warmed up when her mother started crying about the mistakes that she had made with her daughter. Soon, all three of them were chatting as if they were old friends.

Casey proceeded to refill the wineglasses. "You know, Maggie, I have to go back to work tomorrow. I'd feel a lot better if you'd stay with Ann for a while."

Maggie jumped at the chance. "We do have a lot of catching up to do." She looked at Ann. "I'd love to help out."

Ann was quiet for a minute, then returned her mother's gaze. "Well, there still are a lot of Kathy's possessions that I need to box up for her family."

"It's settled then," Casey said.

The next morning Casey left for the airport. A week later, Ann left for Boston, leaving her mother to take care of the sale of the apartment. Each night Casey would call Ann. She flew into Boston as often as she could. Casey never rushed Ann for her decision.

Chapter Thirty-one
(Six months later)

Ann stood with Casey out in the Duncan family backyard in silence. Casey looked like she was high, floating with happiness, the only thing keeping her on the ground were her fingers intertwined with Ann's.

Just then Casey's dad, Ted, quietly walked out and stood beside them. "So, Ann, will you be with us at Christmas?" he asked.

"Well . . ." Ann began, not knowing exactly how to answer the question.

"Dad, I think that's still undetermined," Casey answered for her.

Ted nodded. "Does it have anything to do with—excuse the expression—Casey not being able to keep her dick in her pants?"

Caught off-guard, Ann tried to choke back a laugh.

Casey smiled at her. "I told you, my family doesn't pull any punches."

"That's for sure." Ted put his arm around Ann. "Casey, why don't you give us a minute alone."

Casey looked at her dad suspiciously, then was prodded along with Ted's next statement.

"I'm sure Lila could use some help with the dishes."

Ann gave a nod as if to say "it's okay, I'll be fine," and Casey left.

Ted released his arm from Ann's shoulder and knelt down by the edge of the pool to pick up a leaf floating on the surface. "You know, you're the first woman to ever really get to Casey." He twirled the leaf with his fingers and looked up. "Do you know how I know that?"

Ann shook her head, went over to the chaise lounge and took a seat.

Ted came over and sat down next to her. Still twirling the leaf, he said, "That first family dinner that you missed, we all wondered why Casey came alone. Of course, we would never think of asking her—we learned to keep out of her business long ago. You know, having a famous daughter, you see things in the supermarket tabloids every day . . . some of them ridiculous . . . some of them not so ridiculous . . . Anyway, we never ask her about them." He chuckled. "Unless we read that she's carrying an alien's baby or something . . . then we've got to say something to her."

"Anyway, here we were, sitting around the dinner table, right before I was about to say the blessing, and she just starting blurting things out. She said, 'I know you are all probably wondering why Ann isn't here. Well, I want you to know, I screwed up, and I mean that literally. She caught me with another woman. Nobody special. I let some stranger screw up the only thing that every meant anything to me. Anyway, I just wanted you to know it was my fault. And now Ann has disappeared. I can't find her anywhere. But if I find her, I'll do anything in my power to make this up to her.'" He ran a hand through his hair. "I have to admit, when the tears started"—he cleared his throat as his voice cracked—"we just sat there staring at her. None of us knew quite what to do. We hadn't seen Casey cry in . . . probably fifteen years . . . not even when her mother died . . ."

Casey never talked about her mother, Ann realized.

He turned to look her in the eye. "I've never seen her in such pain in my life. That's how I knew."

Ann nodded. What could she say?

Ted turned his attention back to the leaf, and after a few moments of silence, spoke again. "When you suffered the loss of your . . . previous companion . . . Casey called me. She told me about Boston, what you'd said, and how desperately she wanted to go to you."

Ann was listening intently as she watched the twirling leaf and hadn't noticed that Casey had rejoined them until she heard her voice.

"He gave me the best advice he could offer. He said, 'then go to her as a friend, not as a lover.' And that's exactly what I did. And if that's all we ever have . . . a close friendship . . . I'll still consider it the best gift I've ever received."

Ann now raised her eyes to meet Casey's. Ted rose, gave Ann's shoulder a squeeze and gave Casey a kiss on the cheek, then went back into the house.

Ann picked up the leaf that Ted had finally released on the plastic table beside her and rose. She went over to Casey, leaned back into her arms and cleaned off the leaf with her fingers.

"Are you going to keep that leaf?" Casey asked softly.

Ann nodded. "I think so."

"There are a lot of other leaves out there. A lot of them are cleaner and unspoiled. This one is somewhat tarnished and damaged."

Ann softly smiled, understanding the underlying meaning of Casey's comment. Turning to face her, she replied, "But this one is special. When I look at it, it's like I can see something in it that no one else sees."

Casey's eyes filled with tears. "So you think that you can see past everything that leaf has been through?"

Ann combed the single strand of hair from Casey's face. "I think this leaf is a keeper."

The two of them smiled at each other through their tear-filled eyes and leaned in to kiss. Just as their lips met, another leaf landed on Casey's shoulder. Ann turned to look at the teetering leaf. Casey glanced at it, then at Ann, and laughed as she brushed it away. The gesture was all Ann needed to assure herself that she had made the right decision. "This backyard would be a beautiful place to hold a wedding."

Publications from
BELLA BOOKS, INC.
The best in contemporary lesbian fiction

P.O. Box 10543, Tallahassee, FL 32302
Phone: 800-729-4992
www.bellabooks.com

OUT OF THE FIRE by Beth Moore. Author Ann Covington feels at the top of the world when told her book is being made into a movie. Then in walks Casey Duncan the actress who is playing the lead in her movie. Will Casey turn Ann's world upside down?
1-59493-088-0 $13.95

STAKE THROUGH THE HEART: NEW EXPLOITS OF TWILIGHT LESBIANS by Karin Kallmaker, Julia Watts, Barbara Johnson and Therese Szymanski. The playful quartet that penned the acclaimed *Once Upon A Dyke* are dimming the lights for journeys into worlds of breathless seduction.
1-59493-071-6 $15.95

THE HOUSE ON SANDSTONE by KG MacGregor. Carly Griffin returns home to Leland and finds that her old high school friend Justice is awakening more than just old memories.
1-59493-076-7 $13.95

WILD NIGHTS: MOSTLY TRUE STORIES OF WOMEN LOVING WOMEN edited by Therese Szymanski. 264 pp. 23 new stories from today's hottest erotic writers are sure to give you your wildest night ever!
1-59493-069-4 $15.95

COYOTE SKY by Gerri Hill. 248 pp. Sheriff Lee Foxx is trying to cope with the realization that she has fallen in love for the first time. And fallen for author Kate Winters, who is technically unavailable. Will Lee fight to keep Kate in Coyote?
1-59493-065-1 $13.95

VOICES OF THE HEART by Frankie J. Jones. 264 pp. A series of events force Erin to swear off love as she tries to break away from the woman of her dreams. Will Erin ever find the key to her future happiness?
1-59493-068-6 $13.95

SHELTER FROM THE STORM by Peggy J. Herring. 296 pp. A story about family and getting reacquainted with one's past that shows that sometimes you don't appreciate what you have until you almost lose it.
1-59493-064-3 $13.95

WRITING MY LOVE by Claire McNab. 192 pp. Romance writer Vonny Smith believes she will be able to woo her editor Diana through her writing . . .
1-59493-063-5 $13.95

PAID IN FULL by Ann Roberts. 200 pp. Ari Adams will need to choose between the debts of the past and the promise of a happy future.
1-59493-059-7 $13.95

ROMANCING THE ZONE by Kenna White. 272 pp. Liz's world begins to crumble when a secret from her past returns to Ashton . . .
1-59493-060-0 $13.95

SIGN ON THE LINE by Jaime Clevenger. 204 pp. Alexis Getty, a flirtatious delivery driver is committed to finding the rightful owner of a mysterious package.
1-59493-052-X $13.95

END OF WATCH by Clare Baxter. 256 pp. LAPD Lieutenant L.A Franco Frank follows the lone clue down the unlit steps of memory to a final, unthinkable resolution.
1-59493-064-4 $13.95

BEHIND THE PINE CURTAIN by Gerri Hill. 280pp. Jacqueline returns home after her father's death and comes face-to-face with her first crush.   1-59493-057-0 $13.95

PIPELINE by Brenda Adcock. 240pp. Joanna faces a lost love returning and pulling her into a seamy underground corporation that kills for money.   1-59493-062-7 $13.95

18TH & CASTRO by Karin Kallmaker. 200pp. First-time couplings and couples who know how to mix lust and love make 18th & Castro the hottest address in the city by the bay.
1-59493-066-X $13.95

JUST THIS ONCE by KG MacGregor. 200pp. Mindful of the obligations back home that she must honor, Wynne Connelly struggles to resist the fascination and allure that a particular woman she meets on her business trip represents.   1-59493-087-2 $13.95

ANTICIPATION by Terri Breneman. 240pp. Two women struggle to remain professional as they work together to find a serial killer.   1-59493-055-4 $13.95

OBSESSION by Jackie Calhoun. 240pp. Lindsey's life is turned upside down when Sarah comes into the family nursery in search of perennials.   1-59493-058-9 $13.95

BENEATH THE WILLOW by Kenna White. 240pp. A torch that still burns brightly even after twenty-five years threatens to consume two childhood friends.
1-59493-053-8 $13.95

SISTER LOST, SISTER FOUND by Jeanne G'fellers. 224pp. The highly anticipated sequel to No Sister of Mine.   1-59493-056-2 $13.95

THE WEEKEND VISITOR by Jessica Thomas. 240 pp. In this latest Alex Peres mystery, Alex is asked to investigate an assault on a local woman but finds that her client may have more secrets than she lets on.   1-59493-054-6 $13.95

THE KILLING ROOM by Gerri Hill. 392 pp. How can two women forget and go their separate ways?   1-59493-050-3 $12.95

PASSIONATE KISSES by Megan Carter. 240 pp. Will two old friends run from love?
1-59493-051-1 $12.95

ALWAYS AND FOREVER by Lyn Denison. 224 pp. The girl next door turns Shannon's world upside down.   1-59493-049-X $12.95

BACK TALK by Saxon Bennett. 200 pp. Can a talk show host find love after heartbreak?
1-59493-028-7 $12.95

THE PERFECT VALENTINE: EROTIC LESBIAN VALENTINE STORIES edited by Barbara Johnson and Therese Szymanski—from Bella After Dark. 328 pp. Stories from the hottest writers around.   1-59493-061-9 $14.95

MURDER AT RANDOM by Claire McNab. 200 pp. The Sixth Denise Cleever Thriller. Denise realizes the fate of thousands is in her hands.   1-59493-047-3 $12.95

THE TIDES OF PASSION by Diana Tremain Braund. 240 pp. Will Susan be able to hold it all together and find the one woman who touches her soul?   1-59493-048-1 $12.95

JUST LIKE THAT by Karin Kallmaker. 240 pp. Disliking each other—and everything they stand for—even before they meet, Toni and Syrah find feelings can change, just like that.
1-59493-025-2 $12.95

WHEN FIRST WE PRACTICE by Therese Szymanski. 200 pp. Brett and Allie are once again caught in the middle of murder and intrigue.   1-59493-045-7 $12.95